THE TRUTH GAME

THE TRUTH GAME

Janet Tanner

severn House

This first world edition published 2008
in Great Britain and the USA by
SEVERN HOUSE PUBLISHERS LTD of
9–15 High Street, Sutton, Surrey, England, SM1 1DF.

British Library Cataloguing in Publication Data

Tanner, Janet
  The truth game
  1. Family secrets - Fiction 2. Drowning victims - Fiction
  3. Inheritance and succession - Fiction 4. Domestic fiction
  I. Title
  823.9'14[F]

  ISBN-13: 978-0-7278-6648-6   (cased)

All Severn House titles are printed on acid-free paper.

Typeset by Palimpsest Book Production Ltd.,
Grangemouth, Stirlingshire, Scotland.
Printed and bound in Great Britain by
MPG Books Ltd., Bodmin, Cornwall.

Prologue

They were playing the Truth Game. They almost always did at dinner parties when they had left the formality of the dining room for the faded comfort of the drawing room. Someone must have asked: 'Tell us your most embarrassing moment,' because Katrina could hear Uncle Jack regaling them with one of his interminable stories and everyone else laughing helplessly, though they, like Katrina, had heard the anecdote many times before.

From her vantage point on the stairs she could see him standing in front of the open log fire, brandy balloon in hand, a tall, good-looking man in the black dinner jacket and frilled shirt that her father, Tony, insisted on calling a 'monkey suit', much to her mother's irritation. Katrina giggled as she thought of it, and hugged Jake, the retriever, who had been turned out of his favourite place, curled up on the drawing-room sofa.

Through the partly open door Katrina could also see her father, sitting in one of the pair of vast armchairs which flanked the fireplace, and her mother on the leather pouffe, legs drawn up beneath her long green velvet skirt, auburn hair falling in soft waves around the shoulders of her white silk shirt. She was laughing at Jack's joke. But Katrina's father wasn't laughing. He was staring down at his glass with an expression midway between exasperation and resignation.

Katrina couldn't see any of the others properly – just Auntie Sandra's feet in their high platform-soled ankle strap shoes (Auntie Sandra was Uncle Jack's wife) and the altogether more sensible court shoes which she knew belonged to Aunt Verity. Not that Verity was a real aunt, for which Katrina was eternally grateful. Verity was, she thought, the most boring person she had ever met, though everyone said how *nice* she was, as if they felt obliged to comment on her niceness to make up for the fact that no one actually liked her. Of Hugh, Verity's husband, Katrina could see nothing at all, though she could hear him guffawing loudly, like a donkey with straw up its nostrils. And neither, unfortunately, could she see Liz – her godmother, and an old friend of her mother's – who was over visiting from the States. Though she barely knew her, Katrina adored Liz. In Katrina's eyes she was an impossibly glamorous figure. She was an interior designer and Mummy said she was *famous*. Katrina was determined that when she grew up she would be just like her.

Uncle Jack finished his story just as Jake, tired of being held captive, wriggled free and lumbered down the stairs. Katrina shrank back, afraid someone might look up and see her. But they didn't.

'My turn to ask a question!' That was Auntie Sandra. 'This is a stinker. I want to know which of your children you love the best, and why.'

'Who are you asking?' Liz enquired.

'Not Verity, obviously, since Wendy is her only child.' Sandra giggled. 'And you don't have any at all, that we know of. So I'm asking . . . Trish. Come on, Trish, answer, or pay a forfeit.'

Katrina's heart came into her mouth with a sickening jolt and she shivered suddenly in spite of her warm winceyette nightdress. Perhaps eavesdropping wasn't such fun after all. What a horrible thing to ask! And she certainly didn't want to hear the answer. It wouldn't be her, of course, she was just piggy-in-the-middle, squashed between clever, serious Jessica and Miranda who was devastatingly pretty and enchantingly mischievous. But she didn't want to hear her mother actually say which of them was her favourite. It would be horrid knowing something so important that the others didn't. Katrina sat very still, hugging herself, wanting to run back upstairs to her warm, safe bed, yet unable to move.

'Unlike you, Sandra, I don't play favourites.' Trish was on her feet. Her voice was a little slurred, but Katrina didn't notice it. She was too busy being relieved, and wondering what her mother meant. Which of the boys was Auntie Sandra's favourite – Ash or Alistair? 'If you were hoping to make trouble, you're going to be disappointed. I love all my children equally. All four of them.'

Katrina frowned, puzzled. There was complete silence from the drawing room, even the orchestral version of the theme from *Doctor Zhivago* which had been playing on the stereo had come to an end. Then she heard her father say, 'I think you've had too much to drink, Trish.'

'No, I haven't. And I haven't finished either. This is supposed to be the Truth Game. Well, then, let's have the truth. All of it!'

'Trish . . .' Tony said, sounding a caution.

'Let's have another question.' That was Liz. 'I want to know what you've spent the most money on in one go, and I'm asking – Jack.'

'Oh, that's easy. My marriage licence. The way Sandra spends I've been paying for it ever since.'

Everyone laughed, rather strained laughter. Everyone except Trish.

'You haven't let me finish! It was *my* turn. I want to tell the truth about me, and about all of you. Let's face it, we've all got something to hide. Who shall I start with? Jack? Liz? Verity?'

'Trish, that is enough. You're drunk, and making a fool of yourself.' Katrina's father used the voice he used to her or Jessica or Miranda when they had been very naughty.

'Trish, honey, let's go and make some black coffee.' That was Liz.

'I don't want black coffee.' Trish was in tears now. 'Oh, just leave me alone, all of you!'

She came rushing out of the door, and Katrina scooted up the stairs and out of sight, into her room, into her bed, pulling the covers up to her chin.

Oh, *why* had she been eavesdropping? It had been terrible! Her mother crying and saying those things . . . Katrina's own eyes filled with tears and she pushed her fists into them, trying to blot out the memory, yet still hearing her mother's voice.

'*I love all my children equally. All four of them.*'

But there aren't four of us, Katrina thought, puzzled as well as distressed. There's only Jessica and Miranda and me . . .

She reached for Edward Bear, the battered teddy who shared her bed, cuddling him close. But it was a long time before she fell asleep.

Wells Journal, October 11th, 1983

LOCAL BUSINESSMAN'S WIFE DIES IN DROWNING ACCIDENT

Patricia Morton, wife of local businessman Tony Morton, has died in a drowning accident at her home.

Thirty-eight-year-old Patricia, known to her family as Trish, was found in a lake in the grounds of their home by her husband Tony. He had spent the evening at the Larchdales Golf and Country Club which he co-owns with his ex-professional footballer brother, Jack Morton, and when he returned Patricia was missing from the house. A search of the grounds resulted in the tragic discovery.

The couple have three daughters, Jessica, 17, Katrina, 16, and Miranda, 13.

Police are treating the drowning as an accident. 'It seems likely that Mrs Morton slipped on mud and wet leaves on the banks of the lake,' a police spokesman said.

One

1995

K atrina Morton – Kate to her family and friends – threw her briefcase into the back of her GTi and draped her jacket across it. Then she climbed into the driver's seat, fitted her key into the ignition and leaned back against the headrest, gathering herself together. What a day! A morning of meetings such as she could only have envisaged in her worst nightmares and now, just when she needed time to try and work out what the hell she was going to do, she had to steel herself to attend her grandfather's funeral.

Kate closed her eyes briefly as one set of emotions gave way to another. Saying goodbye to someone she had loved so much would have been bad enough at any time; today, coming on top of everything else it was an ordeal she was dreading. She could scarcely believe that the man she had regarded all her life as both hero and giant was gone. But she knew once she followed his coffin to the corner of the country churchyard where generations of Holbrooks were buried the inescapable reality of it would hit her like a ton of bricks.

It wasn't just losing Grandpa, though that was bad enough. It was also the feeling of desolation that came from knowing a whole era had come to an end. It might be a very long time since she had run to him as a little girl with her troubles, but as long as he had been alive something of the illusion had remained. Now the haven she had been too proud, and too considerate, to seek for years no longer existed, and Kate felt suddenly that she needed it now more than ever.

But somehow she was going to have to cope with her grief, and find it in herself to be pleasant to old friends of Grandpa's she barely knew, and contend with her family, who at the best

of times made her defensive and strung-up. It was all going
to be appallingly, inescapably dreadful.

A soft toot attracted her attention; Kate glanced up and saw
a car hovering alongside her. The driver was pointing to her
parking space, asking if she was vacating it. Kate nodded and
started the engine. She really must get going. She should have
been on her way ages ago – one never knew what the traffic
would be like – and she mustn't be late. She could imagine
the family already gathering – Jessica, her older sister, fussing
as she made sure her sons, Dominic and William, were presentable, and Miranda, younger than Kate by three years, trying
on one outfit after another and groaning that she didn't have
a thing to wear, though her wardrobe was always overflowing
with expensive designer clothes which she couldn't afford.

How ironic, Kate thought, Miranda might be permanently
overdrawn, with huge bills on her credit cards, but at least
she wasn't in the unenviable position of being called in to be
threatened with bankruptcy. At least she wouldn't be informed
by her bank manager – whom she could in any case charm
with a single flash of her navy-blue eyes – that unless she
cleared her considerable debts within the week he would be
forced to foreclose her loan and take steps to recoup the bank's
losses.

A lump that was part panic and part sick dread rose in
Kate's throat, and she swallowed at it angrily, pulling out into
the stream of midday traffic.

She could still scarcely believe that it had come to this, that
she was in danger of losing the interior design business she
had worked so hard to build up, even though for weeks –
months – now, she had felt she was caught in a vortex, being
sucked relentlessly down into the muddy waters of failure.
Ironic, really, that she should have weathered the worst of the
depression only to fall victim to it now. But the years when
the customers had no longer had cash to spare on luxuries such
as new furnishings had taken their toll. The corporate side of
the business had suffered too; few new hotels had opened or
old ones refurbished, and those which did paid her accounts
late or not at all. When one of her best customers called in
the receivers Kate was inevitably one of the losers, but her
own suppliers still had to be paid, and her workforce, and the
interest on her bank loan. Of these three commitments, it had

been the bank loan Kate had put bottom of the list. Now she was paying the price.

How the hell was she going to tell the girls who worked for her that they were out of a job? She'd failed them, just as she had failed her father and Uncle Jack, who had invested in her business in the early days and never yet seen a return. There was no way she could raise the sort of money she needed. It was no use going to her father again, cap in hand. His business, like everyone else's, was suffering from the after effects of the recession, and in any case Kate was too proud to even ask. The failure was hers and hers alone, and there was no way out of it. Unless . . .

Unless there was something for her in Grandpa's will. In his heyday, Robert Holbrook had been a successful building contractor with a virtual monopoly in and around the town. But he had sold out on his retirement twenty years or more ago, and Kate couldn't imagine there could be much left. Dorothea, his wife, had been in a nursing home for years before she died, and everyone knew how much nursing homes cost. And then there was the running of the great barn of a house that he had built when he and Dorothea had married and refused to give up. In any case . . .

Kate shivered violently, disgusted with herself for wondering, however briefly, if her grandfather's will might provide a solution to her problems. She loved him; wanted him to be alive still. How could she even think about profiting from his death? If this was what business did to you, made you think of money first and people second, then perhaps it was just as well she was going bust now, before she was completely corrupted. But the trouble was the business was her whole life. Without it she had nothing. She certainly couldn't count on Chris being there to help fill the empty space. A wave of loneliness and longing washed over Kate, adding to the desolation and anxiety. *Oh Chris, why aren't you here, when I need you so much?*

But the brutal fact was that whenever there was a crisis in her life, Chris never was there. Probably never would be. There had been a time when she'd thought that if she was patient, gave him time to sort out his responsibilities, they would eventually be together. Now she was beginning to doubt that too. Chris might say he loved her, but he belonged to someone else. She had no rights, no rights at all. In this, as in everything else, when the chips were down she was on her own. And she had no one to blame but herself.

Kate, usually so independent, was suddenly achingly lonely. And then determinedly defiant. Forget Chris, forget the business, forget everything except getting to Grandpa's funeral. Whatever the problems in her life, it was time to put them aside and give her full undivided attention to her grandfather's memory and ensure she was there, remembering him with love, when he was laid to rest.

As she hurried up the path of her thirties-style bungalow in a quiet close on the outskirts of town, Wendy Bryant checked her watch. Almost twelve thirty. Oh well, it could have been worse. A couple of prospective buyers had come into the estate agents' where she worked to ask for details of houses just as she'd been on the point of leaving, and with the reams of properties unsold on the books she hadn't dared turn them away. Then the traffic had been appalling – road works and temporary traffic lights *again*. But she was home now. A quick shower, change into her navy pinstripe suit – navy would be suitable, wouldn't it? – drive over to pick up Verity, her mother, and they should still be in good time for Robert's funeral. It wasn't until two, and as long as they were in their seats before the coffin and the family mourners arrived, it should be all right . . .

'I'm home,' she called, opening the door and going in.

No reply, but that was nothing new. Tim never had been one for effusive greetings. She hurried through to the kitchen, dumped the bag of groceries she'd bought at Tesco, and went back along the hall, taking off her jacket and undoing the button of her skirt.

She was getting fat! The waistband of the skirt had been cutting into her waist all morning. She only hoped she could get into the navy suit; she hadn't worn it for ages.

'Tim!' she called again. 'I'll be ten minutes. Are you ready to go?'

Still no answer. Wendy pushed open the living room door and looked in.

Tim was sprawled in one of the chairs. He was wearing a pair of shapeless cords and the sweater which had been irreparably splattered with paint when they'd last redecorated – how long ago? Years, it seemed.

'Tim, you're not ready!' she accused.

'Well nor I am.' His tone was offensive, his voice slightly slurred. With a sinking heart, Wendy saw the tumbler and whisky bottle on the floor beside him.

'Tim! We've got to go to Robert's funeral. We mustn't be late. And what on earth are you doing drinking whisky at this time of day?'

A flicker of aggression crossed his face, once handsome, but now beginning to show the ravages of excess.

'I'll drink whenever I feel like it. I don't need you to tell me what I can and can't do.'

Wendy sighed despairingly. It had been like this ever since he'd been made redundant. She'd known he was drinking too much; what she hadn't realized was just how early in the day he was starting on it.

'They'll smell it on your breath,' she said defensively.

'I doubt it, since I'm not going.'

'Oh, Tim!'

That was another thing; he hardly ever went out now, just sloped about the house in clothes that looked like rejects from a charity shop – Tim, who'd always taken such a pride in his appearance, when he was at work at least. Until six months ago he had been branch manager of the same estate agent she worked for. Then head office had gone on a cost-cutting exercise, hardly surprising, given the state of the market, and decided the branch could run perfectly well without him. Tim had been devastated, especially when he learned the twenty-one-year-old he'd trained himself was now doing his job, albeit for several thousand a year less. It was salt in the wound too that Wendy had been kept on whilst he was kicked out, even though it was a blessing financially. Recently she had begun to feel that the anger and resentment he had at first reserved for Crossways Properties was now directed at her.

'Why the hell should I go to the funeral?' he demanded truculently. 'Robert Holbrook is nothing to me. I don't know why you had to take an afternoon off for it. It's not as if he's a relation.'

'His wife was Dad's second cousin, so he is family,' she argued.

'Your family, not mine. I don't have a family, remember?'

Wendy sighed. Not that again! Tim had been brought up in a children's home and it had left him with an enormous chip on his shoulder.

'And what am I supposed to say when people ask where you are?' she asked.

'Whatever you like. I don't suppose they'll even notice I'm not there. And nor will you, especially if Ash Morton is there.' It was another of his hobby horses; always had been. Today, however, Wendy felt her cheeks growing hot.

'For goodness' sake! I doubt Ash will be there. You know his job keeps him abroad most of the time.'

'But if he is . . . you'll both enjoy the wake, I should imagine. You can't deny that you and he—'

'Don't be so ridiculous!' Wendy snapped. 'You know very well that was all over long before you and I even met. But I haven't the time to argue with you now. I've got a funeral to go to even if you don't.'

She turned away abruptly, leaving the room. But the flush was still there in her cheeks and burning in the fair skin of her neck and chest. Tim was quite right, of course. In spite of her denial, a small treacherous part of her was hoping that Ash would be there. Just as another part, the sensible, thinking part, was hoping he would not. Seeing him would be just too painful.

Oh dear God, how it still hurt! A letter, just a letter, saying he thought it would be better if they didn't see each other again. He hadn't even had the decency to tell her himself. The pain of it reached out to her across the years, the initial disbelief, the dawning realization that it was over. Oh, yes, she had loved Ash for as long as she could remember, and judging by her reaction now she loved him still.

She pushed open the bedroom door. The bed was unmade, the pillows crumpled, the duvet turned back in an untidy heap. Her skin prickled with irritation. Couldn't he even be bothered to make the bed now? She jerked the duvet across the rumpled sheet, stripped off her skirt and blouse and dropped them on top of it. Slovenliness was catching, and besides she had no time to waste. Her mother would be expecting her, probably already had her coat on, ready and waiting. Verity was punctual to a fault.

As she opened the wardrobe door she caught sight of her

face, pale, strained, no sign now of the flush. No colour at all to speak of. I look like a ghost, she thought.

If Ash was at the funeral, perhaps that was exactly how he would see her. A ghost from the past. And if ever he had seen anything in her, he would probably wonder now what on earth it could have been.

She wriggled into the pinstripe suit. Yes, the skirt was a bit tight, but the jacket covered a multitude of sins. She ran a comb through her hair, renewed her lipstick and brushed some tawny blusher high on her cheekbones. It stood out garishly against the pallor of her skin and Wendy pulled a tissue out of the box on the dressing table and wiped it off again.

When she looked into the sitting room on her way out, Tim was still slumped in the chair. He had turned the television on now, but he didn't seem to be watching it. He raised his glass in her direction.

'Have a good time.' His tone, as well as the words, was offensive. Wendy swallowed her anger and left without answering.

Liz Langley eased herself out of the narrow bathtub and stepped on to the small limp towelling mat which she had placed strategically. As she leaned over to pull out the plug the hotel room echoed with loud gurgling. Liz grimaced. Was there no end to the archaic noises this place produced? She had been awake half the night, disturbed by the creaks and groans of ancient timbers settling and knockings in the water pipes, not to mention the sounds of the outside world filtering in through the window – motorcycles like demented sewing machines, car doors slamming, a burglar alarm, a crowd of revellers singing tunelessly, and then, with the dawn, lorries delivering to the shops which lined the street from the market square at one end to the smart new supermarket at the other.

How odd it was, Liz thought, that she had remembered England as being so quiet compared to the USA where she had lived for the past thirty years. Last night, tossing and turning, she had been unable to avoid comparing it unfavourably with the peace of her Florida home, where she could leave the windows open and hear nothing but the chirping of the crickets. Even city hotel rooms were quiet, insulated against the activity on the streets outside, and their comfort went without saying. This hostelry, the best the town had to offer, and given a glowing reference in all the guide-books, was simply not in the same league.

Not, of course, that it was only the noises in the pipes which had kept her awake last night. She'd had quite a bit on her mind too. Coming home for the first time in years had awakened so many memories, disturbed the ghosts she had thought she had laid to rest long ago. And she wasn't looking forward to the funeral, though she'd moved heaven and earth to get here.

'I have to go,' she'd said to Laurie O'Neill, her PA. 'You'll have to cancel all my engagements and put things on hold for a day or two.'

'But Miss Langley, the Benson Corporation contract is coming up. Benny Benson was insistent you should oversee it personally.'

'Benny will just have to accept that my staff are perfectly capable of covering for me or wait until I get back,' Liz had said tautly.

'But really it is most inconvenient . . .'

'Unfortunately, as Scarlett O'Hara said, there really never is a convenient time either to die or to have a baby.' Liz had snapped because she had been very upset when she had received the phone call from Tony telling her of Robert's death, but even as she said it the irony struck her. She had never had a child because there had never been a convenient time, but death couldn't be postponed that way. When the time came that was it, no argument, no procrastination, no excuses.

Liz shivered and towelled herself fiercely. God, it was cold! The central heating which had rumbled and grumbled all night didn't seem to be doing much now and the air felt chill to her skin, warmed by the bath and tanned rich golden brown by the Florida sunshine. Then she let the towel drop and surveyed her reflection for a moment in the mirror which the bath water hadn't even been hot enough to mist over.

Not bad for fifty-three. Waist a bit thicker than it used to be, boobs suffering a little from the effects of gravity, but otherwise still in pretty good shape. She'd worked at it, of course, rising at dawn every morning to swim before going to the office and fitting sessions with her personal trainer into her busy schedule. Even her face looked pretty good, though she had never succumbed to the surgeon's knife, and thanks to a superb colourist her hair was the same bright gold it had always been.

How would the years have taken their toll on the others? she wondered. Tony and Jack were very likely suffering from the excesses of rich food and alcohol that would be an occupational hazard in their line of work. They might have lost their hair, or a good deal of it. Tony was, after all, her age, and Jack older. Remembering Jack's profligate ways it seemed likely he would be showing signs of wear and tear, a shame really, since he had been such a handsome man. But if Tony had lived life at a less reckless pace, which she imagined he had, then perhaps he was the handsome one now.

As for the girls, they had grown from children to women since she had last seen them. Jessica must be into her thirties, Katrina, her god-daughter, was approaching the Rubicon, and even Miranda, whom she remembered as an enchanting child in white tights and black ankle-strap shoes, well into her twenties. Dear God, where had the years gone? She should have made the effort to see them more often, particularly Katrina. She hadn't been much of a godmother. They'd talked on the telephone quite often when Kate had been starting her business since, like Liz, she had gone into interior design. But that was about the size of it.

I failed you, Trish, Liz thought, guilty suddenly. In all kinds of ways.

She closed her eyes briefly, shutting out the faded, chintzy hotel room, and for a moment it seemed to her as if Trish was there, standing beside her. They'd been at school together, friends throughout their formative years, sharing all their secret hopes and dreams and heartaches. But when there had been real problems to face she hadn't been there for Trish. She had gone to the States, obsessed with her career and with things she could never, ever, by their very nature, discuss with Trish. And Trish, dear Trish, had lost her confidante. The things that had happened had driven her to a lingering depression. And in the end she had taken her own life . . .

Liz sighed, slipped into her black silk underwear and a simple black wool shift dress. As she yanked up the zip she moved towards the window, looking out at the scene, once so familiar, now quite alien. The centuries-old buildings which lined the main street, shops, cafés; the market square where stalls mushroomed each Wednesday and Saturday. Home. Except that it didn't feel like home any more.

The church clock was striking twelve thirty. Her taxi would be here soon. Liz sat down on the plush-covered stool in front of the dressing table, tied her make-up cape around her shoulders, and began to make herself presentable for the ordeal which lay ahead.

As she pulled into the drive of the substantial Victorian villa that was her parents' home, Wendy saw the front-room curtains twitch and by the time she had parked the car her mother had opened the front door and was standing on the step.

'Good, you're here. I was beginning to worry. I expected you half an hour ago.'

Verity was clearly ready to leave. She was wearing a boxy black jacket over a black and white tweed skirt; the ensemble emphasized the sturdiness of her body, ample bosom, thick waist and wide hips, and her low-heeled court shoes added little to her five feet two inch stature. She was also wearing a hat, black felt with a small brim, perched like a halo to expose a short fringe of iron-grey hair.

'I've just got to get my bag.' Verity was peering at the car. 'Where's Tim?'

'He isn't coming. I think he felt he'd be out of place. He didn't know Robert that well after all,' Wendy said lamely.

'He *is* your husband, though.' Verity's lips were tight.

She knows, Wendy thought miserably. She knows the problems I'm having. It was practically impossible to keep anything from her mother. She was so perceptive Wendy sometimes wondered if she might be clairvoyant.

'Do you want the bathroom before we go?' Verity was asking.

'No, thanks. I'm only ten minutes from home.' Wendy was amused, in spite of herself.

'Well, yes, but you know how long these things take. It will be a while before you have the chance to go again.'

'I don't need the bathroom, Mum, thank you.'

'There's no need to snap my head off, Wendy.' Verity disappeared into the hall and re-emerged with a black patent bag over her arm. 'We'd better go then. There's going to be a big turn-out today and we might have trouble finding somewhere to park.'

'I'm sure we'll find somewhere,' Wendy said, reversing out of the drive.

'Parking is such a nightmare these days! Would you believe I got a ticket last week in Rosamund Street? Ten minutes over the hour I'd been, that's all – ten minutes. When I came out of the hospice shop there was this plastic package stuffed under the windscreen wiper. I found the traffic warden and gave him a piece of my mind, told him I'd been parking there for years. But it made no difference. He said the ticket had been made out and I'd have to pay. I wrote a good letter to go with the fine, I can tell you.'

Wendy smiled to herself. The altercation between her mother and the traffic warden must have been something to see.

'Dad is making his own way to the church, is he?' she asked. 'He doesn't want us to pick him up on the way?'

'No, he said he'd meet us there. It's only a stone's throw from his office.'

'All the same, if you're worried about the parking, it would have been one car less.'

'I told him that. But you know what he's like. He makes up his own mind.' Her tone indicated she considered Hugh difficult, and his dismissal of her suggestion a personal insult. Hugh usually fell in with her arrangements for the sake of peace. But when he did make up his mind about something, he could also be more stubborn than many a more aggressive man, turning a deaf ear to her ranting and going on in his own sweet way.

'He's upset, of course,' Verity went on, as if she felt the need to excuse Hugh's perversity. 'And who can blame him?'

'Upset?' Wendy squinted a sideways glance at her mother. 'What about?'

'Well, the will of course! Oh, my dear, haven't I told you? Of course, I haven't seen you for a proper chat since poor Robert passed away. Apparently Robert made a new will, and not with your father's office. Now, what do you think of that?'

Wendy was startled. Her father, senior partner in a firm of solicitors in the town, had always dealt with Robert Holbrook's affairs.

'You can imagine what a slap in the face that has been for

your father,' Verity went on, barely pausing to draw breath.
'After all he has done for Robert, to find out that he should
see fit to go to someone else.'

'Poor Dad,' Wendy said. 'Who did Robert go to then?'

'Oh, some upstart who's been *advertising*,' Verity said with
distaste. 'Imagine poaching a client like that! What can Robert
have been thinking of? What disloyalty after all these years!'

'Perhaps like you he thinks it's time Dad retired,' Wendy said
wryly. 'He is going to be sixty-seven next birthday, after all.'

'That is quite beside the point, Wendy. Your father was under
the impression that Robert was his client, and that the document in his strong room was Robert's last will and testament.
And then he received a telephone call from this other man.
Robert had been to see him not long before he died and made
a new will. Naturally, your father feels utterly betrayed.'

'It is strange,' Wendy agreed. 'You don't think that Robert
had gone a bit . . . well, peculiar?'

'My thoughts exactly! But apparently this other man was
adamant that Robert was of sound mind. Now I can only think
there must be something in this new will that Robert didn't
want your father to know about.'

'Good heavens!'

'What else can one think? Anyway, I dare say we'll find
out later. The new man is coming to the house after the funeral
to read the will.'

'That's a little unusual, isn't it?' Wendy said.

'In this day and age, yes. But it seems it was Robert's wish
that the family should all be made aware of the contents at
one and the same time, and since they will all be together
today, that is what was decided upon.'

'There might be a shock or two in store then,' Wendy said.

'Possibly. I do hope not. These things are bad enough when
they're straightforward. What would Dorothea think if she
were alive – or poor Trish. They'd turn in their graves!'

Wendy suppressed a smile. 'If they were alive, Mum, they
wouldn't be in their graves. At least, I hope not.'

'Don't be flippant, Wendy. You know what I mean. Ah,
we're here. Oh dear, look at all those cars! Just as I thought.
Robert was so well known locally . . . There's a space, look!
Quick, before someone else takes it.'

'It's OK, Mum, I've seen it.'

Wendy manoeuvred neatly into the gap, big enough to park a bus in, she thought, never mind her little Fiesta. And thank goodness it was! Her hands were trembling on the wheel, her stomach churning. And she knew that the sudden attack of nerves had nothing whatever to do with the fact that she hated funerals and still less to do with Robert's apparent disloyalty to her father. It was because she was facing the prospect of meeting Ash again face to face for the first time in more than ten years.

Jon Nicholson replaced the law book he had been studying on one of the shelves that ran the full length of his office wall, spun his chair so as to face his desk and reached for the intercom button.

'Julie, could you bring in the Holbrook file, please?'

'You mean Robert William James Holbrook, deceased?'

Jon winced. When he had opened the office here, in the centre of town, Jon had been determined that it would have a modern, informal approach. Julie had come to him fresh from secretarial college and he'd had high hopes of her. But she was beginning to sound like the highly efficient dragon at the firm he'd worked for when he first qualified, and who had refused to allow anyone, even the other solicitors, to enter the domain of the senior partner without first answering to her.

Perhaps it was the exposure to legal jargon that did it, he thought ruefully. Perhaps there was no escape. Perhaps one day even he would fall into the trap, change his sports car for something solid and impressive, buy a set of golf clubs, insist on being called Mr Nicholson and not see anyone without a prior appointment. It was a depressing thought.

A tap on the door and Julie entered, clutching a Manila folder tied with pink tape. 'Robert William James Holbrook deceased,' she said, putting the file on his desk. 'Is there anything else you need?'

'No, thanks. I shall be going out shortly.' He was already reaching for the file, failing to notice the regretful look that crossed her face. Like practically every other unattached female – and some attached ones, too – who came into contact with him, Julie was half in love with Jon Nicholson. Good-looking, with thick dark hair, irregular jaw line and rugby player's physique, not to mention a voice that could make hearts turn over . . . and single.

Julie stood for a moment longer, staring lustfully at his arm, bare below the rolled-up sleeve of his white shirt and tanned to a dark brown from the gloriously hot summer, then gathered herself together and left the office. Jon scarcely noticed her go. His thoughts were on Robert William James Holbrook, deceased.

Frightening how quickly the Grim Reaper could move in. The man who had sat in the client's chair opposite him such a short time ago had looked as if he was good for another ten years at least and probably a candidate for a telegram from the Queen. Though he had admitted to being eighty-three years old he had looked and talked like a much younger man. His hair, though thinning, had been iron grey, not white, his jaw line still firm, his eyes bright and shrewd. And his mind was obviously as sharp as it had ever been. The reasons he had given for coming to Jon instead of the solicitor he had used for most of his life had proved that, and his instructions clear and concise. Altogether Jon had been impressed with him, and gone home thinking that if he could be in such good nick at the age of eighty-three he wouldn't do so badly.

Yet just a few weeks after he had returned to the office to sign the new will he had suffered a massive stroke. After a period in hospital he had moved to a private nursing home and fought like a Trojan to recover some use in his hand and the power of speech. But not even his indomitable spirit could achieve the impossible. On the one occasion Jon had visited him he had been shocked by the change in him, wheelchair bound, unable to control a dribble of saliva from one corner of his now-twisted mouth, frustrated by his inability to find the right words to express what his still-active brain wanted to say.

In the end the inevitable, and Jon thought merciful, had happened. Another stroke, even more devastating than the first. For three days Robert had been in a coma, then he had slipped away without ever regaining consciousness.

What had brought about the sudden decline? Jon had wondered. Had it simply been a time bomb waiting to explode even when he had appeared so healthy? Or had something happened to trigger it? Remembering Robert's confidences, he suspected that might be the case. Stress was bad, even for the young and fit, and however well he had tried to conceal it, Robert had been stressed. And shock, too, could have devastating effects. Had he suffered a shock of some kind as a result of the enquiries he had been pursuing? Jon had wondered about the wisdom of the course Robert was following, but it hadn't been his place to warn him. And even if he had, he doubted Robert Holbrook would have taken any notice. But all the same . . .

Jon flipped open the file and reread the will that made him Robert Holbrook's sole executor. This afternoon, after the funeral, he had to face the family and reveal its contents. It was, he knew, going to be a shock to them. It would very likely open up a can of worms. He only hoped he had tied it up tightly, made sure there were no loose ends for dissenting members of the family to get hold of. He didn't want to end up being sued by one or other of them.

Jon closed the file, retied the pink tape and reached for his jacket. Just time for a sandwich and a coffee, then he'd head straight over to the church. He left the office, ran down the stairs and out into the street, making for the Swan, his favourite hostelry. He wished he could have a real drink rather than coffee, but he wouldn't succumb. Drinking and working didn't mix.

Traffic in the street was virtually stationary. Jon threaded his way between a car and a taxi to cross the road. As he passed the taxi he glanced in and saw a young woman wearing a wide-brimmed black hat, pulled low over her eyes, in the rear seat. Though he could see little more of her, she somehow exuded a glamour rarely seen in a small town such as this. Jon's lips pursed in a silent whistle. The black hat suggested she might be going to the funeral. If so, Robert Holbrook had some very expensive-looking friends and relations.

He pushed open the pub door, saw the crowd inside, and changed his mind. The coffee and sandwich would have to wait. He'd better get straight over to the church. The last thing he wanted was to be late. That would not be a good start, and Jon could not help feeling he needed the very best start he could get.

Two

'Dust to dust, ashes to ashes . . .' The voice of the clergyman was reedy in the dank October afternoon and was accompanied by the rustle of leaves falling from the centuries-old trees which surrounded the newly reopened double plot.

Kate stood motionless, staring down at the single pink rose in her hand and fighting back the tears. She didn't dare look down at the coffin bearing her grandfather's name; wanted even less to meet the eyes of her family, grouped around the grave. The church had been packed – Robert had been well known and well respected locally – and some of the congregation now stood in clusters on the perimeter path, watching from a distance, but Kate was almost unaware of them too.

As the vicar's voice died away Kate was aware of Jessica stepping forward and dropping the rose she held on to the coffin. Kate followed suit, dragging the heels of her shoes out of the soft ground into which they had sunk.

'Goodnight, Grandpa. God bless.' They were the words she had spoken to him every night when, as a child, she'd gone to stay with him and Grandma Dorothea, and now they sprang to her lips as if the passage of the years had never been. As tears filled her eyes, she dropped the rose and saw it settle on the gleaming brass plate.

Miranda was next to perform the ritual, then Dominic and William, Jessica's sons, spruce in their navy blue blazers and dark grey trousers, solemn-faced and angelic for once. Liz, Kate's godmother, followed. That was it then. All over. Kate stood for a moment, looking down at the coffin strewn with roses, drew a deep trembling breath in an effort to gather herself together and moved away.

'Are you all right, Kate?' It was Ash, touching her elbow. Ash, who had flown home for the funeral, and whom she was so glad to see. They had always been close and she had missed him a lot when he had gone to work in the Middle East for a big oil company. Her friends had sighed about it too; Ash was a high-flier, successful, devastatingly attractive – and single. But to Kate he was just Ash, more like a brother than a cousin.

'Yes, I'm all right,' she said with a small, wan smile. 'Or at least, I will be when I've had a drink. I just feel so sad.'

'I know. You thought the world of him, didn't you?'

'Yep.' She bit her lip, glanced towards the knots of mourners still gathered on the path. 'I guess I'd better do my duty and speak to some of those people, thank them for coming.'

'Want me to come with you?'

'Oh, Ash. Yes, please.'

She turned to pick her way across the grass and was startled to see a young woman in a black hat pulled low over her eyes and what looked like a designer suit standing beside the open grave. As Kate watched, she dropped a long-stemmed rose on to the coffin and stood, head bowed for a moment. Kate frowned. Who on earth was it? Her face was almost hidden by the brim of her hat and a pair of dark glasses, but from what she could see of her, Kate didn't recognize her at all. And yet at the same time there was something vaguely familiar about her.

'Ash, who's that?' she asked.

Ash shrugged. 'I've no idea. But then I wouldn't, would I?'

'No, I don't suppose you would.' But her eyes followed the glamorous figure as she stepped back and her curiosity was tinged with discomfort. A stranger throwing a rose down on to Grandpa's coffin? Odd to say the least of it. She made a slight detour on her way to the path and looked down into the grave.

Along with the roses she and the other close family members had dropped on to the coffin, a single long-stemmed bloom stood out, blood-red amongst the pink.

Wendy stood in the drawing room of the house that Robert Holbrook had built for Dorothea, his wife, the year they were married, sipping a glass of sherry and seeing the family gathering through a haze of misery.

Ash was avoiding her. Apart from a curt 'Hello, Wendy' he hadn't spoken to her and when their eyes had accidentally met a moment ago he had looked away too quickly. And it hurt so much! Not that she should have expected anything else, of course. If he could have left her as he had, without so much as a proper goodbye, why in the world should it be different now, when she was married to someone else?

Guilt suffused her as she realized that some small secret part of her had hoped that by some miracle what she and Ash had shared might be rekindled.

Tim was her husband and he'd suffered enough, losing his job, being made to feel worthless, without having his wife in love with someone else added to it. Really she should never have married him, but at the time his attentiveness and persistence had been balm to her broken heart. She'd thought that in time she would forget Ash; she'd been determined to. The trouble was that once he had the ring on her finger, Tim had seemed to change. He was no longer tender and loving, but possessive and abusive. And since he'd lost his job and started drinking things had only got worse, and Wendy couldn't help feeling it was all her fault.

She had to be there for Tim, she had to help him through this slough of despond. But as she gazed at Ash's back, fair hair curling over the collar of his dark suit, Wendy knew that the feelings she had always had for Ash were as deep as they had ever been. Try as she might to get over it, the fact remained, she loved him, and she always would. There was not a single thing she could do about it. It was the cross she had to bear.

'So how are things with you?' Liz asked, joining Kate beside the French windows.

Until now Kate had been so busy playing hostess there hadn't been time for anything beyond the briefest of exchanges; now Liz was anxious to catch up on the latest developments in her god-daughter's life, and, most importantly, the progress of her business. As a successful interior designer herself she had followed Kate's career with interest and knew that she had played her part in Kate's choice of profession.

'It was because of you that I first took an interest in furnishings,' Kate had told her once, and, pleased, Liz had fantasized that perhaps it was her own enthusiasm for the creative art that she had brought as a gift to the child's cradle.

But as a designer, Kate was very much her own woman,

with her own distinctive style. She had done well at college and after the briefest of apprenticeships with an established business she had taken the plunge and set up on her own. In those days she had often phoned Liz for advice, careless of lengthy transatlantic phone calls, but as time went on she had called less and less and it was now six months or more since they had spoken. Because she was busy and successful these days, Liz had told herself. Because the work she did was on quite a different scale to Liz's own projects. Because she'd gained the confidence to make her own decisions. Now, however, she saw a flash of embarrassment in Kate's eyes and realized there was another, less optimistic, reason.

'Actually, things are a bit difficult at the moment,' Kate said as brightly as she could manage. 'What with the recession and everything . . .'

'Ah. That's tough. You want to talk about it?'

Kate hesitated. 'Well . . . I would quite like to pick your brains if the opportunity arises.'

'Perhaps we could have dinner?' Liz suggested.

'That would have been nice. But I think Uncle Jack has organized a family meal for tonight. You're invited, of course, but there won't be much chance for a private conversation.'

Liz smiled. 'Don't worry, we'll think of something. We don't see nearly enough of one another. I really should make the effort to come home more often. Or you could come over and spend some time with me. It's no big deal these days – not like it was when I first went to Florida. Just a few hours on Concorde.'

'I couldn't afford Concorde.' Possibly not even an economy ticket on an ordinary flight, Kate added silently, and felt sick all over again.

'Well, we'll make the most of it while I'm here anyway,' Liz said. 'The trouble is, I've only got a few days. I didn't have time to get things sufficiently organized to be away for longer.'

'It really was very good of you to come,' Kate said.

'I wouldn't have thought of doing anything but. I'd never have forgiven myself if I hadn't been here to say goodbye to Robert.'

'He really was a very special person, wasn't he?' Kate mused.

'He certainly was.' There was a faraway look in Liz's eyes

for a moment, then she was her normal briskly efficient self once more. 'To get back to us. How about we have lunch tomorrow?'

'That should be OK . . .' Kate was shrinking already at the thought of admitting her problems to her gloriously successful godmother. Liz Langley was sought after by film stars and politicians and the filthy rich, whilst she, Kate, had been unable to keep her head above water in an English country town. It made her feel very small indeed.

'Who was that woman at the funeral?' Jack Morton enquired of his brother.

'Which woman?' Tony asked innocently, though he knew very well that Jack had to be referring to the glamorous stranger who had tossed a red rose into Robert's grave as the women and children of the family had done. The same thought had crossed his mind – who the hell was she? But because Tony knew his brother so well he was all too aware that whilst he was merely curious, Jack was interested for quite a different reason.

It had always been thus. In his day, Jack had been a professional footballer and he had taken full advantage of the glamour his career had bestowed on him. He had used it ruthlessly to pull the women he wanted just as he'd used the money he had made to buy the golf and country club in which he and Tony were partners. Over the years Tony had lost count of the women Jack had been involved with yet miraculously his marriage to Sandra had survived. In the early days Tony had covered his brother's tracks for him many times, fielding telephone calls from Sandra, creating alibis, and though nowadays, with Jack approaching the ripe old age of sixty, there were fewer conquests than there had once been, Tony suspected Jack now had designs on the unknown woman at the graveside of his father-in-law.

'Bit of all right, wasn't she?' he said with the slight coarseness which marred his urbane manner.

'She was striking, certainly,' Tony said.

Jack pulled a packet of panatellas from his breast pocket, tearing the wrapper from one with practised ease.

'Looks as if old Robert was a bit of a dark horse, doesn't it?'

'What do you mean?' Tony asked, though he was in no doubt.

'It's obvious, isn't it? She's not family, and none of us knew her. But she knew Robert well enough to throw a rose in on his coffin. She must have been his bit on the side.'

'Robert was eighty-three, for God's sake.'

'So? He was a bit of a one in his time, we all know that. And with all his money . . . Well, it won't be long before we find out if she's got what she wanted. The solicitor will be reading the will soon. You know he went to a different chap, not old Hugh? That's him, over there.'

'Yes, I know.'

'Funny business, if you ask me. Must have had a reason.'

Tony grimaced. Jack seemed to be relishing the possibility of some kind of sensation. But then, he would. It was Jack all over. And whatever shocks might be in store, they wouldn't directly affect him. Robert hadn't been his father-in-law, the grandfather of his children.

For their sakes, more than anything else, Tony fervently hoped there wouldn't be any shocks. The girls had all adored their grandfather, particularly Kate, and it would be very upsetting for them if what Jack was suggesting was true, and some glamorous little gold-digger had got him to change his will in her favour. Besides the emotional hurt they would feel, Tony suspected they could all do with a little windfall. Times had been hard recently, even he and Jack were struggling to keep their business afloat, and the girls had not escaped the chill wind of the recession. Jessica's husband, Adrian, might still be working, but financial consultants were no longer the whiz kids they had been in the eighties, the boys were growing up and costing them a fortune in school fees, and they had negative equity on their house. Why they had to make themselves poor struggling to keep the boys at prep school Tony didn't know; the state system had done well by him and Jack. But there it was, Jessica and Ady had different ideas. As for Kate, though she had never mentioned it, he had heard whispers that her interior design business was in trouble. And Miranda . . . well, Miranda would always need money. She had always been Little Miss Extravagance.

'Talking of paramours, I wonder if he left Liz anything?' Jack was musing as he puffed on his cigar.

'Liz?'

'Liz Langley.'

'I know who you mean. I just don't follow your reasoning. Or why you should mention her name and the word paramour in the same breath.'

'Oh, come on, Tony! He had a fling with her, didn't he?'

'I've no idea,' Tony said coldly. 'And I don't think this is the sort of conversation we should be having when we've just buried the man.'

Jack laughed, squinting at Tony through his cigar smoke. 'Touched a raw nerve, have I? Got a soft spot for her yourself?'

'Don't be ridiculous.'

'You could do worse, you know. I can't understand why you haven't hooked up with someone else in all this time. How many years is it now since Trish died? Ten? Twelve?'

'I don't want anyone else,' Tony said shortly. He checked his watch. 'I think maybe we ought to get on with the reading of the will. That solicitor chap is beginning to look a bit restless.'

He moved away from his brother, crossing the room to where Jon Nicholson stood by the big fireplace.

'Sorry this has taken so long, but I think most of the casual friends and acquaintances have left now. If you want to, we can get the official business over and done with.'

Jon Nicholson nodded. 'Whenever you're ready.'

Tony looked around, checking once again that only family and close friends remained. Then he picked up a knife and banged on the table top.

'If you'd all like to come along to the study now I think we'll get on with reading the will,' he said into the expectant hush.

The study was a big square room on the back of the house that resembled a conservatory. Robert had asked the architect for windows on three sides, with panels of stained glass beneath the traditional clear panes, so that it was the lightest room in the whole house, catching the sun from morning to dusk. It streamed in now from the west, low enough to fragment on the stained panels and mottle the plain hessian weave carpet with a kaleidoscope of bright jewel colours. Tony had arranged for enough chairs to be brought in to supplement the study's sparse furnishings and provide seats for them all, but Ash had opted to perch against the broad shelf of one of the book-cases, Kate was hunched on a pouffe, her arms wrapped around her knees, and Jessica was standing near the window so that she could keep an eye on Dominic and William, who were playing outside in the garden. Jon Nicholson was seated in Robert's swivel chair behind the solid oak desk, the file open in front of him.

'As I expect you all realize, this sort of thing is pretty unusual these days,' he began. 'The public reading of wills went out as a general practice years ago. But Mr Holbrook was insistent that he wanted his family and close friends – "honorary family" as he called them – to hear the contents at one and the same time and in the presence of one another. In fact, it was all I could do to persuade him against making a video so that he could tell you of his intentions himself. He'd seen something like that done in a TV play and he rather fancied the idea.'

Jack chuckled. 'Typical Robert! He always did like being in charge.'

'What a tasteless idea!' Hugh muttered to Verity. He was burning with humiliation that Robert should have gone else-where to make this last will and seething with resentment for the young man who looked more like a rugby player than a solicitor.

Jon Nicholson glanced down at the document, then looked up again.

'As you already know, Mr Holbrook appointed me sole executor. You are probably wondering why he did this, why he came to me at all when you, sir – ' he looked directly at Hugh – 'had dealt with all his legal requirements for so many years. I can only say that he did have a reason, and when you have heard what I have to say, I think the reason will be self-evident.'

At this Verity sniffed audibly and Wendy cringed. But Jon Nicholson appeared undeterred.

'To the will. It begins with the bequests; I'll run through them, though not all the beneficiaries are here.'

He did so and the assembled company listened impatiently as he listed various sums of money that Robert had left to former members of staff, then sat up to take more notice as he moved on to the bequests earmarked for them.

'To my dear friend, Elizabeth Langley, I leave the canteen of antique cutlery and the silver candelabra, that her Florida home may be graced with something of old England,' he began.

Across the room Jack caught Tony's eye and winked. Dear friend my foot, that look said.

'To Wendy Bryant the sum of one thousand pounds and the display cabinet with all its contents which she always admired.'

Wendy was staggered. A thousand pounds! She was touched, too, that Robert had realized how much she loved the pretty bow-fronted cabinet filled with fine porcelain and Bristol Blue Glass which Dorothea had spent a lifetime collecting.

'To my great-nephew Ashley Morton my Douglas motor cycle . . .'

A prize! Ashley thought, surprised and pleased. The Douglas was a classic.

'And to my great-nephew Alistair Morton, the contents of my wine cellar. To my great-grandsons Dominic and William Howard, I leave the sum of fifteen thousand pounds each, to be kept in trust for them until they attain the age of twenty-five years, and their own choice of my collection of silver cufflinks.'

Fifteen thousand each! Thirty thousand plus Wendy's thousand and the bequests to staff . . . Miranda was horrified. She was keeping a mental tally, wondering how much would be left for the rest of them. The house would be sold, of course, and with all its land should fetch a good sum, but by the time the taxman had taken his cut . . . Miranda dug her red-painted nails into her palms and lowered her eyes. She'd thought that after today she might be seriously rich, but it wasn't working out like that. And still the list wasn't finished . . .

'To my son-in-law, Anthony Morton, I leave the sum of fifteen thousand pounds, a small token of my gratitude for his kindness to me. To my trusted friend Hugh Ormrod I leave the sum of ten thousand pounds in an attempt to compensate him for the loss of my business, also my golf clubs, shooting stick and silver hip flask to help him enjoy the retirement he so richly deserves . . .'

Verity sniffed again. Ten thousand pounds couldn't buy back the face Hugh had lost through Robert's defection. Forty pieces of silver, more like!

'And to Verity Ormrod, the Meissen tea service which was once my dear wife Dorothea's pride and joy.'

Oh! Verity thought, slightly mollified. Fancy him doing that!

'And now to the remainder of the estate.' Jon Nicholson poured some water from a carafe which Tony had placed on the desk for him.

Kate laced her fingers together in her lap, unaccountably nervous suddenly. The solicitor had said the reason Grandpa had gone to him would become clear along with the contents of the will, but it hadn't happened yet. Whatever it was must be something that was covered by what the solicitor termed 'the remainder of the estate'. But for the life of her she couldn't think what it could be.

'Unfortunately my beloved only daughter has predeceased me,' Jon Nicholson read. 'This being so, it is my wish that my granddaughters Jessica, Katrina and Miranda be given the opportunity to select whatever items they choose which are of particular sentimental value to them. I sincerely hope they will be able to agree over this and trust them to respect each other's wishes in the matter. This having been done, the remainder of my possessions are to be sold and my assets realized to form the residue of my estate which is then to be divided in equal parts between all the children of my late daughter Patricia.'

'A three-way split, you mean,' Jessica interrupted. Her face was curiously taut and expressionless but her voice was hard and shrill. She had been expecting more, Kate realized, though she couldn't imagine why. Because she was the eldest, perhaps? Or because she was the only one with a family to support?

'I would have thought a three-way split was perfectly fair, Jess,' Tony said, echoing Kate's thoughts.

'Four,' Jon Nicholson said. Very firmly. Very clearly.

There was a sudden hush as if everyone in the room was collectively holding their breath, unable to believe what they had heard. Into it, Jessica hissed: 'I beg your pardon?'

John Nicholson's fingers neatened the lie of the will on the desk in front of him.

'You didn't let me finish reading the clause, Mrs Howard, but perhaps it would be better if I explained it in lay language.

Mr Holbrook believed that his daughter was, in fact, the mother of four children, and it was his wish that his estate should be divided equally amongst them.'

'That's ridiculous,' Jessica said fiercely. 'There are only three of us.'

'That's right,' Miranda echoed. 'Jess, Kate and me.'

'I'm sorry.' Jon Nicholson looked uncomfortable, confronted by a sea of faces whose expressions ranged from puzzled to frankly hostile. 'Mr Holbrook was quite explicit. He was convinced there was a fourth child who had, perhaps, been adopted, and he wanted to make provision for that child.'

The silence descended again, shocked, disbelieving. Then suddenly it shattered and they were all talking at once, gabbling and incoherent. All except Kate. There was a terrible stillness inside her, as if the whole world had stopped and her own heart with it. It was as if she was a child again, peeping through the banisters to eavesdrop on a dinner party. And she was hearing her mother's voice, a little slurred, yet somehow chillingly convincing.

'*I have to tell you I love all my children equally. All four of them.*'

She'd puzzled over it sometimes down the years though she had never mentioned it to either of her sisters. It had been her secret, her glimpse into the mysterious world of grown-ups. And, not understanding, she had come to believe that she had been mistaken, she'd misheard, misunderstood. Mummy had had too much to drink, she did sometimes. She hadn't known what she was saying. Or perhaps it had never happened at all. Perhaps when she'd gone back to bed, she'd fallen asleep and dreamed it. As time passed, she had thought about what she had overheard less and less often until eventually she did not think of it at all. Hadn't thought, now, for years and years. But suddenly here it was again. Not just a hazy memory but an assertion made by Grandpa to his solicitor . . .

'It's not fair! He can't do this to us!' Jessica's shrill voice penetrated the haze of her thoughts and suddenly she was back in the study, back with the incredulity and the wounded feelings and the outrage, a cacophony of arguing voices which had no place in what should be a solemn occasion. Without thinking, almost without knowing what she was doing, Kate leaped to her feet.

'Be quiet, all of you. We've just buried Grandpa, for goodness' sake! Can't we show a little respect for him, today at
least?'

They fell silent and Miranda, at least, had the grace to look
a little shamefaced.

'Kate's right,' Tony said. 'This isn't the time or the place.
I apologize, Mr Nicholson.'

'I'm the one who should apologize for springing this on
you,' Jon Nicholson said quietly. 'But Mr Holbrook was my
client and I was bound by his wishes.'

'What happens now?' Tony asked.

'I shall have to carry out an investigation, set enquiries in
motion with a time limit of a year in which to find this fourth
child. I take it that none of you have any knowledge of him
or her?'

They all nodded, subdued now.

'In that case I suggest we leave it at that for the moment,
and I'll meet with the immediate family privately.'

'Is it going to hold up probate?' Jessica asked sharply. 'If
so, it needs to be dealt with as a matter of urgency.'

'I agree. But I think it might be better to give everyone the
chance to think about this first.'

'There's nothing to think about! The whole idea is simply
preposterous! Grandpa must have taken leave of his senses!'

'I'm sorry.' Jon Nicholson was returning the papers to their
folder.

Kate felt a shard of sympathy for him. It couldn't have
been easy, dropping a bombshell like this. She looked around
at the shocked faces, searching for the one she had always
turned to in times of trouble.

But Ash, champion of her childhood, friend in adulthood,
was nowhere to be seen.

Three

'Well, I must say that new chef of ours has excelled himself. That's the best beef Wellington I've had in a long while, even if I do say so myself.' Jack looked around the table covered in rose-pink damask and set for eleven in the functions room of the golf club which he and Tony jointly owned and glowed with almost inordinate pleasure and pride.

As a boy his bus journey to school had taken him past the self-same golf club; sitting on the top deck, desperately trying to finish his homework or horsing around with the other boys, he had always found time to look down on the smooth green acres. At the time he couldn't understand why it drew him so; football was his game, always had been since the first time he'd kicked a ball in the field behind the row of council houses where they lived. Golf was for old men, rich men. And then one day, thinking that very thought, he had realized just what it was about the golf club that he found so attractive. It had an air of affluence which was totally lacking in his life, a feeling of wealth and success and leisure, all the good things that money could buy and the time to enjoy them.

Jack had looked and known he wanted a part of that life. He didn't want to end up like his father, out of the house at six thirty each morning, catching the coach they called 'the workmen's bus' to the electronics factory thirty miles away and not returning until the rest of the family had finished their tea in the evenings. He was always worn out by then, too tired to do anything but eat the meal which had been kept warm for him over a saucepan of simmering water on the stove, and sink into a chair to read the *Daily Mirror* and snooze for a while. This daily grind went on for fifty weeks of the year, except for bank holidays, and for it he was paid the princely sum of nine pounds ten shillings a week in a brown envelope which he handed over, unopened, to Jack's mother the moment he walked through the door each Thursday evening.

All that work, all those hours, and for what? A pittance that didn't allow him to run a car or buy a television, a vacuum cleaner, or a refrigerator. They did manage a week's holiday on alternate years in a boarding house at Weymouth or Barry Island. But that was about the extent of it. Tony had never seemed unduly bothered; he was quite satisfied with a second-hand Hercules bicycle and a wind-up gramophone instead of a proper record player. But Jack had felt resentful and vaguely ashamed, determined he was not going to spend his life working himself into the ground for enough pocket money to buy a packet of Woodbines and the occasional pint of beer.

From the top deck of the bus he had looked down on the golf club and the nice detached houses on the road beside it and had made up his mind. One day he'd have a lifestyle like that.

Well, he'd done a lot better. His football skills had given him his start; spotted by a talent scout playing for the local team, offered a trial with the City Colts, and progressing fast to League status with the first team. In his day, of course, footballers didn't earn the money they do now, but he'd done OK, and when the time came to hang up his boots he had enough put by to set himself up in business. The golf club had come on to the market the year before he retired and as soon as he heard it was up for sale, he wanted it.

He couldn't take on the running of it immediately, of course, and that was where Tony came in. Unlike Jack, Tony had worked hard at school and gone on to train as an accountant. But he was still employed by the same firm and advancement seemed unlikely. Tony didn't have the drive for it. He was the sort of chap who did his job well and still got passed over, perhaps because he did it *too* well, too quietly, never boasting or drawing attention to himself. Tony would be the ideal care-taker for the club, Jack decided. Not much good on the social side, but he would get down as often as he could to lend his charisma to the scene, and Tony was the perfect choice to manage the business side.

Initially, Tony had turned down Jack's offer. He didn't like the idea of being employed by his own brother. So Jack had come up with the idea of a partnership.

That had been the start, and without a doubt, they were a good team. They even hit it off pretty well most of the time. Four years after taking on the golf club they had opened a health hydro with affordable membership fees, and later two more, both within easy reach of London. But it was the original golf club that was closest to Jack's heart.

Now he looked around the pink-damask covered table and was glad he had suggested that the family should meet here for dinner tonight. But they were all looking so glum.

'What the hell is the matter with you all?' he demanded. 'Anyone would think you'd been to a funeral!'

He laughed loudly at his own joke, hoping to make a crack in the uneasy atmosphere. But for once no one laughed with him.

It was, thought Kate, one of the most uncomfortable meals she had ever had to endure. Whatever Uncle Jack might say, and he did have a very unfortunate way of putting things, a funeral more often than not engendered an atmosphere of solidarity that could be oddly comforting. Though thankfully her experience of funerals was limited, she had always been aware of a drawing together, the need to close ranks with those who were left, the reliving of shared memories, the hoary old jokes retold because they provided relief from the harrowing events recently lived through, the relaxing of one's guard because one was surrounded only by the people one knew best, with whom no pretence was necessary or even possible. Occasionally, after a few drinks, the wake veered towards merriment, unseemly, perhaps, yet somehow rather necessary as a release for all that suppressed emotion.

Not so today. Today had been unspeakably awful from start to finish, and there was no sense of unity now amongst the family gathered around the table. Everyone seemed to have gone into themselves for one reason or another and Kate knew it was Grandpa's will that was to blame.

Surprisingly enough it hadn't been mentioned yet. It was as if they were all avoiding the subject, knowing what a minefield it would be. So far the conversation had all been unnaturally superficial – Jessica relaying anecdotes about the boys; Miranda, who was a buyer for the health hydros, rabbiting on about the range of beauty products she wanted to introduce;

Ash talking about the oil industry and the Middle East; Liz about her business in Florida; Sandra with her sharp little digs; Jack being Jack. Only Tony had been totally silent. He seemed lost in a world of his own, managing only an abstracted response when someone spoke directly to him, or a wan smile that tore at her heart.

Poor Dad! she thought. It must have been a nightmare for him, having this assertion that Trish had another child, with all its inherent implications, brought out in such a horribly public way. Yet it couldn't have been a complete shock to him. He had been there that night when they had played the Truth Game, and Trish had said . . . what she said. If there was anything in it, he must have known, surely, or at least suspected?

As if she had picked up on Kate's thoughts, it was Jessica who raised the subject which could not have been far from any of their minds.

'We really have to talk about this will of Grandpa's,' she said, scrunching her napkin into an untidy ball and depositing it on the table in front of her. 'It's in all our interests to get it settled as quickly as possible. What did the solicitor say? A year to find the missing child? Well, it would take all that and more – considering there isn't one. And I for one don't want to wait that long.'

'Jess . . .' Adrian cautioned.

'I'm sorry, Adrian, I know you think it's vulgar of me to say so, but I'm afraid it's how I feel. How could Grandpa do this to us?'

'It's too bizarre for words,' Miranda said. 'If Mummy had another child, we'd have known about it. Or at least, Dad would.' She turned to him. 'There isn't anything we should know about this, is there, Dad?'

Kate glanced at her father, saw the greyness of his face, and held her breath.

'Come on, Tony,' Jack urged. 'For Christ's sake let's get this out in the open. Surely if there's any truth in it you must have known about it?'

Tony passed a hand across his mouth. 'All I can say is that if Trish had an illegitimate child she never told me about it.'

'There you are then! The whole thing is a load of nonsense. Poor old Robert was off his trolley.' Jack's tone was hearty, dismissive, as if what Tony had said put an end to the matter.

Janet Tanner

'You're quite sure, Daddy?' Kate asked gently.

'Of course I'm sure. If your mother had told me something like that I'd hardly be likely to forget it, would I?'

'Of course he wouldn't!' Jessica said fiercely. 'The whole thing is preposterous. Can't we just persuade the solicitor Grandpa was mistaken?'

'I hardly think so,' Kate said. 'It's there in black and white, whether you like it or not.'

'I suppose you could always contest,' Sandra said mischievously. 'On the grounds that poor Robert was gaga.'

'He wasn't gaga,' Kate said furiously. 'In any case, that would just hold things up more than ever and make a lot of unpleasantness.'

'I must say it sounds pretty gaga to me,' Miranda said. 'I can't believe Mummy had a secret child that none of us knew about. And if she had, Daddy would have known about it.'

'Why?' Sandra asked archly. 'Husbands and wives don't necessarily know everything there is to know about one another.'

'What deep dark secrets have you got that I don't know about then, Sandra?' Jack asked.

Her eyes met his, mildly challenging. 'Not me, darling. I'm not the one with secrets.'

'I thought,' Alistair said hastily, 'that adopted children had no rights to the estate of their natural family.'

'That's not the issue here though, is it?' Ash put in. 'An adopted child might not be able to make a claim on his natural parents, but a person can leave what they like to whoever they like, surely? And in any case, we don't know that the child *was* adopted. He could have been fostered, placed in care, anything.'

'How could you, Ash!' Jessica's eyes were blazing. 'How dare you suggest Mummy would not only have an illegitimate child, but simply . . . abandon it!'

'And in any case, Daddy has said there was no child,' Miranda pointed out.

'No, Tony has said he doesn't know of one. That's not quite the same thing.'

'Ash – how can you sit there and say that?'

'I'm sorry, but we seem to be going round in circles. Tony, I know this is upsetting for you, but the fact of the matter is that Robert seemed certain there was a child, and he was Trish's father. If anyone knew the truth, it seems to me it would be Robert.'

Tony pushed back his chair and got up a little unsteadily.

'You'll have to excuse me. I don't . . .' He broke off, moving towards the door with a sort of desperate determination that suggested he was barely in control of himself. Kate pushed back her own chair, worried, and intending to follow him. But Liz touched her arm.

'I'll go after him . . . make sure he's OK.'

She slipped out of her chair and Kate sat down again, breathing deeply. This whole thing was a total nightmare. She couldn't believe it was happening. And yet at the same time it was as if she'd always known that one day it would come to this.

'I think,' Jessica was saying, 'that it's absolutely necessary that we retain a united front on this and fight, fight hard. We don't want probate being held up and we certainly don't want our share of the estate reduced. God knows, it's not exactly a fortune. By the time all the bequests have been paid out and the inheritance tax, what's left will hardly be worth dividing in three, let alone four. I was hoping there'd be enough to ensure the boys got a decent education, but now—'

'Jessica!' Adrian admonished, and Kate finally exploded.

'How can you be so mercenary? How can you sit there talking about your share of the inheritance when Daddy is so upset and we've just buried Grandpa?'

'We haven't all got thriving businesses, Kate. Some of us are struggling to make ends meet . . .' She shrugged off Adrian, who was now glaring at her, clearly worried as to what she was going to say. 'It's true, Adrian. I know you don't want people to know it, but it's true. God knows where next year's school fees are going to come from. It's all very well for Kate . . .'

'Perhaps,' Kate said coldly, 'I need the money more than you think. But I'd like to think I have enough decency not to squabble and speculate at a time like this. I'd like to think I have more respect, and consideration for other people.'

'It's our inheritance!'

'No,' Kate snapped. 'It was Grandpa's money to do with as he liked. He must have known something we don't, and if

Mummy did have another child, that child is your half-brother or sister. For all you know they might need the cash more than any of us. Have you thought of that?'

'No,' Jessica said. 'I haven't. For one thing I don't believe it and for another I really don't care. I don't want to discover some seedy person I don't even know is my brother or sister and you can't expect me to care about their problems.'

'Not surprising, since you don't even care about ours. All you are concerned about, Jess, is yourself – and your sons.'

'And that's as it should be,' Jessica said shortly. 'Wait until you have a family of your own, then you'll know just how much they matter. *If* you ever have a family. *If* you can tear yourself away from your business for long enough to get married and have children.'

'Don't you think,' Ash said, 'that it might be an idea to cool this? In a minute somebody is going to say something they will regret.'

'I should think,' Sandra said sweetly, 'that has probably happened already.'

'I haven't said a single thing I'm the least bit ashamed of,' Kate said. 'Though I should be surprised if the same goes for my sister. I don't like this any more than you do, Jess, but I'm sorry, I can't just bury my head in the sand. I don't believe Grandpa was wandering when he made that will. I think he knew exactly what he was doing. And we have a duty to see that his wishes are carried out.'

'No matter how much Daddy might be hurt in the process?'

'Unfortunately, yes. I couldn't be comfortable with myself unless I did everything possible to find out the truth. I can't grab what doesn't belong to me as you seem ready to do. I shall get in touch with the solicitor tomorrow and tell him I'll help him in any way I can.'

'I suppose you fancy him. That's what's behind all this,' Miranda said spitefully.

'That,' Kate said tonelessly, 'is the nastiest remark I've heard in a long while.'

'She didn't mean it,' Ash said placatingly.

'I think she probably did, but it reflects a good deal more on her than it does on me.' Kate got up. 'I'm going home. I've had about as much of this family as I can take for one day.'

'Kate, don't go like this,' Ash said.

'It's all right, I don't include you, Ash, in my general disgust. But if I don't soon get some fresh air I think I shall suffocate, and in any case, I have to be up early in the morning.' She slipped on her jacket and left the room. Behind her the arguments started up again, the shrill, outraged voices of Jessica and Miranda dominating.

Thank God she was out of it! Thank God she didn't have to live in their pockets, though she had the feeling she would have to see a great deal more of them before this was over.

The corridor, thickly carpeted, the walls hung with pleasant, unchallenging watercolours, was empty. No sign of her father and Liz. She'd have to find them. She couldn't leave without saying goodbye. What a day. What a pig of a day! It had ended every bit as badly as it had begun.

Oh, Chris, she thought, as she so often did, where are you? What are you doing right this minute? Having a nightcap in front of the television with your wife sitting there beside you, the picture of domestic bliss . . .? But for once, utterly wretched though the thought made her feel, it lacked some of its usual sting. For once she had other things on her mind, more pressing and even more painful.

Liz had found Tony in his office, standing at the open window and taking great gulps of cold night air. She hesitated in the doorway, realizing he didn't know she was there, then tapped on the wood panelling.

'Tony, are you all right?'

He straightened, looking round and loosening his tie. 'Depends what you mean by all right. If it's my health you're enquiring after, I should think I'll survive.'

'Well, for a minute in there I did wonder,' she said, trying to lighten the situation and realizing immediately how crass she sounded. 'I'm sorry, Tony. This is all perfectly dreadful for you, isn't it?'

'It's not exactly a picnic,' he said bleakly.

He sat down heavily in the chair, elbows resting on the desk, head in hands. He looked defeated and weary, Liz thought. Earlier that day she'd been delighted to see how little he'd changed. Now, suddenly, he looked his age, and more.

'The girls are upset,' she said inadequately. 'They don't know what they're saying.'

'Oh, I think they do.' He leaned back, but his eyes still avoided hers. 'They're upset, of course. Bad enough to find out they've got a lot less coming to them than they expected, and they're probably going to have to wait for it, worse still to discover they might have a sibling they knew nothing about.'

Liz slipped into the chair opposite him.

'And have they?'

'I don't know, Liz. And that is the truth.' But there was an undertone in his voice which might have been uncertainty. Liz leaned forward.

'You never suspected she might be hiding something?'

'Oh . . .' Tony sighed, shaking his head. 'There were times when I wondered. Not that, specifically, of course. I had no reason, except . . .' He broke off, his eyes going far away, as if he were remembering something, then it was gone. 'No, it was just the way she went into herself sometimes, disappeared to a place where I couldn't reach her. But you know what Trish was like, Liz. You know how introverted she could be when the mood took her.'

'I remember her as a very sunny person.'

'Well, yes. But these moods of hers . . . they just swallowed her whole, sometimes. They'd last for days on end, she'd just walk about in a dream and cry for no reason, and pace the house when she should have been asleep.'

'And you never asked her what the matter was?' Liz asked.

'Oh, I'd ask her. I'm not totally heartless. But she'd never tell me and I didn't press her. I suppose I didn't want to rock the boat. I thought . . .'

Liz could guess what Tony had thought. That Trish was hankering after someone else. His own brother. Tony knew, just as she did, that Jack had been Trish's first love. No doubt, loving her as he had, he had thought he could live with that. Just as long as he didn't have to hear from her own lips that she still cared for Jack, wanted him enough to sink into the depths of depression.

'I thought letting her work through it on her own was for the best.' Tony laughed bitterly. 'But I was wrong, wasn't I? If I'd talked to her, tried to help her, perhaps things wouldn't have ended the way they did.'

He bowed his head and Liz leaned across the table, taking his hands in hers.

'It probably wouldn't have made any difference at all,' she said. 'I'm sure it was an accident, just as the inquest found. Trish slipped on leaves and fell into the lake. I accept she'd probably been drinking and was too woozy to save herself. But you'd done everything you could to cure her of that.'

'It wasn't an accident,' Tony said heavily.

Liz sighed. She knew what Tony meant. Truth to tell she'd never really believed Trish's accident had been an accident at all; that the coroner had gone for the verdict he had in the absence of any evidence to the contrary out of deference to the family's feelings.

'You still can't blame yourself, Tony,' she said. 'If Trish did take her own life – and I don't accept that she did – then her mind was made up and there wouldn't have been anything you could do to stop her.'

Tony shook his head. 'There must have been something I could have done. If I'd realized just how desperate she was . . . tried to help her instead of simply ignoring it. I wasn't there when she needed me. I failed her.'

Liz bit her lip. 'I guess we all failed her. But it's too late to worry about that now. Twelve years too late.'

'Why the hell did Robert have to do this now?' Tony exploded suddenly. 'Why couldn't he let her rest in peace?'

'Knowing Robert, I expect he did what he felt he had to do.'

'Probably. But I just don't understand. What are the girls going to think? Hearing that their mother . . .'

'The girls, as you call them, are grown women. They know, just as you do, that Trish was only human.'

'As if it wasn't bad enough that she committed suicide.'

'I know.' She squeezed his hands again. 'But they loved her Tony. In the end that's all that matters. Whatever the outcome of all this, they'll get over it, and they won't love her any the less because of it.'

'I suppose you're right.' He sighed, getting a grip on himself. 'This solicitor chap will investigate, but he won't find anything. How could he?'

'Exactly. If you don't know and I don't know, who on earth would? There's probably nothing to find out anyway.'

But she didn't believe it, and she knew he didn't either.

A tap at the door. Kate was standing there, looking embarrassed.

'I just came to say goodnight.' She hesitated, looking at Tony anxiously. 'Are you all right, Daddy?'

'I'm fine,' Tony said. 'Liz and I have been talking, that's all.'

'I really do have to go.'

'Me too.' Liz stood up. 'I think I'm suffering from jet lag. I'll ring for a taxi.'

'There's no need for that. I can give you a lift,' Kate offered.

'Oh, that would be great,' Liz said. 'I'll just get my coat.'

In the doorway Kate turned to look back at her father. 'Daddy, are you sure you're OK?'

'I told you. I'm fine. Just get off, Kate. Don't worry about me.'

But that, Kate thought, was easier said than done.

'Daddy is really upset, isn't he?' Kate said.

'Yes, he is rather.'

'I must take my share of the blame for that, I suppose, for giving credence to what Grandpa said. I wouldn't upset Daddy for the world, but I can't just dismiss it the way Jess and Miranda seem to want to.'

'No, that wouldn't be you, Kate. I'm sure your father knows that.'

They were back in town, parked outside the hotel where Liz was staying.

'Liz, you don't know anything about this, do you?' Kate asked. 'I mean, you were Mummy's friend . . .'

'No, this has been as much of a shock to me as to everyone else.' Liz hesitated. 'I can't help thinking, though, it might be best for everyone if it was just allowed to die the death. Even if there is a child, what chance is there of finding him – or her – after all these years? It's only going to cause untold misery to everyone, perhaps unearth all kinds of things that are best kept hidden.'

'What kind of things?' Kate asked sharply.

'Oh, I don't know. But everyone has skeletons in their cupboards. I don't imagine this family is any different.'

In the light thrown by the streetlamps, Kate looked at her narrowly.

'You *do* know something, don't you?'

'No,' Liz said, too quickly. 'I just think it's best to leave the past where it belongs.'

'Grandpa didn't think so, obviously. And I can't help thinking it would be what Mummy would have wanted too. If she did have an illegitimate child and gave it up, I think she lived to regret it. Perhaps in the end it was what drove her to do . . . what she did. And I feel we owe it to her to try to make amends.'

'You don't think . . .' Liz hesitated, uncertain how to put this. 'You don't think that perhaps the living are rather more important than the dead? Your mother is gone now, Kate. Nothing can touch or hurt her any more. But your father, your sisters . . .' She broke off again. She had been going to extend the list of people who might be hurt if this Pandora's box was opened, but this wasn't the right moment. Say too much too soon and it would only make things worse rather than better.

'I know, I know.' Kate sighed. 'But I overheard Mummy say something years ago. You must have heard her too. You were there, at a dinner party. I was only about six or seven, and I was on the stairs, eavesdropping. She said she loved all her children equally – all four of them.'

'Oh my God,' Liz said softly. 'Yes, I remember that night. And you were listening to everything that was said?'

'Yes. I haven't thought about it for years, but now it makes sense. Though I can't understand why Daddy should be denying all knowledge. After that outburst, I'd have thought he'd have questioned her at least, if he didn't know anything about another child.'

'Trish was rather drunk that night,' Liz said. 'He probably didn't take too much notice of what she said.'

'Well, maybe. But still . . .' Kate was silent for a moment. 'Anyway, I do believe that if we have a half-brother or sister somewhere we should try to find them. I guess they'd be in their mid to late thirties by now, which narrows it a bit.' A sudden thought struck her. 'Oh my God! The woman at the funeral! The one nobody knew, who dropped a flower in Grandpa's grave . . . you don't think it could be *her*?'

'If it was, there'd hardly be a mystery,' Liz reasoned. 'It would mean, surely, that your grandfather had already found her, or she had found him, so he would have included her by name in the will.'

'Not necessarily. Perhaps he'd found her only just before

he had his stroke and didn't have a chance to get it altered. She'd be about the right age, wouldn't she?'

'Perhaps. But there could be another reason entirely for her being there. I expect there were things about your grandfather you didn't know too,' Liz said gently.

'Oh . . . this just gets worse and worse!'

'I'm going to have to go to bed,' Liz said suddenly. 'I'm exhausted.'

'Sorry . . .'

'It's all right. You wanted to talk to me about your business and we haven't even touched on that.'

Kate grimaced. 'Suddenly that seems very unimportant. It won't be in the morning, I suppose, when I have to face it all again, but right now it's sort of unreal. So is everything else really. It's like a bad dream.'

'I know. Go home, Kate, and try to get some sleep. Give me a call tomorrow and we'll arrange a meeting.' Liz unfastened her seat belt, got out of the car and stood watching as the tail lights disappeared down the street.

She felt she needed a drink but it was too late to buy one now, and the White Hart didn't run to minibars in the bedroom. In any case, she wasn't sure it would help. Jet-lagged and exhausted she might be, but she thought it would be a very long time before she was going to get to sleep.

As Kate left the town, turning on to the almost deserted road home, she heard her mobile phone begin to ring. She pulled into the side, rummaged in her bag and clicked the 'receive' button.

'Kate – it's me.'

'Chris!'

'Just a quick call. Anna's in the bath, but she might come down at any time. How was it?'

'Oh, Chris, it was awful. I can't talk about it now. Will I see you tomorrow?'

'I'm not sure. I might be able to get out of the office for a half-hour.'

'*Great.*'

'Don't be like that, Kate. You know the score. And I will try, I promise. If only you knew how much I want to see you.'

'If you'd only get around to telling Anna we wouldn't have

to sneak around like this.' To her annoyance, Kate found she was very close to tears.

'I will tell her. When the moment's right. How many times do I have to say it? Look – I'm going to have to go. I think I can hear the water running away. I'll try to see you tomorrow. Love you.'

And he was gone. Kate banged the mobile down on the seat beside her and put her foot down hard on the accelerator. She shouldn't be driving this fast on a dark narrow road, especially when her eyes were full of tears. But quite honestly she didn't care. It was the only release she had for all her pent-up emotions.

Four

L iz had been right in thinking she wouldn't sleep. She had
run a bath and soaked in it, trying to relax, but it hadn't
worked. The muscles of her neck and chest still ached with
tension and her mind was buzzing. She felt dreadfully sorry
for Kate and for Tony and she could even feel sympathy for
Jessica and Miranda. They had not behaved as well as they
should over all this, but she could see what a shock it had
been to them.

Most of all, though, her thoughts were with Trish. The deep-
rooted sense of guilt had never quite left her in the years since
Trish's death. Now, in the light of the revelations the day had
brought, it was sharper than ever.

I wasn't here when you needed me, she thought. Something
happened that changed you for ever, something that in the
end you couldn't live with. You couldn't bring yourself to tell
Tony the truth, but if I had been here, I think you would have
told me because we were always close. And besides . . . I knew
the way it was with you and Jack. If you hadn't had to suffer
alone, perhaps you would be alive today.

Perhaps. So many imponderables, so many things she
could only guess at, but one indisputable truth. Trish had
been in love with one brother, married the other. Had she
also had his child? Was that what was on her mind when
she descended into her silent black moods? Had Tony
guessed, and that was the reason he had never delved too
deeply into the cause of them? Was he, even now, trying to
avoid the truth? She didn't know. All she could see was the
sixteen-year-old Trish, her face aglow with love for Jack
Morton.

'Liz, what do you think? He's asked me out! Oh, Liz, isn't
it super? I wonder where he'll take me. Not that it matters.

I really don't care. What should I wear, though? My gingham skirt and the three-tier petticoat underneath? Or do you think my pedal pushers would be better? I don't want to look *fast* . . .'

'I don't suppose he'll even notice what you're wearing,' Liz said. 'Boys don't.'

They were in Trish's bedroom. Liz was staying over as she often did at weekends and the two girls would talk long into the night when Robert and Dorothea thought they were asleep.

'Besides,' Liz added, 'I should think you've got more to worry about than what to wear. Such as, what is your father going to say when he knows it's Jack Morton you're going out with?'

Trish's face fell. 'Oh, no! He's not going to let me go, is he?'

'A professional footballer? No, I don't think he is.'

Robert was notoriously protective of his pretty daughter with her big blue eyes and cute little tip-tilt nose. Liz had found out just how protective when he'd driven past one Sunday afternoon a year earlier just as the two of them were leaving the Black Cat Coffee Bar. They were not supposed to go there, they knew. The Black Cat had once been a transport café, but was now the haunt of the wilder youth of the district and gangs of leather-clad bikers. It was harmless fun, drinking endless cups of espresso coffee and listening to the hit-parade records on the jukebox, but the place did have something of a reputation and Trish's parents had barred it as unsuitable.

That Sunday afternoon they were lingering outside chatting to a group of boys when Robert happened to pass by. The big grey Humber Hawk lurched to a stop and reversed back along the road, tyres squealing.

'What do you two think you are doing?' Robert demanded in a voice like thunder.

The lads dispersed like magic, leaving Trish and Liz shaking in their shoes.

'We were just having a coffee,' Trish gulped.

'You can have a coffee at home.' Robert threw open the rear door of the car. 'Get in, both of you.'

He drove them home without another word, and they thought

the worst of it was over. They were wrong. Back at the Cedars they were ordered into the drawing room and Dorothea was summoned.

'They've been in that café place,' Robert told her. His fury was still barely contained. 'I caught them with Teddy boys.'

'They weren't Teddy boys, Mr Holbrook,' Liz said, feeling bound to explain. 'Teddy boys have DA haircuts and wear drapes and brothel-creeper shoes.'

'*What* shoes, did you say?' Dorothea looked shocked. 'And what is a DA haircut?'

Liz bit her lip. After the gaffe about the brothel-creepers she certainly didn't want to explain what DA stood for.

'You will not go there again,' Robert said. 'I will not have my daughter associating with boys like that. Do you understand?'

They nodded, chastened, though they felt Robert was being very unfair. Possibly Dorothea thought so too but with Robert in this mood she knew better than to say so.

They did go to the Black Cat again, of course; they were just careful not to get caught.

The following year, when they were sixteen, the rules were relaxed a little. The Black Cat was still forbidden territory, but they were allowed to go to the Piccolino, which, having no jukebox and no bikers, was considered by Robert to be permissible. Besides espresso coffee it served snacks – Liz and Trish particularly liked the sardines on toast that dripped with butter, and the spaghetti Bolognese topped with frizzled cheese and served in earthenware bowls. And it was here that Trish had met Jack Morton.

Jack had come in with three other boys, all extremely 'dishy', with hair that looked as if it had been styled rather than cut into a short-back-and-sides by the local barber or greased into a DA, and instead of the usual blue jeans they wore cavalry twill trousers, tweed jackets and white shirts. Trish was instantly smitten, though Liz had her reservations. Jack Morton was a little too sure of himself for her liking.

Over their second cup of coffee, the boys started chatting them up and Liz realized why he seemed to think he was so great. Though he was a local lad, Jack was signed up with a professional football club in the city, some twenty miles away. Though she knew very little about football she had heard of

Jack Morton; everyone in town had. He was regarded as the hottest young talent in the team.

But because he was local, she also knew that he came from the not-very-salubrious council estate. Cavalry tweeds or not, he was not the sort of boy Robert would consider suitable for Trish, and the fact that he was a professional footballer just about put the tin lid on it, as her mother sometimes said. There was no way Robert would allow Trish to go out with him, and Liz hoped for all their sakes that he wouldn't ask her. But he did.

'You'll have to help me!' Trish said to Liz. 'If I can't go out with him, I'll just die! Please Liz, think of something! If you're my friend . . . please, please!'

Though Trish was less than happy about it, they came up with a plan. Pretending to go to the tennis club, they left the Cedars at six thirty dressed in their whites and carrying their racquets. But unknown to her mother, Trish also took with her a leopard-print top with a deep V-neck at the front and a stand-up collar at the back, her pedal pushers and a bag containing blue eye shadow, shocking pink lipstick and a cake of mascara that you had to spit on. She changed in the Ladies, half afraid someone who knew Robert might come in and catch her at it, and so aquiver with excitement and nervousness that she had to have three goes before she got the mascara on without leaving black smudges under her eyes. Then she went off to meet Jack Morton and Liz spent the evening in the clubhouse hoping no one would ask her why she was on her own.

Trish had said she would be back by ten, but she wasn't. Nor even a quarter past. Liz was very jumpy; she was beginning to think Jack Morton must have abducted Trish in his smart little Sprite, until Trish appeared, bubbling and excited.

'I have had the most fantastic time! We went for a drive up to Deer Leap.'

'And?'

'What do you mean . . . and?'

'He didn't try anything, I hope.'

'No, of course not,' Trish said, but Liz noticed she went a bit pink, and thought she might not be telling the truth.

'Are you going to see him again?'

'Yes, on Sunday. Oh, Liz, I think I'm in love . . .'

*   *   *

It couldn't last, of course. Jack Morton wasn't used to girls who had a ten-thirty curfew to meet. He began to lose patience and Trish and Liz had to be ever more devious in their efforts to fool Robert and Dorothea. The solution was for Trish to stay the night with Liz instead of the other way round; Liz's mother seldom asked questions. But Liz was beginning to get fed up with the whole charade, and with Trish's obsession with Jack Morton.

'You're going to have to tell your parents,' she told Trish. 'We can't go on like this for ever.'

'I couldn't!' Trish said, appalled. 'They'd go ape if they knew. They'd stop me seeing him for sure. And if I don't see him, I'll just die!'

'I've had enough of it,' Liz said. 'I'm not telling any more lies.'

'Liz . . . please, *please*!'

Liz, feeling utterly trapped, was trying to get up the courage to tell Trish that she was absolutely not going to cover for her any more when the decision was taken out of her hands. Jack had decided that pretty as Trish was, she wasn't a whole lot of fun and he'd be better off going out with girls who knew the score and who didn't have parents who imposed restrictions on them. He stopped calling Trish, and for a while, at least, it was over.

They had left school when it began all over again. Liz was going to a college of art to do a course in interior design and Trish had a place in a local secretarial college. For the first time in years they had their own separate lives, but they still kept in touch, writing long letters, talking on the telephone, and spending their holidays together.

When Trish wrote that she had met up with Jack again and they were giving things another go, Liz's heart sank. But at least now she did not have to be involved in the subterfuge; Trish had reached an age where her parents no longer insisted she live by their rules, and in any case Liz was too far away to be able to serve as an alibi.

At first Trish was ecstatic; she was still crazy about Jack. But before long her letters were full of tales of woe and Liz felt sure it was going to end in tears. All too often he let her down or even failed to turn up for a date, and Trish was miserably certain he was going out with other girls besides herself. In particular, she was worried about Sandra Barlow.

Sandra had been brought up on the same council estate as Jack, but at the age of fifteen she had gone to London to dance or model, no one was quite sure which, and there was a certain amount of gossip which said that what she was doing was even less respectable. But whatever might be said about her, there was an aura of glamour about Sandra and when she came home to visit, dressed to the nines and swinging a long umbrella (the ultimate fashion accessory), everyone sat up and took notice.

Jack had been seen in town with Sandra on more than one occasion, Trish told Liz, so distraught that she was in tears on the telephone.

'I don't know why you put up with the way he treats you,' Liz told her. 'You should tell him to take a running jump. He's never going to change, and you'll never meet anyone else if you just keep hanging on for him.'

'I don't want anyone else,' Trish said tearfully. 'At least he always comes back to me.'

'You'd do better to go out with Tony,' Liz suggested. Tony Morton, Jack's younger brother by a year, had taken a fancy to Trish, and Liz was of the opinion he was a much safer bet.

'I don't want to go out with Tony. He's nice, and I do like him, but . . . oh, he's not Jack.'

Liz sighed and gave up. She had tried very hard to be understanding, but she had had almost more than she could take of the never-ending saga. And then something happened that changed her life, and everything, for ever. She fell in love with the unlikeliest, most unsuitable person imaginable. She fell in love with Robert Holbrook, Trish's father.

She had always been very fond of him, of course, even though he was so strict with her and Trish. But it came as a total shock to her when she realized the feelings she had for him were far from the ones she should have for the father of her best friend. She couldn't stop thinking about him; he seemed to have got inside her head and under her skin. All she wanted was to be in his presence, but when she was, it wasn't enough. Never enough. For the first time Liz understood the obsession that kept Trish hankering after Jack no matter how badly he treated her. But now, more than ever, she didn't want to think about Trish. It was too uncomfortable by far.

The crazy fantasy had started when Robert had called her one evening on the communal telephone which served all the student bedsits in the house where she lived in term time and asked if she would like her first professional commission. At first, Liz had thought he was joking. In fact, he was perfectly serious. His building firm had won the contract for a small development of houses on the outskirts of town and now that the first one was nearing completion he wanted to decorate and furnish it as a show house. And he had thought it would be an ideal first step on the ladder for Liz, who was now in the second year of her two-year course.

Liz was overawed by the prospect, but also excited. She took a train home that weekend, Robert met her at the station and drove her straight to the new development, much of it still a sea of mud, littered with cement mixers, piles of sand and mounds of bricks. But as he had said, one house was nearing completion, a square, impressive-looking house with a nod towards the Georgian. Liz had spent the entire journey studying brochures and the file of cuttings she'd assembled over the past two years, pictures of interiors of all kinds clipped from magazines, articles about the latest trends, selecting and rejecting colour schemes, ambiences. Now she went from room to room making copious notes, her excitement growing.

'White units would really give the kitchen a feeling of space and light . . . a roller blind at the window, I think . . . blue, perhaps. And magnolia for the walls. The lighting will be important and it needs to look good from the outside as well as the inside, so that when prospective buyers come on a dark evening that first glimpse through the window makes them feel they really want to live here.'

Robert smiled. 'You see, Liz? I knew you could do it. Now, I'm going to take you out for a spot of lunch. Dorothea and Trish have gone to Bristol shopping. So I thought we could go to the Dog and Duck. They do quite a reasonable bar snack.'

Already drunk on the euphoria of working on her first proper prospect, Liz giggled. Strict Robert taking her to a pub!

As they left the house, balancing along the plank laid across the unmade-up garden, Liz almost slipped. Robert's arm shot out to steady her and in that moment, something very odd happened to her heart. Not just her heart, but every one of her senses. It was over so quickly it might never have happened at all, but the sudden awareness made her legs go weak so that she almost stumbled again. She simply could not believe the way she was feeling, as if she had just fallen off a very high cliff. As they ate chicken-in-the-basket in the Dog and Duck she found herself looking at him shyly through quite different eyes. She'd always thought of him simply as Trish's father, someone of a different generation; now she realized he didn't look old or fatherly at all. He was still handsome, his face weathered to a healthy tan from spending so much time out of doors, his thick dark hair streaked with silver, which made him look distinguished. He was wearing cords and a waxed jacket over a roll-neck sweater which, she thought suddenly, made him look hunky. And there was something utterly *solid* about him that was lacking in boys of her own age.

She told herself, of course, that she had gone mad, it was just too ridiculous for words, but all the telling in the world made no difference. Liz just couldn't stop thinking about him and remembering the way she had felt when his arm had gone around her to stop her from falling. She threw herself into her plans for the show house not just because it was an exciting project now, but because she was doing it for him and nothing mattered but that she should do a really good job and impress him with her flair.

At first all went well. Liz's college tutors allowed her to concentrate on the show house instead of the scheduled assignment because it was real, and offered advice when she needed it. And then, quite suddenly, everything was going wrong. The fabric she had ordered for the master bedroom was no longer obtainable, there was a delay in delivery of the carpet for the lounge, the colour of the emulsion for the bathroom walls was ever-so-slightly out of kilter with the sanitary ware so that, to Liz's eyes, at least, it jarred horribly.

'I've messed it up,' she said to Robert, standing in the bathroom with her hands over her face because she couldn't bear to look at that horrid clash of colour. 'I'm really sorry. You trusted me and I've messed it all up.'

'Of course you haven't,' he said. 'You've done a great job.'

'No, I haven't,' she said, and burst into tears.

'It's going to be fine,' he promised her, but it was as if the bubble of excitement and emotional euphoria of the past weeks had suddenly burst, and she couldn't stop crying.

'Oh, come here, you silly girl. There's nothing to cry about.' He pulled her towards him so that her face was buried in his chest, the zip of his waxed jacket biting into her cheek and Liz was suddenly aware of nothing but the electric impulses that were darting through her veins. She burrowed into him, tightening her arms around his waist, aware now of nothing but her longing to be close to him. He was stroking her hair; his mouth pressed against her forehead. The world seemed to stand still; it was as if she were suspended in space. She lifted her face, looking up at him, waiting for him to kiss her, and . . .

He released her, so abruptly that it shocked her and the space between them became a yawning chasm. 'Time I was getting you back to your train.' There was a hard edge to his voice that reminded her of the tone he used to use when he was angry with Trish. Liz wanted to cry again, but pride forbade it. She bit down fiercely on her lip and turned away, gathering herself together when all she wanted to do was curl up, crawl into a hole and hide. Embarrassment was flooding through her in hot waves. She'd given herself away. He was going to ignore it, but he knew how she felt about him. How awful was that? It was only years later that Liz wondered if he'd felt that electric attraction too, and it was himself, and not her at all, that he was angry with.

Shame was her overriding emotion now; though she was still crazy about him she couldn't bring herself to face him. Going back to complete the furnishing of the house was torture; the ease between them had gone for ever, replaced by a wall of awkwardness. Liz knew Trish wondered why she didn't go home much any more, but there was no way on earth she could tell her. She simply made excuses, and the closeness she and Trish had always shared suffered too. And still, though she knew it was hopeless blind infatuation which could never go anywhere she couldn't get Robert out of her head, or her heart.

The opportunity for a clean break came as a complete surprise. One of her tutors had a friend in Florida who was looking for a young assistant, someone with talent and flair, and the tutor recommended Liz without hesitation. Liz wasn't sure she wanted to go to Florida, but it was a chance she couldn't turn down, and besides it would place her on the other side of the world from Robert. If I can't get over him there, I never will, Liz thought. She went.

She and Trish still corresponded, though not as often as they had used to. The endless saga of Trish and Jack Morton continued, the most on-off relationship Liz could imagine, and eventually Trish wrote that Jack had married Sandra Barlow. But to Liz's surprise the tone of the letter was more resigned than heartbroken, as if all emotion had been wrung out of her by the turbulent years and she no longer cared very much one way or the other.

It was still a surprise, though, when she got engaged to Tony, and Liz hoped that Trish was going to marry him for the right reasons. When the date was set, Trish asked Liz to be her bridesmaid, and she went home, terrified at the prospect of having to face Robert again. But somehow it was oddly all right.

As for Trish, she seemed happy enough with Tony, bright, sparkling like crystal, the old Trish, basking in his adoration. But there was also a reserve that had not been there before, something hard and hidden. Trish had changed in a way that Liz found inexplicable.

Now, soaking in her bath, Liz thought of it, and knew that the change in Trish had come about because of something which had happened to her, and of which she, Liz, knew nothing.

A child. Trish had borne a child and given it away, and the experience had made her a different person. I wasn't there when she needed me, Liz thought. I wasn't there for her then, and I wasn't there for her ever again. For nigh on twenty years she lived with all that pain bottled up inside and no one to share it with and in the end she couldn't take it any more. Trish died in the cold, murky waters of the lake, and her secret died with her.

Except that it hadn't. Robert's will had opened up a Pandora's box and all kinds of mischief were escaping to destroy the carefully constructed illusion. Bad enough for the children to discover that their mother had a past of which they knew nothing and they had a sibling of whom they knew nothing. But for Tony the revelations must be infinitely worse.

Liz was horribly certain that if Trish had given birth to an illegitimate child, there was only one person who could have been the father.

Jack. The love of Trish's youth, perhaps the love of her life.

Jack, Tony's own brother.

Five

The Westminster clock on the mantelpiece downstairs was chiming midnight. Wendy threw back the duvet, got out of bed for the third time in the last thirty minutes and padded across to the window. The curtains were still half-open; she'd left them that way so that she'd see the moment a car turned into the close, but outside everything was eerily still in the orange glow of the streetlamps. No one walking their dog for the last time before going to bed; no one putting out milk bottles; no lights in any of the other houses; no cars. And no Tim.

Where on earth *was* he? Wendy wondered distractedly. It was four hours now since he'd gone out, taking her car. He'd made the excuse that he wanted to buy cigarettes, but Wendy had suspected that it was really a fresh bottle of whisky he'd been desperate for. The one he'd been letting into this morning was standing empty beside the waste bin in the kitchen.

She hadn't wanted him to take her car; she suspected he was probably over the limit.

'Why don't you walk?' she'd suggested. 'It's not far to the off-licence, and it's quite a nice night.'

But as usual these days he had become stroppy. 'Surely you don't begrudge me borrowing your bloody car? Bad enough I have to ask. What's it coming to, eh? No job, no car . . .'

'Of course I don't mind you using my car, but you have been drinking,' Wendy said tentatively.

'Oh, give it a rest! You sound like a cracked record. I'm not drunk, nowhere near. And I've had it up to here with you suggesting I am.'

'Oh, for heaven's sake!' Suddenly Wendy had been too weary to argue any more, and in any case, he had already helped himself to her keys from the hook in the kitchen and was on his way out of the door.

Now, however, she wished fervently she'd tried a bit harder to stop him. Supposing he'd had an accident? Or been breathalysed? Or both? She guessed she'd have heard by now if it had been serious, but if Tim lost his licence on top of everything else it would be the last straw, and besides, if he was fined, where on earth would they find the money to pay it? With only her wage nowadays they were stretched to the limit. At least she had the legacy from Robert when the will was finalized, but there were so many things they needed. And she could well imagine how Tim would resent her paying it out of that. She hadn't even plucked up the courage to tell him about it yet. She thought he would resent that too.

Wendy chewed her lip, beside herself with anxiety. No point going back to bed. She'd never get to sleep until he got in though she was so tired she felt slightly sick and her head had begun to ache, an ominous throb and a red-hot needle piercing her right eyebrow, which usually heralded the start of a migraine.

She wasn't very warm, either. She fetched her dressing gown from the hook on the bedroom door and slipped it on. The bedroom was illuminated suddenly by the lights of a car heading straight down the close. She dived back to the window, heart pumping with relief. But the car did a swooping arc in the turnaround and passed her gate, pulling up outside one of the houses further down. Not her car. Not Tim. Just one of the Gunning girls being dropped off by a friend after a night out.

Where *was* he? Something had happened. It must have done.

She went into the kitchen, swallowed some aspirin with a glass of water and returned to the window. Was that car headlights? No, just the tree at the end of the close blowing in the wind and making the light of the streetlamp splinter and shiver.

'How can you do this to me?' she whispered through gritted teeth. It didn't used to be like this. Is it any wonder I can't stop thinking about Ash and wishing . . .

But in her heart she knew it wasn't just Tim's behaviour that was making her long for Ash. It was that he was special. Always had been. Her eyes misted a little, and she found herself remembering the first time she had met Ash Morton.

It was the Christmas when she was seven years old. She, Verity and Hugh had been invited to the Cedars for one of the big family parties that used to be an annual event in those days. The house had been overflowing with people she scarcely knew because she and her parents had only just moved back into the area, though their roots were here and Dorothea Holbrook, whom she was expected to call 'Auntie Dorrie', was a distant cousin of Hugh's. Across the years, Wendy found she could remember every detail – the smell of oranges and pine-cones, the log fires blazing, the tall tree with its twinkling coloured lights and bags of chocolate coins in silver paper and delicate glass ornaments that shattered if you so much as touched them, the cards propped up on every available surface, the sack of presents which Robert, dressed as Father Christmas, would distribute, the crackers and indoor fireworks and scraps of tissue paper which burned away to make fragile flowers of ash. And the games. Running from room to room trying to collect the pieces of pictures which had been cut up, jigsaw fashion and scattered about the house, 'Man and his Object', 'I went to market and I bought something beginning with . . .' Charades, sardines . . . Oh, yes, sardines.

She was hiding in one of the bedrooms, squashed under the bed between a tin trunk and a pile of blankets zipped into a plastic storage bag, hoping she wouldn't be found too soon because she really wasn't very good at games and it would be nice to do well just this once, when she heard somebody come into the room. She lay very still, listening to whoever it was opening cupboards and closing them again. And then a bit of fluff got up her nose and before she could stop herself, she'd sneezed.

The person stopped again, right by the bed. She knew it was one of the boys because she could see his brown lace-up shoes. Then the coverlet was lifted and she saw Ash's face peering in at her. 'Found you,' he said.'

She was glad it was Ash, or Ashley as his mother Sandra called him. His brother Alistair, who was younger than she was, had pulled her pigtails when he thought nobody was looking; she didn't much fancy being squashed under the bed with *him*. Or, truth to tell, any of the other boys who had been invited to make the party go with a swing. Wendy wasn't used to boys. She had no brothers and since she went to a convent school there were no boys there either, except in the nursery class.

'Move over then,' he said.

It wasn't easy; she tried to push the bag of blankets to one side, but it was squashy and heavy, and Ash moved the trunk instead. Just as he was doing it they heard footsteps on the landing, and he dived under the bed with such haste she was almost suffocated by the blankets.

'Sorry,' Ash said, when the footsteps had gone away again. 'I didn't hurt you, did I?'

'No,' she said, suddenly feeling very excited and warm inside without knowing why.

'I'm Ash,' he said.

'I know. Where do you go to school?'

'The local primary. What about you?'

'The convent school. I went to a convent school in the Midlands where we lived before, too, but it was nicer than this one.'

'Do those weird nuns teach you?'

'Yes. Why do you think they're weird?'

'Those funny things they wear. They look like black bats.'

'Ours don't wear black, they wear grey. And the ones who teach don't wear habits and wimples. Just ordinary skirts and a veil.'

'Still weird.'

'I suppose. I don't know why they send me to a convent. We're not Catholic or anything. And when the girls who are go to Mass those who aren't have to stay in the classroom and have an extra lesson.' She paused. 'I haven't made any friends yet, either. All the others know one another, and I don't.'

More footsteps outside. They lay very still. The footsteps went away and Wendy was glad. It was nice here, talking to Ash. Much nicer than being downstairs with all those people she didn't know very well.

'This is fun, isn't it?' she said.

'Is it? I think it's a stupid game really. But we always have to play it.'

'Oh,' Wendy said, feeling crushed.

They were discovered soon afterwards by Jessica and Katrina, who were charging about together. Katrina banged her head on the iron bedstead and started crying loudly and that was the end of the game. They had to go downstairs for tea – ham sandwiches and mince pies and thick slices of Christmas cake. Afterwards Aunt Dorrie played carols on the piano and the all had to sing, Uncle Jack told a joke she didn't understand and Auntie Sandra was cross with him, and Auntie Trish, who was very fat because, Jessica had told her, she was soon going to have another baby, had asked her all sorts of questions about her new school and how she liked it, and Alistair had pulled her pigtails again, and all the time she had looked longingly at Ash and wished they were still alone upstairs, squashed under the bed.

It was, she thought, a desire which had not faded with the years, but only intensified. But it had been a very long time before anything like it happened again.

They saw one another, of course, at family gatherings, but their paths really didn't cross that much. Ash passed his eleven-plus and went to the local grammar school, Wendy stayed at the convent, moving from the preparatory into the high school. At sixteen, she left and got a job with an insurance company, a little before Ash, who was a year older, went off to university. Wendy still idolized him from afar, but it wasn't until Trish's funeral that they had got together.

Wendy hadn't wanted to go but Verity had insisted that she must. It was a terrible occasion; Uncle Tony and the girls were all understandably in deep shock, and the tragedy of what had happened had numbed everyone so that they barely knew what to say to one another. When they had returned to the house, Wendy had escaped into the garden and Ash found her there, kicking at the leaves that had begun to fall from the trees to make deep drifts on the lawn.

They stayed there a long while, talking and in a funny sort of way, it was just like being under the bed together again; the two of them isolated from the rest of the family. They talked more deeply than they had ever done before, made ruminative, perhaps, by the awful thing that had happened to Trish. And when Verity appeared in the doorway, calling for Wendy, Ash touched her arm.

'I'd like to see you again, Wendy. Shall we go out for a meal or a drink sometime?'

Wendy's heart sang. She could feel the fair skin of her neck growing pink, but for once in her life she didn't care.

'I'd like that,' she said.

The two years that Wendy was with Ash were the happiest of her life. He was doing his degree at Exeter, so it wasn't that far away, and they were able to spend most weekends together. Though she could hardly believe that someone as wonderful as Ash wanted to be with *her*, yet at the same time there was a sort of rightness about it, an inevitability, as if it had always been meant to be. He even talked about getting engaged when he finished at university, and asked Wendy what sort of ring she'd like. They looked at some in jeweller's shop windows, though she never actually got around to trying one on. That was in her imagination only, how the sapphire and diamond cluster would look on her finger, and how happy she would be when Ash slipped it on.

Then, just when all seemed set fair, her whole world fell apart. Ash wrote her a letter – *a letter, for goodness' sake!* – calling the whole thing off. He'd realized it was all wrong. *They* were wrong. He was too young to be tied down. They both needed their space . . . And that was it.

Wendy was absolutely devastated, and even more so when he finished his course and left to start a job in the Middle East with an oil company without even coming home. It was over. There was a gaping hole in her life, and a place in her heart that no one else could ever fill.

'Oh, shit!' Wendy said now, wondering how it could still hurt so much when plainly Ash didn't give a fig for her. But it did, oh, it did!

There were lights on the road outside; lost in her thoughts she hadn't even noticed them. Now she realized a car was pulling into the drive – her car. Tim was home, thank God! At least he hadn't been involved in an accident. Wendy sighed, retied the sash of her dressing gown, and went down to the hall to greet him.

'What the hell are you doing, still up?' Tim demanded when he closed the door behind him and saw her standing there.

'I couldn't sleep,' she said. 'I was worried about you. You only went out to buy cigarettes, and that was hours ago.'

'Oh, putting the stop watch on me now! I don't need your permission to change my mind, do I?'

'Of course not. But I thought something had happened to you. You'd been drinking, and you were driving my car.'

'Now we're getting down to it! It was your precious car you were worried about, not me.'

'No!' Wendy said crossly. 'Well, yes, I was hoping you hadn't done anything to it. We'd be sunk if you did. But it was *you* I was worried about.'

Tim snorted, taking off his jacket and aiming it at the hall-stand. It missed, falling into a heap on the floor, but he didn't bother to pick it up, just left it there and pushed past her to go into the front room. Wendy followed. Tim had the side-board open and he was getting out a fresh bottle of whisky. So, he'd had one here all the time. That hadn't been the reason he'd gone out.

'Where have you been?' she asked.

He poured some whisky into a tumbler and gulped at it like a man who has just found an oasis after being lost in the desert.

'If you must know, I went to see your precious Ash. Oh, there's no need to look so worried. He wasn't there. None of them were. The house was in darkness – well, not quite dark-ness, those stupid lights that they have on time switch kept going on and off at different windows. But they were all out.'

'I think they were having a family meal at the country club.'

'Oh, a party, eh?' Tim laughed rudely. 'Good for them! I expect they're all a good deal richer than they were yesterday. Pity old Robert didn't leave some of it to you.'

Actually he did . . . Wendy bit back the words. She didn't feel like telling Tim about her thousand pounds when he was in this mood.

'Well, even if he had, I don't suppose it would have done me much good. I don't want handouts from you.'

'I don't give you handouts, Tim. We share things, I thought.'

'Oh, yes, like the bloody car. When I want to use it, though, it's *yours*, isn't it? *Where have you been with my car?*' he mimicked.

'Oh, Tim, I'm sick of this! But whilst we're on the subject, please will you either give me back the keys or put them back where they belong yourself? I shall need them in the morning and I don't want to have to hunt for them.'

'Have your bloody keys!' He threw them at her. They narrowly missed her face. She picked them up wearily.

'Have you really been over at the Morton house all this time waiting for Ash to come home?'

'Yep.' He had finished his whisky and was pouring another.

'I don't understand you. Why on earth were you so keen to see him?'

'Why do you think? To tell him to leave you alone, of course. And perhaps sock him on the jaw while I was about it.'

'Oh, Tim, how many times do I have to say it? There is nothing between me and Ash. I haven't seen him for years until today, and we didn't exchange more than half a dozen words. You really have to get it out of your head that there is something going on. It was all over a long time ago, before I even met you.'

His eyes met hers; there was something in them she couldn't read. Then: 'In that case, why did he phone you this evening?' he asked.

Wendy went blank with utter astonishment. 'What are you talking about? He didn't phone me.'

'Yes, he did. While you were in the kitchen making supper.'

'That was *Ash?*' She'd heard the telephone ring; when she'd asked Tim who it was he'd said it was a wrong number. 'Why didn't you tell me?'

He shrugged. 'What was I supposed to say? Oh darling, your boyfriend is on the phone for you?'

'What did he say?'

'Nothing. I didn't give him the chance. I told him to bugger off.'

'Oh, Tim!' But her heart had begun to thud treacherously hard. 'I'm going to bed if you're not,' she said, turning away. 'I have to be up early in the morning.'

'Yes, some of us have to work, I know.'

She ignored the jibe. 'Don't you think you ought to come to bed too?'

'What's in it for me if I do?'

'Tonight – nothing. I'm tired and you're . . .'

'Drunk? Good excuse, isn't it? Not that you need an excuse. But, fucking hell, neither do I! You're my wife, and if I want to make love to my wife . . . Have to go down on my knees and beg, do I? I'll bet bloody Ash Morton wouldn't have to. I'll bet you'd offer it to him on a plate.'

'Oh, grow up,' Wendy said contemptuously. Her head had

begun to ache again and she was trembling with tiredness and frustration. She turned for the door but his hand shot out, imprisoning her shoulder and turning her to face him.

'What did you say?'

'I said grow up.' But she said it more quietly, more tentatively. There was something in his face she didn't like at all. 'Let me go, Tim. You're hurting me.'

'What the hell do you mean – grow up?'

'You know very well. You're behaving like a child. I know things have been rough for you lately, but don't take it out on me.'

'You cow!'

He lashed out furiously. She was too taken by surprise to duck or dodge. Her neck cracked with the force of the blow and she gasped with shock and pain, her hand flying to her cheek and feeling the warm blood on her fingers.

Involuntary tears filled her eyes; still cringing she looked up at him and saw that his furious expression was now one of blank disbelief. His hand was still raised, suspended in mid-air as if it had been turned to stone.

'You hit . . . me,' she whispered.

'I didn't mean it! Wendy, I'm sorry!'

'I should think you are . . .' The words were disjointed, she still couldn't catch her breath properly and her mouth felt stiff; it was an effort to make the muscles work. She could feel blood trickling between her fingers now, down her chin.

'I'm so sorry . . .' His hand was reaching out for her.

'Stay away from me!'

But he didn't. He just stood there, blocking her way. She tried to push past him but he caught her in a bear hug, holding her throbbing face into his chest. For a moment she stood impassive, not wanting to be in his arms, but too weak to fight him and too afraid to protest in case she set him off again.

'I didn't mean to do that – it's that bloody Ash. I can't bear to think of him with you . . .' He was stroking her hair now; something inside her recoiled from the touch of his fingers.

'Let me go, Tim. I want to go to bed.'

He ignored her, tilting her head back, kissing her forehead, her cheek, her poor sore mouth. She jerked her face away, seeing the scarlet stain on his shirt that was her own fresh blood, feeling with revulsion the urgent desire stirring his body.

He was yanking at the sash of her dressing gown, tearing it open. Beneath it she was wearing only a thin nightdress with shoestring straps. He pushed the dressing gown off her shoulders and buried his face in her breasts.

'Tim – stop it!' She tried to free herself, but her arms were pinioned now by the sleeves of her dressing gown and when he raised his head, she saw with a dart of fear that the crazed look was back in his eyes.

'For once, Wendy, you will do as *I* want.' His voice was a thick snarl.

He turned her, driving her across the room to the sofa, scrunching her nightdress up, ramming his hand between her legs. Wendy was outraged but also panicked into submission, too afraid to struggle much in case he hit her again.

'Tim . . . please, no!' she whispered.

He eased back; she thought for a moment that he was going to stop, but what he was doing was unfastening his trousers. He fell back on to her with a groan, more like a wild animal than a man to whom she had been married for almost eight years, pinioning her, thrusting into her with a ferocity that made her feel he was ripping her apart. She lay sobbing beneath his heaving body, part of her distanced, so that she seemed to be watching from above, part of her utterly, totally there, humiliated, violated, hurting.

When it was over he rolled away. His face was glistening with sweat and with her blood, the face of a stranger. She lay without moving, still spreadeagled on the sofa, then, defensively, she pulled her nightdress down over her legs.

'Don't ever do that to me again!' she wanted to say. But the words were locked inside; she didn't dare speak them. Her mouth was throbbing, the soft tissues deep inside her burned fiercely. But neither, she thought, were as bad as the pain in her heart.

Six

Liz had slept late. When she woke and checked her travel alarm she was startled to see that it was almost ten. Her body clock was upside down, she decided. Jet lag never seemed to affect her when she flew from England to the States, but the other way round and she was totally out of synch for days.

She pushed back the covers and padded across to the dressing table where a kettle stood on a tray along with a cup and saucer and a selection of tea bags, sachets of coffee and plastic pots of milk. No use calling room service, obviously, and she would have missed breakfast by now. She switched on the kettle and went into the bathroom, running the cold tap and splashing water on to her face. It looked puffy this morning with dark circles under her eyes and the lines between nose and mouth horribly pronounced. Liz grimaced at her image. Perhaps she should think about having a face lift after all!

By the time she returned to the bedroom the kettle had boiled. She made herself a cup of black coffee and topped it up with cold water from the tap.

At least there was a telephone in the room, one that provided a direct line out if you dialled the right prefix, and later on she intended to call her office and check that everything was running smoothly. But it was still the middle of the night in Florida. Right now there was another call she wanted to make.

She finished her coffee, tore open another sachet and made another cup. She was beginning to feel halfway human now. Leaving the cup on the glass-topped dressing table she picked up the telephone and dialled the number of the golf and country club.

'Is Mr Morton in this morning?' she asked when the receptionist answered.

'Which Mr Morton?'

'Tony.' Actually she was hoping to be able to speak to Jack

too at some point, but she was hoping she could do that without making an issue of it.

'I'll try to find him for you.'

A few moments later Tony was on the line. He sounded tired she thought.

'Tony, it's Liz. I was wondering if I came over whether you could spare the time to have lunch with me.'

'Oh – yes.' He sounded surprised. 'Why not?'

'My sentiments exactly,' Liz said. 'I'm at a loose end and I really don't fancy eating lunch alone.'

'Can you get here?'

'Of course. I'll take a taxi. I'm going to have a wander round town, look up old haunts. Shall I see you about one?'

'Yes, fine. I'll look forward to it.'

'So shall I,' Liz said. And realized with a slight sense of shock that it was no less than the truth.

Kate pushed the pile of papers away from her across her desk, rested her head on her hands and closed her eyes. Rarely, if ever, had she felt so totally swamped, unable to think straight. The whole of her life, it seemed to her, had taken on the aura of a nightmare. She had scarcely slept last night, her brain fluttering like a caged bird between everything that was happening – her business problems, the will and the reactions it had provoked, the fear that something she didn't want to know was lurking, the driving need to do what she believed was right, whatever the cost. And underlying it all the bleak knowledge that somehow she had to find the willpower to end things with Chris.

She should never have allowed herself to become involved with a married man, she knew. It went against everything she believed in, and her common sense too. The trouble was that when she had fallen in love all that had gone out of the window. She had kidded herself that it was special, different, that she and Chris were soul mates. She had believed him when he said his marriage was already as good as over, and he would leave his wife for her. But of course that hadn't happened and she had gradually come to realize it never would. In a perverse way she wasn't even sure she wanted it to; she didn't think she could bear to be the cause of the break-up of a family.

But for once she had other, more pressing things on her

mind. A business to get back on track for starters. Kate sighed and pulled the pile of unread mail towards her once more. A cheque from one of her clients – well, that was something. But not enough. Not nearly enough. She needed all the people who owed her money to pay up and still it would be difficult to get back into the black.

She glanced around her cluttered little office, minding dreadfully that soon, short of a miracle, it would no longer be hers. She could probably get another job, she thought, maybe as a design consultant with a fabric firm or a paint manufacturer, or if the worst came to the worst she could work alone, making curtains and loose covers on her own sewing machine on the kitchen table, but it wouldn't make up for what she was losing, and wouldn't be any help to all the people she was letting down. She'd be a bankrupt, the bailiffs would change the lock on the door of her shop, block out the windows with sheets of paper, tear out all the fittings she'd had installed with such pride and stick up a notice board 'Premises to Let'. Behind the locked door the dust would gather on what little was left when the vultures had taken their pickings – the mock-up swags and tails, the samples of lace curtaining, the wallpaper and carpet books, the swatches of fabric. And the girls, her girls, would have nothing but their P45s to show for their loyalty. That was the worst thought of all.

The telephone at her elbow began to ring, making her jump. She reached for it, trying to inject some quality of efficiency and confidence into her voice.

'Kate Morton.'

'Hold the line please, Miss Morton. I have a call for you from Mr Nicholson.'

Mr Nicholson, Jon, the solicitor Grandpa had turned to rather than let Hugh Ormrod know what was on his mind. During one of her periods of wakefulness last night she had made up her mind to ring him today; now here he was ringing her. Telepathy, perhaps? Anyway, it was one less call to be charged to her phone bill.

She doodled on the corner of a letter while she waited. At least the telephone wasn't playing music at her. She always found that irritating; this morning it would have been insupportable.

'Miss Morton. Sorry about that. My secretary has this habit

of getting the person I want to speak to before buzzing back
to me. I'm trying to break her of it, but so far I haven't had
much success.'

'No problem,' Kate said automatically. 'What can I do for
you?'

'I'd like to arrange to see you and your sisters as soon as
possible so that we can discuss the way forward. I've tried
telephoning Mrs Howard – Jessica – but I haven't been able
to reach her.'

Typical of Jess! Kate thought. Making a fuss about wanting
to get things sorted out urgently, and then not being available.

'She's probably helping out at the hospice shop or something. She does a lot of charity work,' Kate said. 'But I do
know she's very anxious to get things moving with regard to
the will.'

'Yes, I gathered,' Jon Nicholson said dryly. 'I am trying
not to let the grass grow under my feet. I'm taking steps to
try to trace the missing beneficiary.'

'Such as?'

'To begin with I'm placing notices in the press. But to be
honest, I'm not overly optimistic about the chances of a
response to that. It's a bit hit and miss. And if the child was
adopted, as I should think it almost certainly was, then the
name of Morton would mean nothing whatever to them unless
they have applied for their original birth certificate. Quite a
few adopted children do that these days, of course, but I can't
help feeling that if that were the case they would have surfaced
before now, tried to make contact with their natural family.
And from your response yesterday I take it nothing like that
has ever happened.'

'Not to my knowledge, certainly.'

'And you haven't remembered anything else that might be
significant, I suppose?'

'No, nothing. I talked to Liz Langley, too. She was Mum's
best friend when they were young, and I thought she might
know something. But she was as much in the dark as the rest
of us. And I'm pretty sure Dad doesn't know anything either.
I'll talk to him when I get the chance, but I suspect that if
there was a child it was before they were married and she
never told him about it.' She hesitated, then, feeling duty

bound to somehow excuse her mother, went on: 'I know you'd think she would have, considering all the years they were together, but secrets have a way of getting stuck, don't they? You don't say anything in the beginning because you can't bring yourself to for one reason or another and then it just gets harder and harder because it's not only the secret itself but the fact that you didn't share it.'

'Yes, I suppose so,' Jon Nicholson said vaguely. 'Anyway, to get back to business. The other thing that needs sorting out is the house. I've already asked a local estate agent to give me a valuation. The sooner we get it on the market the better. Property is very slow to move these days, especially the more expensive ones. And we shall need to arrange for a house clearance, unless you want to take care of that yourselves.'

Kate gulped. The thought of the things that had made up Grandpa and Grandma's home being piled up in an auction room, picked over, and perhaps knocked down for a song made her feel very hollow and miserable.

'There's no urgency about that, of course,' Jon Nicholson was saying. 'A house always looks more attractive to prospective buyers if it's still furnished. But it might be an idea to sort through any personal effects. And there is the matter of the gifts, the cufflinks for your nephews and so on. Perhaps we could arrange to meet at the Cedars to sort that out fairly soon.'

'Yes, of course,' Kate said. 'I could make it at the weekend and I should think Jess and Miranda could too. Or would that be difficult for you?'

'I don't normally work at weekends, but . . .' he hesitated. 'I could manage Sunday I should think.'

'That would be perfect,' Kate said gratefully. 'I'll talk to Jess and Miranda and get back to you.'

Her eye fell on the pile of bills on her desk, and, hating herself for sounding every bit as mercenary as Jessica, she said tentatively: 'The missing beneficiary. Is it going to hold up probate while we try to find him or her?'

'Not necessarily. We can go ahead on the basis that you are entitled to a quarter share of the estate. Then, if at the end of the twelve months I have still been unable to trace the missing beneficiary, the fourth share can be divided equally between the three of you.'

'I see,' Kate said, ashamed at the relief she couldn't help feeling.

'Not, of course, that there will be very much to distribute until the house is sold. Unless there are assets I don't yet know about. I have asked Hugh Ormrod to let me have any relevant papers he might have in his strong room.'

I'll bet Hugh will love that, Kate thought. She put the phone down and sat for a moment with her hand resting on the receiver. Perhaps if she were to tell her bank manager she was expecting a legacy he might be prepared to hold off a bit longer.

It was as she was dialling the number of the bank that she remembered she hadn't said anything to Jon Nicholson about the mystery woman at the graveside. Was it possible that she might be the missing beneficiary? It didn't seem likely, since if she were and had been in contact with Grandpa, surely there wouldn't have been all this mystery. But all the same, Kate thought they should probably try to find out who she was.

Not now, though. The most pressing thing at the moment was trying to buy a few days' grace for her business.

Liz's taxi dropped her off outside the golf and country club at twelve ten. Flags on white-painted poles fluttered in the October sunshine outside the doors to the main reception area; inside, beyond the floor-to-ceiling glass doors, a plump woman in her forties sat behind a reception desk.

'Mr Morton is expecting me,' Liz said when the woman looked up at her enquiringly. 'Mr Tony Morton.'

'Oh, I think Mr Morton has gone to the bank.'

'Never mind. I'm early.' This was just the opportunity Liz had been hoping for. 'Is Mr Jack Morton around?'

'I think so, yes. Who shall I say . . . ?'

'Is he in his office?'

'He was ten minutes ago.'

'In that case I'll just go up,' Liz said.

She turned to the stairs, smiling to herself. The receptionist would probably warn Jack before she made it to his office, but she had no intention of announcing herself.

Jack's office was next door to Tony's; she had noticed his nameplate on the door last night. As she had expected, the receptionist had obviously buzzed straight through to him; by the time she had climbed the stairs he was in the doorway, looking out. He was wearing a boldly striped shirt rolled back at the wrists and a matching tie loosened sufficiently at the neck to show the top button. He looked, she thought, extremely handsome in a rather rakish way.

'Liz – it's you! What are you doing here?'

'Having lunch with Tony. But he's out at the moment, and I wanted a word with you, Jack.'

'You'd better come in.'

The office, though identical in lay out and decor to Tony's – same barley-white walls and chocolate brown carpet, same view across the gold course from windows hung with the same chocolate brown curtains – nevertheless bore the hallmark of a totally different personality. Whereas Tony's office was remarkably impersonal since he had occupied it for so many years, Jack's was very much his own. A framed photograph of him in his footballing days accepting a silver cup from some dignitary dominated one wall, a portrait of Sandra sat on his desk alongside an executive toy, a dinner jacket and white shirt with black tie draped around it hung from a peg behind the door. It swung perilously as he closed the door behind them.

'Drink, Liz?'

'Not for me, thanks. My body clock is telling me it's still only breakfast time.'

'Well, I shall have one.' He opened a mini fridge and took out a bottle of lager, glistening with condensation. 'I like to keep my own supplies up here. Don't want the bar staff knowing every time I fancy some refreshment.' He poured the beer, settled himself in his leather-tooled chair, and regarded her steadily. 'To what do I owe this pleasure? It's not a social call, I imagine.'

'No.' Liz smiled wryly. She and Jack had never shared social intercourse. His flamboyance had never cut any ice with her, and she thought he resented the fact that she had been Trish's confidante. 'No, it's not a social call, and if you don't mind I'll come straight to the point. I'd like to get it over with before Tony comes back from the bank, or wherever it is he's gone. It's about Trish.'

He frowned. 'Why in the world would you want to talk to me about Trish?'

'Oh, Jack, you know very well why. I don't have to spell it out, surely?'

He chuckled. 'You want to know if I know anything about this fourth child. You think that if there was one, I'm the father.'

Unexpectedly, Liz felt her cheeks turning pink.

'It wouldn't be so impossible, would it?' she said. 'No, actually I don't want an answer to that. There are some things I'd rather not know. But I am very concerned . . .'

'Christ, Liz, you've got a long memory! Whatever there was between me and Trish finished years ago – years before she died. She married my brother. End of story.'

'Yes, she did marry your brother, and that is exactly what is worrying me. Tony adored her, Jack. I don't want to see him hurt. This will of Robert's has opened a Pandora's box. It's bad enough for Tony that all kinds of aspersions are suddenly being cast, but things could get much worse, couldn't they, if . . .'

'Don't you think you might be worrying unnecessarily?'

'Possibly, but I do care very much about this family and I think it would be best for everyone if all the speculation were allowed to die the death. There's a very real risk of people being hurt if skeletons begin falling out of cupboards. I think you know what I mean.'

'Oh, I know what you mean, all right. And I think you have the most colossal cheek. You have lived in America for a very long time now. We have all been managing perfectly well in your absence, though I can't see that you have been greatly concerned about it one way or the other. Now you come back and start preaching like some latter-day saint, sticking your nose into things that don't concern you, and haven't concerned you for years.'

'I'm sorry you see it like that,' Liz said tightly. 'It's just that I'm worried about Tony and what it will do to him if—'

'You need not worry about him,' Jack interrupted her. 'He's not nearly as fragile as you seem to think. In fact, I would say my brother is pragmatic to a fault. Shall I tell you what I think? I think that if there was a child, Tony must have known about it. Trish couldn't have kept it from him all those years. No, what he's worried about is other people knowing. And caring too much what other people think is one of the biggest curses going. I thought that sort of hypocrisy went out of fashion thirty years ago. It seems I was wrong.'

Liz pushed back her chair. 'And it seems I was wrong to think you might actually have some consideration for your brother's feelings, and those of his daughters.'

Jack huffed, rising along with her. 'Oh, shit, Liz, I'm sorry. But you do have a way of getting up my nose. You always did.'

'There, at least, we have something in common.' Her eye fell on Sandra's photograph in its silver frame on his desk. Jack was a fine one to pour scorn on hypocrisy! 'You won't mention this conversation to Tony, I hope?' she said.

'I'm not a complete bastard, Liz, whatever you might think.'

She smiled wryly. 'No?'

Her hand was on the door handle, easing it open, when he said: 'And by the way, I really don't know anything about this mystery child.'

She looked back at him. With his beer in his hand and an expression of bonhomie and studied honesty on his still-handsome face, he should have been convincing. But for all that, Liz was not at all sure that she believed him.

'What did you and Jack find to talk about?' Tony asked, filling Liz's wine glass from the bottle of Chablis on the table between them. 'I didn't think there was much love lost between the two of you.'

'Oh, we just chatted,' Liz lied. But she was cursing silently; the receptionist had obviously made it her business to tell Tony she had visited Jack in his office.

'How are you today, anyway?' she asked.

'I'm OK.' But he looked tired and strained. 'I'm sorry about last night. Well, I'm sorry about the whole thing. This isn't much of a homecoming for you.'

'I came for Robert's funeral, Tony. I never expected it to be a picnic.'

'Well, it's certainly not that! I just don't understand why Robert should have done such a thing. After all these years, why rock the boat?'

His choice of phrase puzzled her, but she simply said: 'You know what Robert was like.'

'Yes. But Jess and Kate and Miranda . . . they're the ones who have always been there for him. They could do without all this. Did you know Kate's business is in trouble?'

Liz sighed. 'I suspected it.'

'Me too. She's been playing her cards very close to her chest, but I had heard rumours. With all the business people who are members here it's impossible not to. Anyway, she phoned me this morning. Said she wanted to warn me there might be stormy times ahead. She's still trying to be optimistic, of course, but I can read between the lines. She's very worried. And the hell of it is I can't do any more to help her out. We have our cash flow problems too. Our saving grace is that we own our own premises, but it's not easy. Nothing is these days. And I can't see Jack sanctioning a handout even if I could rustle something up.'

'No,' she said wryly. 'Sentimental, Jack is not.'

'You wouldn't be able to help her out, I suppose, Liz?' he asked tentatively.

'Kate wouldn't accept help from me,' Liz said. 'She's fiercely independent.'

'Yes, she is. But I was thinking that if the business goes under. I just wondered if you might be able to—' He broke off, clearly embarrassed.

'If Kate finds herself out of a job, then I could certainly find a place for her – if she wanted it. I'm not sure she would.'

'No, I'm not sure, either, but bless you anyway, Liz.'

The waitress, neatly attired in black skirt and white blouse, arrived with their lunch orders – battered cod for Tony, a large mixed salad for Liz.

'Anyway, what do you say we forget our problems for the moment and enjoy our meal?' Tony suggested.

Liz smiled, looking at him across the table and thinking how lucky Trish had been. She hadn't appreciated him . . . or had she? In the years between had she finally got over Jack and given Tony her undivided love? If so, it was somehow all the more tragic that circumstances were now conspiring to throw a shadow over his most precious memories.

'Here's to sorting everything out as speedily as possible,' Tony said, raising his glass.

'I'll drink to that,' Liz said, doing the same. But silently she was adding: And sorting it out, if possible, without anyone getting hurt!

At one o'clock precisely Wendy left her office to buy a filled roll from the sandwich bar on the corner. It was a daily ritual unless she was detained dealing with a client, but today she was dreading facing the cheerful, talkative woman who served in the sandwich bar. She was bound to ask what Wendy had done to her face, and though she had already had to make up a story for the benefit of her colleagues, she shrank from the prospect of having to go through it again, trying to sound convincing.

Tim had been asleep when she'd left this morning and she had been glad. She didn't know what she would have said to him if he'd been awake. She didn't want to have to even look at him.

Halfway through the morning her mother had telephoned.

'I was wondering if you and Tim would like to come over for lunch on Sunday. Your father would be pleased to see you. It would take his mind off this Robert business.'

'Oh, Mum, I don't know what we're doing yet,' she hedged.

'Well, let me know, will you?' A pause. 'You haven't heard any more about it, have you?'

'Sorry?'

'I'm thinking about this fourth child business. I wondered if anyone had been in touch with you with any more thoughts on what happened to it.'

'No.' Wendy's mind had been far from the problems of the Holbrook and Morton families. 'Why would anyone get in touch with me?'

'Well, I suppose they wouldn't. I'm just so curious about it all I am grasping at straws. It is such a mystery, isn't it? One can't imagine . . .'

'Mum, I have to go,' Wendy said, finding her mother's interest distasteful to say the least of it. 'I'll let you know about Sunday.'

But she knew they wouldn't go. For one thing, Tim wouldn't want to, for another her lip would probably still be swollen. She didn't want her mother to see it.

Now, she turned up the collar of her jacket, trying to bury her face in it and pretend she was escaping the October wind,

which was keen in spite of the sunshine. She wasn't sure she'd
be able to manage a crusty French roll today. Perhaps she'd
have a sandwich instead, something very soft that would slip
down easily.

'Wendy!'

She stopped dead in her tracks, her heart thumping. Ash.
Ash, wearing a dark green Barbour over a thick jersey, blocking
her path.

'Good heavens!' she said. Her voice sounded unsteady.

He was staring at her. 'What on earth have you done to
your face?'

'Oh . . .' Her hand flew to her mouth, covering it defensively. 'It's too silly. I walked into a door.'

'How in the world did you manage that?' She could see
from his eyes that he didn't believe her.

'Drunk again, I expect.' She laughed apologetically.

'Drunk, you? Never!'

'No, it just sort of stuck . . .' She hesitated. 'Did you phone
me yesterday?' she asked before she could stop herself. 'Tim
said . . .'

'I did, yes.' He looked a bit awkward. Wendy was surprised;
awkwardness wasn't something one associated with Ash.

'Was Tim rude to you?' she asked.

'Let's just say he made it quite clear it wasn't convenient.'

'I'm sorry.' She could feel the flush creeping up her cheeks.
'You'll have to excuse him. He's been very touchy since he
lost his job. It's a horrible thing to happen to anyone, and Tim
. . . well, he's taken it very hard. It seems to have resurrected
all his old in-securities. You know, the baggage he carries
from being raised in a children's home.'

'Wendy,' Ash said, giving her a very straight look. 'Tim
didn't do that to you, did he?'

'No! Of course not!' But the flush was turning fiery red;
she could feel it burning in her face and neck.

'If he did . . .'

Wendy had never seen Ash look so furious and his tone
was a low snarl she couldn't ever remember him using before.

'He didn't,' she said hastily. 'He wouldn't. Why did you
ring me anyway?'

'I just wanted to talk to you. We didn't get the chance at
the funeral.'

'Oh, I see.' She didn't know whether to be pleased or disappointed.

'Look, if this is your lunch hour, why don't we go somewhere and have a coffee?' Ash suggested.

Her heart leaped. *Oh yes, please!* she wanted to say, but she didn't dare. If someone saw them, if Tim should come into town for some reason and bump into them, he really would think there was something going on. Even seeing them talking in the street would be enough for him.

Her guilty thoughts were making her jumpy; she looked over her shoulder, half expecting to see Tim there.

'I'm sorry, I can't. They're expecting me back at the office.'

'Oh, right.' For a moment he looked crushed, and her heart leaped again. Then suddenly she was angry, with herself, and with him too. He had dumped her unceremoniously, and she had married someone else. End of story. He had no right to churn her up all over again. As for what he'd said about not having the chance to speak to her at the funeral, that was rubbish. He'd had every chance, and simply chosen not to.

'I really have to go, Ash,' she said. 'It was nice seeing you.'

'And you. Wendy . . .'

For a moment, something hovered in the air between them, unsaid. Wendy turned away, biting her lip, and then wincing because she had forgotten how tender it was. At the door of the sandwich bar she turned, looking back. But Ash was nowhere to be seen. Wendy felt totally bereft suddenly, emptiness and longing aching inside her.

It was only when she came out of the shop again, clutching her pack of egg-and-cress sandwiches and thanking her lucky stars that she hadn't been served by the chatty woman, that it occurred to her to wonder just what Ash had been doing in town, in the street where she worked, at just the time she went out every day to buy lunch. Was it possible he'd been there on purpose? That he'd been heading for the estate agent on purpose, even?

You never give up, do you? Wendy said to herself crossly. It's no wonder Tim hit you. You really are asking for it . . .

But try as she might, she couldn't stop thinking about Ash, and wondering what he would have said if she had gone with him for a coffee. And she couldn't stop remembering his violent reaction when he'd thought Tim had hurt her. In a bleak, horrible world it was like holding out your hands to a roaring fire and feeling the comforting glow of warmth, like seeing the first snowdrop against the barren wintry ground. For all her good intentions, Wendy could not bring herself to let it go.

Jessica dialled the number of Hugh Ormrod's office and unbuttoned her coat as she waited for someone to answer. The phone had been ringing as she came in the door after finishing her stint at the charity shop; it had been Kate, asking her if they could meet Jon Nicholson at the Cedars on Sunday, and when they'd finished talking, Jessica hadn't stopped to take her coat off before putting in the call to Hugh. She was too wound up about it all; she wanted his advice, and she wanted it *now*.

'Jessica, my dear. How can I help you?' Hugh's voice conjured up an image, thin like his face and sharp aquiline nose, thin like his long fingers with their perfectly manicured nails and the little line of black hairs that ran from knuckle to knuckle.

'Oh, Hugh, I've just had Kate on the phone. Apparently this new solicitor person wants us to go through Grandpa's things with him and choose whatever we want before the rest is sold off. Quite honestly, I feel we need to be represented.'

'But that is all in accordance with the terms of the will, Jessica. I'm sure Mr Nicholson can be trusted to carry out your grand-father's wishes.'

'But . . .' Jessica floundered helplessly for a moment. 'With all the complications, don't you think it would be best if we had an independent adviser? And who better than you?'

There was a small silence, then Hugh said, rather stiffly: 'Under the circumstances, I really don't think I should get involved. I'll tell you what I'll do, I'll have a word with our Mr Lightfoot. As I become less active in the firm, he's the one who is taking over my clients. I'm sure he would be pleased to help you.'

'But, Hugh, you're the one we know. The one who knows us.'

'Precisely. I really think it would be for the best.' His tone was final.

'Oh,' she said, defeated.

'I sent all the papers concerning your grandfather's affairs to Mr Nicholson by courier this morning,' Hugh continued, clearly relieved to have extricated himself from an awkward situation. 'Everything concerning your grandfather's investments. His stocks and shares, National Savings Certificates, bank details, deeds . . .'

'The deeds of the Cedars, you mean?'

'Yes. And the land he owned.'

'Land?' Jessica said sharply. 'What land?'

'The land he acquired at one time with the intention of developing it. Quite a considerable acreage, with outline planning permission already granted. For some reason he never got around to it. He retired and sold the business, but he kept the land. It seemed like a good investment to him, I expect – it was growing steadily in value at that time – the boom years.'

Jessica's skin had begun to prickle with excitement. 'And now?'

'Still worth a tidy sum, I'd say. Especially if the economy starts to pick up. There's quite a shortage of land for building on around here. The outline planning permission might have been for luxury four-bedroom detached houses with good sized gardens and double garages, but in the present climate I doubt there'd be much difficulty getting it changed to a cluster of starter homes.'

'I see,' Jessica said tautly. But for the first time since the reading of the will, she was smiling.

So she'd been right to seek independent advice. Perhaps, with this Mr Lightfoot's help, it would be a good idea to contest. After all, it seemed that there was a good deal more at stake here than they had realized.

Seven

There were two cars already parked on the broad gravel turn-around outside the Cedars when Kate raced her GTi up the drive – Jessica's Renault, and a car she didn't recognize: a red BMW sports which she presumed belonged to Jon Nicholson.

Why did she always have to be late? she wondered, irritated with herself. Today it was because she'd hung on and hung on hoping Chris might telephone. He often did on Sunday mornings when he went out to buy the Sunday papers. But the telephone had remained obstinately silent.

As she parked next to Jessica's Renault, Dominic and William came running around the corner of the house. Today they were dressed in jeans and sweatshirts, but the jeans were neatly pressed, with creases. Dominic was carrying a battered yellow frisbee; Kate recognized it as one that Robert had bought years ago and kept at the Cedars for them to play with when they came on visits.

'Hello, boys,' she said. 'Have you been here long?'

'Ages. It's really *boring*,' Dominic said, and William added: 'We had to choose cufflinks.'

'Wasn't that fun?'

'No. Bor-*ing*! Who wants *cufflinks*?'

'You probably will, when you're older.'

'I won't. I'll never wear *cufflinks*.'

'Neither will I.'

'Yes, you will,' Kate said, 'and then you'll be really glad you've got something that belonged to Great-grandpa.' The boys looked unconvinced. 'Is Auntie Miranda here yet?' Kate asked.

'Yes, she came with us. We picked her up,' Dominic offered.

'Come on, Dom!' William was tugging at his brother's sleeve. 'Let's go and swing on the rope Great-grandpa put up for us in the tree!'

Kate smiled to herself. She wouldn't mind betting Jess didn't know about *that*.

'Just be careful, fellas,' she called after them as they raced off across the leaf-strewn grass. She shook her head, watching them go, then climbed the steps to the house. The front door was on the latch. She pushed it open and went inside.

Surprisingly, since it was only two days since they'd held the funeral wake here, the house had a cold, shut-up smell as well as a feeling of emptiness. No one had lived here, of course, since Robert had his first stroke, but presumably it hadn't been so noticeable on Thursday, when the drawing room had been overflowing with mourners and the caterers had occupied the kitchen. Now there was no escaping it, and remembering how warm and welcoming the house had always been when she was a child sent a jar of sadness through Kate. In those days there had always been roaring fires in the huge open grates on cold mornings such as this, and the smell of the Sunday roast wafting out from the kitchen.

'Hello?' she called. 'Where is everybody?'

'Kate, is that you? We're in the drawing room.' Jessica's voice. Kate followed it.

'Hi. Sorry I'm late.'

Jessica was standing by the fireplace clutching a large Victorian porcelain vase to the waxed jacket she was wearing over her Laura Ashley jumper and Liberty print skirt. 'It doesn't matter. We started without you.'

Kate glanced at the vase, and at the silverware piled on the table where Miranda, in a fluffy powder-blue tunic and matching leggings, hovered possessively.

'So I see.'

'We didn't think you'd mind,' Miranda said. 'You won't want any of these, will you? They wouldn't fit in with your decor.'

'I thought the point was to choose things to remind us of Grandma and Grandpa, not divide up the spoils,' Kate said rather tartly.

'In that case you can have Grandpa's old gardening jacket,' Miranda said, intending to be sarcastic. 'He loved that jacket. I lost count of the times Grandma put it in the sack for Oxfam and he took it out again.'

'Actually, I *would* quite like it,' Kate said. She was remembering a frosty Guy Fawkes Night, long ago. Grandpa had always had a bonfire for them and lots of fireworks which, although they were less impressive by far than the ones at the Round Table displays their parents took them to, were also much more exciting because they were theirs alone. They'd had Golden Rain and Silver Fountains and Mount Vesuvius stuck in flowerpots on the garden bench, rockets in milk bottles, Catherine wheels pinned to the fence, and squibs which always seemed to hop in Grandma's direction, making her squeal and yell at Grandpa to be more careful.

This particular Guy Fawkes Night, Kate had insisted on wearing her new cagoule instead of a warm anorak and by the time proceedings were still only half over she'd been shivering so much that her teeth were chattering, and trying not to let it show because she knew her mother would be cross with her. But Grandpa had noticed. He'd gone into the garden shed on the pretext of getting another box of matches, and when he'd come out he'd brought his gardening jacket and wrapped it round her shoulders. 'Look after this for me, will you, Kate?' he'd said, putting his finger to his lips in a conspiratorial way, and she'd said: 'All right, Grandpa,' and snuggled into the thick tweed that felt scratchy and comforting against her chin, and smelled of tobacco and petrol and garden peat.

'Kate – I was joking!' Miranda said now, her voice incredulous. 'What on earth would you do with Grandpa's old jacket?'

Kate sighed. 'I don't know really. I'd just like it. It's got happy memories.'

'There's no point being sentimental,' Jessica said briskly. 'Everything has got *memories*, but we can't possibly keep it all. We need to pick out the things of value and get rid of the rest.'

Kate wanted to say that it was the belongings that had made up Grandma and Grandpa's lives that were of value. They were the things that mattered, really, they had far more meaning than the stocks and shares which Hugh had kept in his strong room, or even the silverware that Miranda had obviously got her eye on, yet they would probably end up in black plastic bin bags at the town rubbish dump.

'Have you any thoughts on what you would like, Miss Morton?' Jon Nicholson asked. 'Apart from the gardening jacket, that is?'

He was sitting at the table with a sheaf of papers spread out in front of him, making what looked like a list. Today, in an enormous Aran sweater and green cords, he looked less like a solicitor than ever.

'Not really,' she said. 'I'll have a look round later on. And by the way, do call me Kate. Miss Morton sounds dreadfully formal, and there are two of us.'

'Yes, but he already calls me Miranda, and I call him Jon.' Miranda looked at him through her thick lashes as she said it. She fancies him, Kate thought. Not that it meant anything, necessarily. Miranda couldn't resist flirting with any personable male under the age of ninety, and sometimes she didn't even draw the line at that.

'Mr Nicholson – Jon – was just telling us that the estate is considerably larger than we realized,' Jessica said, looking smug. She set the vase down on the table beside Miranda's haul of silver ware, having now stated her claim to it. 'When the papers arrived from Hugh Ormrod, there were deeds for building land which none of us knew anything about.'

'I suppose there was no reason why we should know. It was Grandpa's business, after all.' Kate turned to Jon, wishing Jessica didn't get up her nose so. 'You haven't made any progress in finding the missing beneficiary, I suppose?'

'Oh, not that again!' Jessica snapped. 'I can't think where on earth Grandpa got such a ridiculous idea from. He didn't explain himself to you, I suppose, Jon?'

'I'm afraid not. I simply took his instructions. I did point out the difficulties, of course, which is why the will is worded to give me twelve months to use my best endeavours to find the fourth child. But I do know that your grandfather was hoping to resolve matters himself. He told me he was setting enquiries in motion and as soon as he had something concrete he would let me know.'

Jessica froze and her eyes widened in what looked very like horror. 'Grandpa was making enquiries himself?'

'Yes. Unfortunately he had his first stroke not long after we had that conversation. I didn't know about it at the time, of course. I simply assumed he was beavering away and would contact me in due course. By the time I heard he was ill and went to see him, he was far too ill for me to be able to ask him anything.'

'So what happens now?' Miranda asked.

'Well, I've placed notices in the press . . .'

'You've done *what*?' Jessica exploded.

'Placed notices . . .'

'Yes, I heard you. I just couldn't believe my ears. *What* press? Where are these notices going to appear?'

'*The Times. The News of the World . . .*'

'*The News of the World?* I don't believe this!'

'And local newspapers.'

'Local! This gets worse and worse! You mean local people are going to read about our private business?'

'I'm sorry, Mrs Howard. I am afraid I am required by law . . .'

'Law! Grandpa loses his marbles, and you are required by *law* to turn it into a circus!'

'Jessica, for goodness' sake!' Kate said. 'It's not his fault. He's only doing his job.' She turned to Jon Nicholson, who was looking extremely uncomfortable. 'I know you don't hold out much hope of learning anything new from the notices – even if the child were to see them they wouldn't necessarily know they were the person referred to. But it did occur to me that you might very well get some impostors coming forward in the hope of coming into some money they have no right to.'

'That is a possibility, yes.'

'So how will you go about proving whether or not they're genuine?'

'That should be relatively straightforward,' Jon Nicholson said. 'I shall require a birth certificate as proof of identity. As you know, adopted children can apply for their original birth certificates these days, and if someone is able to come up with one that states Patricia Holbrook or Patricia Morton was their natural mother, then that would be fairly conclusive.'

'And if no one comes forward, what then?' Kate asked.

'Well, assuming that if there was a child it was adopted, I propose trying to identify any agencies your mother may have used and asking them to check their records. The files are confidential, of course, and they would never divulge where a child had been placed. But I think that in a case like this they might make contact with the adoptive family, put them in the picture, and see if the child would like to come forward. The problem is knowing where to start. I can get a list of agencies operating in this area in, say, the early sixties, but it might take some time. There were quite a few of them, I imagine. In those days, before the changes in the abortion law, adoption was a good deal more common than it is today. It would help if we could narrow it down a bit. What religion was your mother, for instance?'

'What on earth has religion got to do with it?' Jessica demanded.

Kate shot her a look. 'Presumably because the different churches had their own agencies?'

'That's right. It was looked on as a way of ensuring the adoptive child was given the sort of upbringing it could have expected with the natural parents.'

'Our mother was C of E,' Kate said. 'She didn't often go to church though.'

'But it would probably rule out the RC agency.' Jon Nicholson was scribbling on a large pad with a fountain pen.

'I should think so, yes,' Kate agreed. Grandma had been rather anti-Rome, and Robert something of an agnostic.

Not that Robert had had anything to do with it, she reminded herself. Or had he? Had he known all along that Trish had put a baby up for adoption? Confidentiality would have meant that even if he had known which agency Trish had used, he wouldn't have known what had become of the child. But if he had known all along, why had he changed his will only months before he died? Because it had been preying on his mind, perhaps, and eventually he'd felt bound to make provision for the lost grandchild?

'From what he said I rather got the impression that Mr Holbrook intended employing a private detective,' Jon Nicholson continued. 'If he did, I'd like to know who it was, and what, if anything, they turned up.'

'Nothing,' Jessica said flatly. 'There was nothing to turn up.'

Jon Nicholson rolled his pen between finger and thumb, looking apologetic.

'To be honest, I can't help wondering if something did come to light, something which upset Mr Holbrook so much that it was the trigger for his stroke.'

'Oh my God!' Miranda said. 'Surely not?'

'It's only surmise, I admit, but he seemed in such good health.'

'What rubbish!' Jessica stormed. 'A stroke can happen to someone of his age at any time. Particularly someone who liked his drink as much as Grandpa did.' She broke off, colouring a little as the others stared at her incredulously. 'Well, he did!' she added defensively.

'Not to excess,' Kate said.

'And how often were you with him lately?' Jessica asked tartly.

'I used to come over and see him whenever I could.'

'Flying visits, maybe. You weren't there in the evenings when he was alone. He telephoned me one night, quite late, and he was positively rambling. I couldn't make any sense of what he was saying, though he seemed to think it was important.'

Kate was suddenly remembering what Jon Nicholson had said about Robert's investigations. 'What did he say?' she asked sharply.

'I don't know. I told you, he was rambling.'

'But you must have at least tried to understand, asked him why he needed to call you late at night.'

'Of course I asked him. It didn't make any difference. He seemed to be on a voyage into the past. He was just going on about things that happened years ago, and then he got on to Mummy killing herself and he was crying, and I simply couldn't stand it. I mean, I have my feelings too, and he was just drunk and maudlin.'

'How could you not tell us about this?' Kate said angrily. 'If I'd known he was in such a state I'd have . . .'

'Yes? What would you have done? St Katrina to the rescue, I suppose.'

'Oh – shut up!' Kate crossed to the window, looking out at the sunlit lawn, trying to ingest some of the peace and sunshine to take the sting out of the fury she was feeling. Grandpa had phoned Jess, terribly upset about something, and she'd simply hung up on him. Why didn't he phone me? Kate thought, hurt as well as angry, and then crumpled inwardly as it occurred to her that he might have done, and she had not been there. Perhaps it had been one of the occasions when Chris came to the flat and they took the phone off the hook so that their precious shared time would not be interrupted. Oh dear God, she was as bad as Jess – worse. She hadn't even picked up the phone to him . . .

'And with hindsight you don't think anything he said might be relevant?' Jon Nicholson was asking. 'You don't think any of it might have meant he had found his missing grandchild?'

'Of course not!'

'Well, we don't seem to be getting very far with this.' Jon Nicholson capped his fountain pen and laid it on top of the pad. 'I suggest we move on, or we'll be here all day. You ladies are going to do some sorting out, aren't you? I trust if you find anything that is any way relevant you will let me know about it.'

He was looking at Jessica as he spoke, a very straight look, a little like a stern schoolmaster, Kate thought, and stifled the urge to giggle. Modern and slightly unconventional Jon Nicholson might be, but he was certainly no pushover, and Jess, used to riding roughshod over the men in her life, would be in for a shock if she thought he was.

'With your permission, I'd like to look through your grandfather's papers myself,' he said, and again Kate bit back a smile. 'With your permission', indeed! As he was sole executor of the estate, she rather thought it was they who should be seeking *his* permission to poke about the house.

'I could help you,' Miranda suggested. 'I'm not really dressed for ferreting around in dusty rooms.'

Jon Nicholson smiled at her charmingly. 'Thank you, but I think I can manage.'

'You can come with me, Miranda,' Jessica said. 'I want to do the bedroom before outsiders get in there. As far as I know, all Grandma's clothes are still there, as well as Grandpa's. You can help me bag them up for Oxfam.'

'I'll take the other bedrooms,' Kate said. 'I'll just do a quick sort-through for the most personal things. I've got some boxes in the car. I'll go and get them.'

'Oh – could you spare one for me to put my silver things in?' Miranda asked.

'I expect so,' Kate said. 'It's a pity you didn't think to bring some yourself, though. There was a limit to the number I could pinch from Waitrose.'

She went out to the car. She could hear the boys shrieking with laughter somewhere in the garden, and a light aircraft chugged overhead in the clear blue sky. Life going on as normal all around, whilst she and the others were caught in

this unreal vacuum. Everything she had taken for granted for
so long had turned to quicksand. Kate sighed, brushed her
hair out of her eyes and opened the boot of the car to get out
the boxes. Two had contained crisps, and one soap powder.
Miranda could have the soap powder one; it wouldn't matter
if it made her silverware smell scenty.

By the time she went back into the house the drawing room
was empty. Jon Nicholson must have gone to the study to
make a start on Grandpa's papers, and Jess and Miranda
upstairs. Kate left the soap powder carton on the table beside
Miranda's silver and went upstairs herself.

The house boasted five bedrooms besides the big master
bedroom which Robert and Dorothea had occupied. Kate went
quickly through the first two, packing the photographs which
stood on the dressing tables and tallboys into one of her boxes
and flipping open drawers and wardrobe doors to check inside.

The drawers were mostly empty, ready for use by visitors, though it was now many years since Robert and
Dorothea had done much entertaining. Kate remembered
how inviting those empty drawers had always seemed when
she had come to stay as a child, and how excited she had
felt unpacking her small case and stacking T-shirts and shorts
on the pretty scented paper liners, and tucking lace-edged
lavender bags between her underwear. A few lavender bags
remained, dry and crumbly now, but still faintly perfumed.
She sniffed one and stuffed it into her pocket as a keepsake.

The wardrobes, too, were empty, except for Grandma's fur
coat, covered with a polythene cleaners' bag and smelling of
mothballs. Kate laid it on the bed. Something else for Oxfam
– unless Jess wanted it, of course. Nobody really wore furs
nowadays, but she couldn't imagine Jess being squeamish
about animal rights if she thought the coat would look good
over an evening dress for one of the annual dinners she and
Adrian attended.

Kate bypassed the bathroom and went into the third
bedroom. Like the others, the bed was made up with a mound
of pillows beneath a quilt, but Kate guessed it was even longer
since anyone had used it, and in spite of the same almost
unnatural air of neatness there was also a more personal feel
to the room. Kate knew the reason. This had been her mother's
room until she had married, and afterwards Dorothy had still

regarded it as such. No visitors were ever allowed to use it unless the house was overflowing, and the things Trish had left behind were still here, little treasures she had not wanted to take with her to her new home but which she had not wanted to throw away either. A battered leather jewellery box containing necklaces with broken clasps, some beads unthreading from their string, a plastic brooch in the shape of a heart with her name, Patricia, painted on it, a handful of badges, Girl Guides, GFS (Girls' Friendly Society, Kate remembered), Cadbury Cubs. A handkerchief sachet filled with little handkerchiefs and another lavender bag tucked between them, a long-legged china foal, a wild-haired troll wearing a tiny jumper Trish had obviously knitted for her. There was a photograph of Trish aged about eight wearing a swimming suit and eating an ice-cream cone, another, when she must have been in her teens, sitting on a park bench in a froth of gingham, broderie anglaise and paper nylon petticoats. She had been so pretty! Kate thought wistfully. So happy. No shadow of foreboding. Not the slightest indication that one day that happy, smiling girl would take her own life.

A lump rose in Kate's throat. This was the room where her mother had dreamed her childish dreams, grown through adolescence to womanhood. The long mirror on its oak stand had seen her dressed for her first date, and as a bride. She had left this room for her marriage to Tony and never come back. Who knew what her thought had been that day? What secrets the creaking boards could tell if only they could speak?

And had this room also seen her anguished over the expected birth of an illegitimate child? Had she cried here for the baby she would never see grow up? *I love all my children equally . . . all four of them . . . Oh Mum, Mum, what did you bear alone? I want to know. I want to share it with you . . .*

Kate gave her head a small impatient shake and loaded the jewellery case and the trinkets into the cardboard box along with the photographs. She didn't know what she'd do with them, they'd probably end up in her little loft, but she couldn't bring herself to throw them away.

The corner alcove of the room had been blocked in with white-painted wooden doors to form a cupboard. Kate pulled them open by the small brass knobs and a musty smell rushed out. Damp. This corner of the house, right over the front entrance porch, was unmistakably damp. Probably everything inside was ruined. Well, that would make it easier to throw the stuff away.

Some clothes were hanging from the cylindrical metal rail, early sixties style suits with boxy jackets and short straight skirts, a turquoise blue linen duster coat, a pale, waisted tweed. As Kate has suspected, they were all spotted with mould. No use for Oxfam or even a costume museum. She pulled them out, wrinkling her nose, dumping the hangers in a heap on the floor and folding the clothes into an untidy pile. Some hats she found on a shelf went the same way, a large-brimmed white one, trimmed with navy ribbon and net, probably bought for a wedding, a straw sun hat, a tiny feathered band, very fifties, a Jackie O pillbox. Kate was surprised there were so many of them, she couldn't remember her mother ever wearing a hat. On the floor were a couple of pairs of shoes, also spotted with mould, a paper carrier bag containing more clothes, and an oval box, black and white houndstooth check with a red leather trim and handle. A vanity case, Kate thought, and wondered how she knew what it was called. She pulled it out and dropped to her haunches, flipping open the catch and lifting the lid. She half-expected it to contain cosmetics, but it did not, apart from one old lipstick and a small pot of bright green eyes shadow. There was a pencil, a clip-on earring, a tiny notebook, unused, and several wallets of snapshots and negatives, a bundle of letters and cards tied together with a piece of pink wool, and some typed Manila envelopes.

Kate rocked back on her heels, wondering what to do. The photographs, fine. But the letters – that was something different. They would almost certainly be private, and Trish would have been horrified at the thought of anyone else reading them. Under normal circumstances Kate would not even have considered doing so, she'd have burned them, unopened. But if Trish had had an illegitimate child whilst living in this house, then these letters might just contain something in the way of a clue.

Kate put the letters on the floor beside her, putting off the moment. Instead, she flipped open one of the wallets of photographs. They were all sticking together from the damp and she had to peel them apart, then she peered, fascinated, at the images of her teenaged mother, with hair backcombed into a beehive, some alone, some with friends.

She replaced them in their wallet and opened another. A

young man, tall, good-looking, casually dressed; Kate frowned as she recognized him. Uncle Jack in his footballing days. She'd seen photographs of him before, of course, but now she was struck anew by just how handsome he had been. She flicked through the photographs, expecting to find one of her father, but there were none. Just Uncle Jack, Uncle Jack and Uncle Jack again, in various poses in various places. Except for one – of her mother, sitting on a grassy bank, her full skirts spread out all around her, smiling into the camera with an expression that could only be described as coquettish. Kate's frown deepened. Surely that bank was precisely the same one she had noticed in one of the photographs of Jack? She turned back to it, lay the pictures side by side and compared them. Yes, definitely the same spot, the same light – the photographs must have been taken on the same day, but there were none of anyone else. Jack and her mother had been alone on that grass bank; they had simply swapped places and taken each other's picture.

For no reason she could explain, the shock was enormous. She'd known, of course, that her mother, Tony and Jack had all been friends, but somehow she had always imagined that the friendship with Jack had been because he was her father's brother. Now, for the first time, she realized there had been more to it than that. It didn't necessarily mean anything of course, and even if Trish had been involved with Jack it wasn't unusual for siblings to date the same person. She and Jess had had at least one boyfriend in common. No, the really surprising thing was that she could never recall having heard it mentioned. One would have thought that at some time over the years some reference would have been made to it, however jokingly. But it never had.

Perhaps, Kate thought, the old relationship was a sore point with at least one of them. There really could be no other explanation for the deafening silence.

She replaced the photographs in the wallet, and returned to the bundle of letters. Now, more than ever, she really didn't want to read them, aware of being very close to a past she would rather not know about. She'd check the Manila envelopes first, she decided. They weren't likely to be personal – were they?

She slipped the first sheet of paper out. The letterhead was that of a firm of solicitors in Bristol, and it was offering her mother a job – her first job – as a junior secretary. She smiled to herself as she read the terms and conditions; ten days holiday a year and a weekly salary of five pounds seven shillings and sixpence. Five pounds seven shillings and sixpence! She replaced the letter, took out the next one. Same letterhead, same typewriter, even, by the look of it. But a very different content.

Yes, the writer agreed that Patricia could take unpaid leave to enable her to look after her sick cousin in Worcester, and yes, her position would be held open for her. Kate stared at the letter. She had begun to tremble. Paid leave to look after a sick cousin in Worcester? What cousin? She didn't know of one. She checked the date. June, 1964. Oh dear God, it fitted.

Kate sat back on her heels, staring into space, at the dust motes dancing in a shaft of sunshine. Worcester. Was that where Trish had gone to have her child? But why *Worcester*? Was there a mother and baby home there? Or was it a red herring, simply conjured up as a suitable location for the fictional cousin? Whichever, if the letter regarding her leave of absence was here in the vanity case there was a good chance that any other correspondence relating to the birth was here too. And perhaps the adoption . . . Kate's fingers tingled suddenly as if the pile of letters had become charged with electricity.

The Manila envelopes seemed the best bet – local authorities and courts would certainly still have been using them in those days if private firms of solicitors were. But to her disappointment none of the envelopes revealed any more than she already knew. Two more letters from her employers, one asking Trish if she had any idea when she would be returning to work, the other confirming the date of her return to the office – September, 1964 – and both, curiously, addressed to Trish here, at the Cedars. Clearly she had not given her employers any forwarding address in Worcester or anywhere else. The other Manila envelopes were stamped Inland Revenue and contained code numbers and some communications regarding the fact that Trish had not been in receipt of a salary between June and September.

Kate put them all back in the vanity case and turned to the handwritten envelopes. She wriggled them out of their ribbon of pink wool, flicking through to check the postmarks. If the baby had been born in 1964 there was no need to pry into letters written earlier. Perhaps she could find out what she needed to know without violating her mother's privacy totally.

She did not have to look very far. Half an hour later she packed the letters together again, keeping out just one or two, which she put with the ones in the buff envelopes. The rest went into the bottom of the cardboard crisp box, out of sight beneath the photographs. Then she went downstairs to the study, where Jon Nicholson was wading through a pile of paperwork.

'I think I've found something,' she said. 'I think the place to start searching may be Gloucester.'

'Gloucester? Why Gloucester?' Miranda asked.

Jon Nicholson had called the others down when Kate presented him with her evidence; clearly shaken, they were questioning her finds furiously.

'Because Mummy was there for three months in 1964,' Kate said.

'Why should that mean anything?' Jessica wrapped her arms around herself in a gesture that was curiously defensive. 'She might have been working there.'

'But she wasn't. She was on paid leave, supposedly looking after a sick cousin in Worcester.'

'So why Gloucester?' Miranda asked again. 'Why not Worcester?'

'I've no idea. But that's where she was.' Kate tossed an envelope down onto the desk. 'This is just one of a number of letters from Grandma to Mummy care of a Mrs Millett at Number Fifteen, Osborne Terrace. To me that sounds like digs. I think she must have gone there to hide away until the baby was born.'

'Why didn't she go to a mother and baby home?' Miranda asked.

'I don't know that either. Perhaps she thought she had a better chance of keeping it a secret if she . . .'

'Now, just a minute!' Jessica interrupted. 'Aren't you making a pretty big leap here? Why should you assume Mummy went there to have a baby? Do the letters mention such a thing?'

'Not in so many words, well, not the ones I've looked at

so far, anyway,' Kate admitted. 'But there are plenty of references to "when all this is over and you come home", that sort of thing.'

'For heaven's sake, that could mean anything!'

'I'm sorry, Jess, but it's good enough for me.'

'Well, it would be, wouldn't it? You seem determined to go along with this fantasy, Kate. It's almost as if you wanted it to be true. And you're twisting everything to make it fit. I'm sorry, but I simply cannot understand why you should want to believe all of this. If Mummy did have a baby, what possible good can it do to rake it all up now?' She grabbed the top letter from the ones Kate had laid on the desk, ripping it across and across again. 'That's what I'd like to do with them all, and anything else that supposedly adds substance to these ridiculous claims.'

'Jessica!' Kate cried, appalled.

'Now see what good it is to you!' Jessica was still tearing at the letter with a sort of frenzied determination. 'Try to stick *that* back together if you want to use it as evidence.' She raised her hands high above the desk and tossed the shreds of paper so that they rained down like confetti.

'You shouldn't have done that,' Jon said, fairly mildly, Kate thought, but for the first time she felt some sympathy with Jessica. Hadn't she wanted to destroy the photographs and letters before anyone else could see them? And what had she done? Produced them as evidence for her case. Suddenly she felt slightly ashamed of herself.

'Mrs Howard, I realize this is upsetting for you,' Jon Nicholson was saying. 'But you really are not helping yourself or anyone else by all this, and whatever you might think, I have a job to do. I must ask you to respect that.'

'Respect?' Jessica was beside herself. '*Respect* – for someone like you? Seducing Grandpa away from the person who's represented his legal interests all these years, scheming with him, poking around . . . What's your interest in it, I'd like to know? It's not going to turn out that it was *you* who was adopted in Gloucester or Worcester or bloody Timbuktu in 1964, is it?'

'Jessica!' Kate exploded, horrified.

'Oh, yes – *Jessica*!' she mimicked, reaching for the other letters, but this time Jon Nicholson was too quick for her. He caught her wrist, looking at her directly and sternly, so that for a ludicrous moment they resembled a pair of arm wrestlers locked in combat.

'I don't advise that, Mrs Howard.' His tone, too, was stern. 'I'll pretend I didn't hear the accusations you just levelled against me. But I can't promise to turn a blind eye if you try to destroy any more papers which belong to this estate. I am, let me remind you, its executor, and you, it seems to me, are trying to interfere with the due process of the law.'

'You pompous bloody ass!' Jessica wrenched her hand free. 'I don't have to stay here and listen to this. As for you, Kate, I don't know what's got into you. Well, you and Miranda can do what you bloody well like. I'm going!'

She marched out; a moment later they could see her on the steps calling angrily for the boys.

'I've never heard Jess swear before!' Miranda said, awed.

'She's upset,' Kate said. 'For someone who is usually buttoned-up and proper, she certainly knows how to make a scene when she feels like it. I'm really sorry, Jon. She had no business saying things like that.'

'I've heard worse,' he said with a rueful grin.

'And ripping up that letter . . .'

'We've already established it didn't actually contain what you might call incontrovertible evidence.'

'I'd like to have seen it though,' Miranda said wistfully.

'It really didn't say anything,' Kate reiterated. 'And the others are all in the same vein. Grandma obviously wrote to Mum regularly, at least once a week.'

'Are there any letters from Grandpa?'

'Not that I found,' Kate said. 'Nor from anyone else, come to that.'

It seemed the whole thing had been a very well-kept secret.

Ten minutes later, Jessica was back. 'I went without my vase.'

'It's quite safe, put aside and waiting for you,' Jon said.

She hesitated in the doorway. 'I'm sorry. I shouldn't have said what I did, though I refuse to apologize for ripping up the letter. I'd have done the same to all of them if you'd let me get my hands on them.'

He smiled. 'I quite understand.'

'Do you? Really?'

'Of course I do. I'm not entirely without feeling. But as I told you, I have a job to do.'

She sighed. 'I suppose you do.'

'Then can we work together without fighting?'

'I suppose so.' Her jaw set. 'But if you think I am going to help you find this fictitious child, then I'm afraid you are much mistaken.'

'Let's forget about it for the moment, then, shall we? Look – I'm trying to make head or tail of these books of your grandfather's. Trying to find some record of all that land Hugh sent me the deeds for, and all sorts of other things, and getting nowhere. Do you think perhaps you could help me?'

With a sigh Jessica took off her coat and hung it over the back of a chair. She was flattered by his request, but she had not the slightest intention of showing it.

'All right,' she said. 'What do you want to know?'

'He really is quite a personable man,' she said to Adrian later. 'The trouble is, he's still insisting on finding the fourth beneficiary. And he hasn't the first idea about Robert's affairs. There would never have been all this trouble with Hugh.'

Adrian refrained from pointing out that it was clearly Hugh's familiarity with the family that Robert had wished to avoid. But he didn't want to involve himself in another endless discussion about it. He was already sick to death of the subject.

'I'm sure you were able to put him straight, Jess,' he said, without looking up from the business section of the *Sunday Times*.

'I think so, yes.' She frowned. 'Adrian – you're not really listening to me at all, are you?'

'Of course I am.'

She shook her head impatiently. She didn't believe him. But it was a tribute to Jon Nicholson's tact that it did not occur to her than Adrian might not be the first one who had tried to pull the wool over her eyes that day.

Eight

K ate had been home for about an hour when the telephone rang. She reached for it, cradling the receiver under her chin whilst at the same time taking a frozen cod and prawn fricassée out of its wrapper.

'Hello?'

'Jon Nicholson here. I know we've only just parted company, but I really do need to talk to you, and I'd rather it was face to face. Could you spare me an hour if I was to come over to you?'

Kate chewed her lip. 'To be honest, I'd rather not this evening. I've been out all day and I do have things to do. I haven't even eaten yet.'

'Supposing I was to buy you supper? Would that help?'

Kate hesitated. The cod and prawn fricassée didn't look madly appealing in its frozen gelatinous state, and besides she was curious to know what it was that he wanted to talk to her about that was so urgent.

'All right,' she said. 'Just as long as you come over to Bleadon. There's no way I'm driving all the way back to Market Denton tonight.'

'Done. I have your address. Is it fairly straightforward to find?'

'Oh, there's no need for that. There's a good Indian restaurant in the High Street, the Rajpoot. I could meet you there. You do like Indian, do you?'

'I do. Will we be able to get in without a booking?'

'On a Sunday night, I should think so. I'll call them and make sure though if you like. What shall we say – half-past seven?'

'Fine.' He sounded vaguely put out; because she had taken over the arrangements, she thought, smiling to herself. There was something faintly old-fashioned – and rather nice – about the way he'd assumed he would pick her up. But she had no intention of allowing that. She was too fond of her independence.

Kate finally made it to the restaurant, a bit late because just as she was leaving Chris had rung, and then she'd remembered she'd promised to phone Liz and tried, without success, to get hold of her. Jon Nicholson was already there when she arrived, sitting in one of the little red velvet booths and sipping what looked like beer.

'Sorry I'm late,' she said. And then: 'Oh dear, that's twice today I've had to apologize. I seem to be making a habit of it.'

'That's all right. I appreciate you turning out again, especially at such short notice. Would you like a drink?'

'Oh, I'd love a gin and tonic. Except . . .' She broke off, remembering with regret that she had insisted on driving herself. 'Perhaps I'd better not.'

'Had you been drinking before you came out?'

'Of course not!'

'One wouldn't hurt then, surely? We can order iced water to go with the meal. I always think anything else is wasted on curry, anyway.'

'Oh, I guess so. And something tells me I'm going to need a drink. You've found something out, haven't you? That's what you want to talk to me about.'

'Shall we order first?'

'OK.'

They perused the menus briefly; Kate, who usually maintained that choosing and anticipating were equally as pleasurable as actually eating, was scarcely able to concentrate on the list of exotic dishes. By the time the waiter returned with her gin and tonic they had decided to do it the easy way and go for the set meal for two. The waiter departed carrying the menus and Kate sipped her drink as if it were a life saver, looking at Jon over the rim of her glass.

'Well?'

'A couple of things. As I thought, your grandfather had been employing a private detective. I found a business card amongst his papers – a Mr Knott with an address in Victoria Street. It's a flat above one of the shops there, I suspect. I'll check it out first thing tomorrow and see if I can get him to tell me the result of his investigation.'

Kate looked at him narrowly. 'What makes you think there was a result?'

'There was also an account from this Mr Knott, dated just a few days before Mr Holbrook had his first stroke. It wasn't specific, in fact it was very vague. On purpose, I imagine. "For services rendered" covers a multitude of sins, and when people consult private detectives, they usually require a high level of confidentiality. But "for services rendered" suggests to me that the investigation had reached a successful conclusion.'

'He'd found Mummy's missing child, you mean?'

'It has to be a possibility, doesn't it?'

'Hmm. Had Grandpa paid the account?'

'It's not been receipted, but it looks like a copy to me. I should imagine your grandfather returned the original with his cheque; I'll sort through his bank statements and cheque-book stubs tomorrow and see if I can tie it up. But I would have thought if it hadn't been paid the chappie would have sent a reminder by now. There was no sign of one, and in any case, if there had been it would have alerted whoever was looking after things after your grandfather was taken to hospital to the fact that something a little bit out of the ordinary had been going on.'

'Adrian – Jessica's husband – was doing all that,' Kate said. 'He's in the finance business, and he thought he was one of the executors of Grandpa's will. Well, he was, on the old will.'

'I see.' He wondered if that went some way to explaining Jessica's hostility. Perhaps. But it was more than that; more a stubborn refusal to accept that her mother could have had secrets of which she knew nothing. 'It's possible, I suppose, that a reminder did come and he paid it and kept quiet about it. Perhaps he didn't want to upset your sister. She is quite volatile, isn't she?'

'About this, yes. She's not usually. But then, usually she is in control. I think she feels a bit helpless at the moment.'

Jon smiled wryly. 'Anyway, I didn't think it wise to raise the subject again whilst we were at the house today. Didn't want her rushing off in another huff, which is why I decided to let discretion be the better part of valour and brief you privately.'

'But I don't quite see why it was so urgent,' Kate said. 'Or why you couldn't have told me about it over the telephone, for that matter.'

'Well . . . there is actually something else besides.' He hesitated, fiddling with his glass and looking uncomfortable. 'Does the name Tamsin Wells mean anything to you?'

'Tamsin Wells . . .' It was ringing bells, but it didn't make any sort of sense. 'You mean the *model* Tamsin Wells?'

'Yes. I found an autographed photograph of her in your Grandfather's desk, and it occurred to me that . . .'

'The woman at the funeral!' Kate said disbelievingly. 'Yes, you're right! Now you come to mention it, I think it might have been her! I thought there was something familiar about that woman, but I just couldn't place her.'

'Why should you? I don't suppose any of us were expecting to see a famous model there, and I'm not at all sure I would have recognized her anyway, even without the hat and the dark glasses. They all tend to look alike to me.'

'Not Tamsin Wells! She's really beautiful.'

It was a nationally accepted fact. Tamsin Wells, one of the faces of the nineties. Best known as the girl who advertised the Gazelle car, the girl who drove it around mountain passes, who parked up on the shoreline with the waves lapping the wheels to watch the sun go down in a scarlet orb into a violet sea, who leaned against the bonnet, caressing it with sensuous pleasure, but who never, ever so much as looked at a man. Tamsin Wells, the Gazelle girl, ultimate sex symbol, desirable and unattainable.

The waiter was hovering now, unloading a hot plate and a carousel of mixed dishes on to the table. Kate waited until he had finished and glided away before she went on: 'Surely you're not going to suggest that Tamsin Wells is Mum's missing child? My half sister? That is bizarre. Impossible!'

Jon helped himself to an onion bhaji. 'Why impossible?'

'Well, just look at me! I couldn't possibly have a half-sister who looked like that!'

'Why not?'

She laughed. 'It's all right, you don't have to be kind. But I'm sorry, I just can't believe it. Not Tamsin Wells.'

'Have some food.' Jon manoeuvred the serving spoon closer to her. 'It's one explanation of her being at the funeral, you must admit. Suppose, for argument's sake, the private detective traced her and they were in contact. She could have sent your grand-father the photograph not long before he had his stroke. Perhaps they never got around to meeting in person.'

'I thought you had a theory that whatever it was Grandpa found out was the cause of his being taken ill. You're not suggesting that a photograph was enough to cause that?'

'No. It would have to be something else, something we don't know about. And I could be barking up the wrong tree altogether. There could be another, quite different reason for her being at the funeral.'

Kate, a spoonful of fragrant rice halfway to her plate, froze. 'That she was a friend of his, you mean?'

'Well, yes . . .'

Kate deposited the rice on her plate, dipped into a vegetable korma. 'You needn't look so guilty about suggesting it. It's been perfectly obvious from the start the mystery woman had to be one or the other. No one dresses up in black and turns up to throw a rose into the grave of a perfect stranger, unless they happen to be a sandwich short of a picnic. No, the shock is that she's who she is. How on earth did Grandpa meet someone like that?'

'Assuming that she's a friend and not the missing grand-child? I have no idea. He never mentioned her to me, not in passing, and not as a beneficiary.'

'Which is a bit strange if she was a friend,' Kate mused. 'He seems to have left something to just about everybody else, even if it's on the keepsake level. I have to admit it seems to point to her being . . . well, the person she might be in the first place. Mummy's adopted child. And I guess she'd be about the right age, too. I mean, she's not one of those very young models, is she? The fact that she's older has always been one of her selling points.'

They ate in silence for a few moments, then Kate asked: 'So what happens now?'

'I shall get in touch with Miss Tamsin Wells and try to fix up a meeting with her.'

Kate put her fork down. 'I don't think I shall mention this to Jessica until we hear what she has to say. She's likely to go ballistic.'

He grinned. 'Yep. We shall have to take cover in the trenches.'

'I'm so sorry.'

'Goes with the territory.'

'I'll bet you're wishing you'd never heard of Robert Holbrook, or Market Denton, even. You haven't been here long, have you?'

'About two years.'

'And before that?'

'Can't you tell from my accent? Monmouth is my home. Just across the border, the bit that calls itself Wales but still feels like England. Except that we are all rugby mad, and if you happen to be in Cardiff Arms Park for an international you would be left in no doubt where our loyalties lie.'

'So why come to Denton?'

'The firm I work for decided to expand, and market research showed that Market Denton was a likely place. Only the one old established firm – and premises came up at just the right moment. I was asked if I'd like to set up an office here, and it seemed like a good idea at the time. I don't have family ties to worry about as some of the other likely candidates did – children settled in their schools, that sort of thing. I'm a free agent. So – I accepted the challenge. And here I am.' He reached for the serving spoon. 'Can I help you to something else? This dish is chicken, quite spicy, but very good.'

'I couldn't eat another thing,' Kate said. 'You finish it.'

'Sure?'

'Quite.'

She watched him demolish what was left on the platter with relish, and smiled to herself. Jon Nicholson clearly liked his food. It was probably all that rugby . . .

'You're in business, aren't you?' he asked, laying down his fork at last.

'Mmm.' Kate's good humour disappeared, leaving her feeling flat and apprehensive. The prospect of having to go back to her studio tomorrow was not a nice one. Whereas once she had itched to be there, now it meant dealing with the piles of bills, placating the bank manager, putting a brave face on for the girls in the workroom and waiting for orders which no longer seemed to come. How the hell was she going to cope with it, presiding over the failure of a business which was her whole life?

'Unless you have any more shocks in store for me, I really think I ought to be getting home,' she said.

'I don't think I can rustle any more up,' Jon said lightly. But for a brief moment Kate thought that he looked distinctly regretful.

Sandra Morton returned the walkabout telephone to its cradle and went back into the big, light room that she always called the 'lounge'.

The lounge, furnished from end to end in cream, was Sandra's pride and joy, the room she had dreamed of in the days when home was a boxy little council house, and it had been the selling point, as far as she was concerned, when she and Jack had first viewed the house. With the money he was making as a professional footballer burning a hole in his pocket, Jack had fancied something solid and impressive, a miniature version of a stately home. But Sandra had found all the old houses they had viewed dark and claustrophobic. This one, brand new, with its huge open-plan rooms and ceiling-to-floor windows leading out on to wide manicured lawns, had made her feel good, pampered and happy and excited and content. Sometimes, over the years, Jack had suggested moving, but Sandra had always dug her heels in. Nothing would persuade her to give up her private palace for a great mausoleum of a place like the Cedars, which she knew Jack coveted.

'What on earth,' Sandra enquired now, of no one in particular, 'is the matter with that woman?'

'What woman?' Ash asked. He was sprawled on the cream leather corner sofa with several sections of *The Sunday Times* spread out around him.

'Verity Ormrod. That was her on the phone. She really is a pain in the ass.' Sandra dropped into one of the enormous squashy chairs, kicking off her fluffy mules and tucking her feet up beneath her. She was wearing burgundy velour leggings and a big cream silk overshirt, and her hair was caught up with rhinestone-studded combs. In a soft light, if one did not stare too closely, she looked about twenty-five – thirty at most.

'What did she want?' Ash asked, looking at his mother narrowly over the top of his paper.

'Goodness knows, I don't. She was rabbiting on about this will of Robert's, asking me if I knew what had happened about it. She's upset because Hugh wasn't trusted with it, I suppose, but why on earth she should want to talk to *me* about it, I can't imagine.'

She reached for her cigarettes, a pack of slim elegant More, and her lighter, equally slim and elegant. 'I told her, I haven't the slightest interest in whether Trish had an illegitimate child or not, which made her splutter a bit, since she is obviously agog to know the truth. It's always the way, isn't it? It's always the holier-than-thou types who are absolutely avid for any snippet of scandal. She wants to be censorious, I expect, whilst all the time pretending to be sympathetic. Personally, I have no time at all for that sort of attitude, especially when poor Trish is no longer here to defend herself. There but for the grace of God go many of us.'

Ash, who was reflecting on Trish's assessment of Verity, said nothing. The holier-than-thou types. It seemed to him that was a fairly accurate assessment of Wendy's mother. As for the bit about 'there but for the grace of God', that was predictable too. Since he had learned to count nine months back from his birthday he had known it was less the grace of God which had made him legitimate than a hastily arranged marriage ceremony.

'I had my suspicions, of course,' Sandra confided. 'Years ago at a dinner party we were playing the Truth Game. I asked Trish which of her children she loved best, and she replied that she loved all four of them equally. It was passed off at the time that Trish had had too much to drink, but it seemed a strange mistake for anyone to make, drunk or not.' She inhaled thoughtfully. 'Verity was there that night. I'm sure if I remember it, she must too. But she's not letting on.'

There was still no response from Ash and for a moment or two Sandra was silent, lost in her thoughts. Then she went on: 'She really is a ghastly woman, Verity. Quite ruthless somehow beneath all that sensible tweed and Laura Ashley cosiness. And poor Hugh is totally under her thumb, of course. Always has been. And she still treats Wendy like a child, too. Interfering where she shouldn't and fussing and worrying about her. The girl is over thirty years old, for heaven's sake. But Verity the mother hen can't let go.'

'She's worried about Wendy?' Ash asked sharply.

'Oh, she seems to think there is something wrong just because she invited Wendy and Tim to lunch today and they didn't go. She has this idea that Tim is giving her little girl a hard time. It doesn't seem to occur to her that poor Tim has problems of his own. It must be pretty unpleasant for him to have lost his job and have to be supported by his wife, especially since she's still employed by the very people who chose to give him the boot. If he's taking it out on Wendy, it's hardly surprising.'

'He doesn't hit her around, does he?' Ash asked.

Sandra looked at him narrowly through her cigarette smoke. 'What makes you ask that?'

'Oh, no reason.'

But she knew he wasn't telling the truth.

'I'm sure Tim wouldn't do anything like that,' she said.

'He'd better not be, is all I can say.'

A frisson of alarm prickled in Sandra's veins. She knew her son, knew that tone of voice. She also knew that he still had strong feelings for Wendy.

'Leave well alone, Ashley,' she cautioned. 'Interfering between husband and wife is not a good idea, and will only end in tears. Wendy will sort out her own problems; there's nothing you can do about it.'

He didn't reply, but his face still wore that dark, brooding expression and there was a steely glint in his eye. He bundled the various sections of the Sunday paper together into an untidy heap on the coffee table and got up, heading for the door.

'Where are you going?' she asked sharply.

'For a drink with Alistair. We arranged it this morning.'

'Oh, for a moment I thought . . . What time will you be home?'

'I don't know. Not late I should have thought.'

'Have a good time, then.'

When he had gone, Sandra stubbed out her cigarette and almost immediately lit another. She presumed Ash was telling the truth when he said he was going to meet his brother; it was the sort of alibi that could be checked too easily to be invented. But she felt uneasy, all the same. Much as she was enjoying having her elder son at home, she couldn't help thinking it might be rather a relief when the leave he had taken came to an end and he headed back to the Middle East. Well away from Wendy Bryant and the hold she still had over him.

When they left the Rajpoot, Jon insisted on walking Kate back to the pay-and-display where she had parked, though his own car was squeezed into a kerbside space almost right outside the restaurant.

'There's no need, really. I'll be fine,' Kate said, but he over-ruled her.

'Sorry to disagree, but I'll feel a lot happier if I know you're safely on your way. I'm afraid this town is as bad as any other when it comes to gangs of yobbos, and that pay-and-display car park is very dark.'

'Well, if you insist.' Much as she liked her independence, there was something rather nice about someone being concerned for your safety, Kate thought. Especially one who looked as if he could fell a couple of thugs with a left and a right and then catch any who were making a run for it with a flying rugby tackle. That was not something she could imagine Chris doing in a million years. He wasn't a New Man exactly, not the quiche-and-sandals type, but he wouldn't be one to wade in either, and she'd always thought that was a sensible attitude. Now she glanced at Jon Nicholson and felt a twist of something that felt suspiciously like old-fashioned attraction.

For goodness' sake! she scolded herself. That single gin and tonic seemed to have gone to her head. Or perhaps it was the spicy food. Was curry supposed to be an aphrodisiac? She couldn't remember.

They didn't meet any yobs, or 'yobbos' as he called them, only a couple of rather merry louts with their arms round one another, singing loudly and kicking a lager can, but Jon was right, the car park was badly lit and Kate remembered the last time she'd used it late in the evening she'd found it vaguely threatening. For a moment she couldn't see her car, and forgot the rather treacherous feeling of attraction she had experienced towards Jon in a great wash of panic. It wasn't there. Her lovely little GTi had been stolen. And all the things she'd brought from the Cedars were still in the boot, too, all the photographs and letters . . .

Then she saw it, hidden behind a huge chunky Volvo, and breathed again.

'Oh, I thought my car had gone . . . I'm always doing that! It's small enough to disappear behind practically anything. Or else I go to the wrong row, or the wrong floor in a multi-storey.'

Jon laughed. 'Well, you're all right this time. Joy riders are awfully fond of GTis, though. If it worries you, you should get something old and heavy and slow.'

'Who wants something old and heavy and slow?' Kate asked. 'And you don't practice what you preach, do you? That is an extremely racy car you have if I'm not mistaken.'

'Yes, I must put my hand up to that. One day I'll move on to the sort of solid respectable model solicitors are supposed to drive, I suppose. In the meantime I comfort myself that nothing is safe from the car thieves if they make up their mind to it. I had to defend a lad the other day on a charge of taking and driving away a milk float.'

'Defend. In court?'

'Magistrates' court. I was duty solicitor.'

'I didn't realize you did court work. I thought . . .'

'That I did only probate? In a small firm like ours one has to be a bit of a jack of all trades. I have a specialist for Family Law, and a very experienced conveyancing clerk, and eventually I shall take someone on to deal with the probate too, though as you know, at the moment I'm covering it myself. And very glad I am too that it was me your grandfather came to.'

She glanced at him. 'I'd have thought you'd got yourself rather a poisoned chalice there.'

'Maybe. But it also means I met you.'

Kate was totally unprepared for that. It had never occurred to her that the attraction she had experienced might be reciprocated, or even to ask herself why he had felt the need to take her out to supper in order to brief her on something that could just as easily have been reported to her by telephone in the morning. Suddenly her cheeks were hot.

'Do you say that to all your clients?' Embarrassment made her tone hard and a little shrill.

'Not all of them, no.'

'I'm glad to hear it.' She could still feel the flush burning in her cheeks and she turned quickly away, fitting the key into the lock on the car door. 'Thanks for seeing me back to my car. I'll be fine now.'

'That's OK then.' But he sounded a little taut, too. The ease between them had disappeared as if by magic.

She got into the car, started the engine. As she drove out of the dimly lit car park she glanced in her rear-view mirror. He was still standing there under the single lamp standard, hands in the pockets of his jacket, watching her go. She was, she realized, not only fazed, but also slightly regretful. She'd put him in his place, and for a crazy moment she wished desperately that she had not.

That blew that, Jon thought ruefully as the tail lights of Kate's car disappeared into the night. Well, you couldn't win 'em all, and it looked as if Kate Morton was going to be one to put down to experience. A pity though. It was a long time since he'd felt quite so attracted to a woman. In fact he'd barely looked at one since Megan . . .

The familiar knot, weighing heavily like a badly digested meal, was suddenly there in his stomach. Megan, lovely, laughing Megan, with her long straight hair and her huge sparkling eyes; Megan, small and warm and soft, with whom he had fallen in love without thinking about it and certainly without telling her. He'd been so involved with his studies and his rugby he'd taken her for granted, and taken their future together for granted too. In his head he had made vague plans, how he would ask her to marry him as soon as he was qualified but not before, because he could hardly afford to live on his student grant, let alone buy a decent ring, and he wanted to do things properly. Megan deserved it.

The trouble was the chance to buy Megan a ring had never come. One day she was poorly, with a feverish cold and a headache, the next she developed a rash and was rushed into hospital where, less than seventy-two hours later, she was dead. Meningitis, they said. Viral meningitis. Jon had been devastated. It was only when she was no longer there, sitting on his bunk bed listening to him quoting reams of definitions, or putting Wham! tapes into his machine when he wanted to listen to Queen, or twisting her arms around his neck with that teasing look in her eyes, that he realized just what he had lost. She had gone from his life and a light had gone out.

The pain had begun then and it had never really gone away. It wasn't just the loss, it was the guilt too, that came from never really telling her how he felt about her, and knowing that now he never could. He'd graduated, gone home to Monmouth, gone through the motions. But a part of him was dead with Megan and though he did not dwell on it, he nursed an inner certainty that there could never be anyone else for him who could come close to matching her.

Now he stood in the car park, hands thrust into the pockets of his jacket, and thought with some surprise that for the first time in years he had actually been affected by a woman on a basis that was not purely physical. When Kate had left this afternoon, he had actually wanted to see her again, soon, and not in his office. Which was why he'd suggested meeting this evening, using the estate as an excuse. As they'd talked, he'd had the feeling she liked him too, which was why he'd risked an overture which stepped outside the professional. Well, it seemed he'd been wrong. She'd given him a very cool brush-off. And it had stung. Maybe just his pride, maybe something more.

But the job wasn't over yet. There were still a lot of ends to be tied up. Jon realized that in spite of the knock-back, he was still hoping he could find a way to get through to Kate Morton.

Tim Bryant was standing at the bedroom window looking out.

'Who the hell is that—'

'What?' Wendy, sitting on the stool at the dressing table to remove her make-up, glanced round, puzzled.

'There's a car parked just opposite. It's been there for the last half-hour.' Tim sounded put out, angry even, and Wendy's heart sank. He'd been pretty amenable the last few days. It was as if striking her had shocked him into realizing he really couldn't go on drinking and hating, and she thought he was sorry, too, for what he had done. Now, though, his voice was slightly slurred again as well as annoyed, and she wondered if he'd been knocking the whisky back again when her back was turned.

'Sophie Gunning has a boyfriend,' she said, trying to calm

the situation. 'He was parked there for ages the other night. I expect he's there again.'

'No, there's somebody sitting in the car.'

'Sophie Gunning and her boyfriend. Saying goodnight.'

'What do you take me for? A fool?' Tim snarled. 'It's that bloody Ash Morton, isn't it? I'm going out to give him what he's asking for!'

'Don't be stupid, Tim.' As he passed her, she caught at the sleeve of his towelling robe to stop him.

What happened next took her completely by surprise. Tim swung round, lashing out, and before she knew it Wendy found herself toppling backwards off the stool, and landing in a heap on the fluffy rug, gasping with shock, pain, and sudden over-whelming fear. She covered her face with her hands, and his slippered toe kicked viciously into her stomach. She doubled up, groaning, and he kicked her again.

'You knew he was there, didn't you, you bitch?' He aimed another kick at the small of her back, and stormed out.

Wendy heard the bolts being drawn on the front door but she couldn't move. She lay where she had fallen, curled into a frightened ball of pain. Her sobs were ragged, each shaky breath a knife thrust of agony. When she heard his footsteps on the stairs, returning, she tried to struggle to her feet, drag-ging herself up by holding on to the edge of the bed, but all the use seemed to have gone out of her arms and legs, and she collapsed on to the rug again.

As he appeared in the doorway she shrank into herself, looking up at him like a hunted animal.

'Wendy?' He sounded startled, as if it was a surprise to him to see her lying there. He came towards her and she cowered away, expecting him to kick her again. But he didn't. He simply leaned over her, looking down at her with a perplexed expression.

'What in the world is the matter with you?'

'You . . .' Her voice cracked. 'You hurt me, Tim!'

'Oh, Wend, I didn't mean it. Get up!' She stared at him in disbelief, struggling into a sitting position and hugging herself with her arms. 'I'm sorry,' he said, but with more aggression than regret. 'I thought it was that bloody Ash Morton out there, after you again. I was wrong. It was just some young lad.'

'I told you that,' she managed.

'Oh, I know what you *said* . . . but you make me so angry! Why do you do it—?' And then: 'Oh, Wendy, don't cry!' He dropped to his knees beside her, rocking her into his arms, covering her face and hair with kisses. Wendy was too shocked, too frightened and full of despair to even protest.

Nine

'Tamsin, honey, are you awake?' The low voice of George, her partner, crept into Tamsin Wells' semi-conscious.

She opened her eyes experimentally, squinted as the October sunshine, slanting in through a gap in the curtains, pricked them painfully, and closed them again. She'd been very late home last night after doing a stint of duty at the Mill House Hostel for the homeless; she felt muzzy and her head was aching. She was aware too of an insidious anxiety that crept in her veins like a murky tide. It had infiltrated her dreams and was still with her now. The Mill House was in deep financial trouble; unless it raised a substantial amount of funding soon it would have to close.

They'd asked her if she could see her way to helping out as she had done in the past, but this time Tamsin wasn't sure she could, or at least, not with enough cash to make the difference. Successful she might be, her face known to millions as the girl in the adverts for the Gazelle – 'the most desirable car in the world' – but she was not rich any more. Bad advice resulting in a series of bad investments had seen to that. She needed a new contract to keep her own head above water, never mind bailing out the Mill House, and she wasn't sure it was going to happen. She was very afraid she'd had her day and was about to be replaced by a new face, someone younger and fresher. Truth to tell, she'd been amazed when she'd landed the contract in the first place; she'd thought she was already too old. But they hadn't wanted one of the very young girls; she'd matched the image they wanted to portray. The trouble was time had moved on, and so had she. Well, if it all ended tomorrow she couldn't complain. She'd had a good run. But it hurt to see projects like the Mill House go down the pan and not be able to do anything to help.

The Mill House was close to Tamsin's heart. Raised in care

herself, she empathized totally with the homeless. *There but for the grace of God* . . . she thought whenever she saw some pathetic figure huddled in a doorway. And was thankful that places like the Mill House existed to provide those who needed it most with at least some temporary shelter.

She often visited the Mill House in the late evening when they were at their busiest, dressed in jeans and a lumber jacket, her glossy hair tucked under a baseball cap. Sometimes she sat down and chatted to those who needed a friendly ear, sometimes she washed dishes, sometimes she joined the soup run, taking comfort out on to the streets for those who had not found their way to the old, overcrowded building. She did it because she wanted to, and because she felt her own good fortune invested in her a special responsibility for others who had not been so lucky. And she found the most enormous satisfaction, and a sense of peace with herself, from her involvement, besides feeling the friendships she had made with the other volunteers were worth more than any in her rather superficial world.

She couldn't bear to think that the Mill House would have to close its doors, but she didn't know what she could do about it. Front a campaign for funding, perhaps? It was a possibility, but she shrank from making public what she had always ensured was a private commitment. And there was no guarantee it would bring in the funds required. The dilemma smouldered away at the edges of her mind as she fought her way back to full wakefulness, and saw that George was holding out the walkabout telephone to her with a resigned expression.

'For me?' she asked. Her voice was still thick with sleep.

He covered the receiver with his hand. 'Marjie Baines. Shall I ask her to call back?'

'Yes . . . no, I'd better take it.'

Marjie Baines was her agent; she'd been waiting for this call. 'Just give me a minute.'

She rubbed her eyes gently, then opened them again behind the screen of her fingers. Even without the sun in them they felt gritty and heavy. Perhaps she should put a stop to these late nights. She couldn't seem to take them as well nowadays as she'd used to, and in her profession looking good wasn't just a matter of vanity, it was necessity, and the older you got and the more competition there was, the more necessary it became. But what was the point of any of it if you couldn't live your life the way you wanted to, do the things that were important to you?

She pushed her fingers up into her glossy chestnut hair, easing the heels of her hands away from her eyes and then reaching for the phone that George was holding. He handed it to her, then sat down on the edge of the bed, looking at her expectantly. She made a wry face back at him. She didn't mind him listening to her conversation. They had no secrets where her work was concerned.

'Hi, it's Tamsin,' she said into the mouthpiece.

'Tamsin.' Marjie's voice was crisply efficient. Obviously *she* hadn't been up half the night. 'I owe you an update.'

'You've talked to the Gazelle execs?'

'Yes.'

'And?' Tamsin was aware she was holding her breath.

'Nothing yet. They haven't got round to making up their minds about the new campaign.'

'They might be going to replace me, you mean.'

'Not necessarily. They're still discussing different approaches, apparently. If they stick with the Gazelle girl, I should think without doubt it will be you. You *are* the Gazelle girl. But there's a possibility they might change tack entirely, go for something high tech. So much is becoming possible, these days.'

Tamsin was aware of a sinking feeling in the pit of her stomach. She'd always known it couldn't last for ever, but it wasn't pleasant, facing the reality that the years of security were over.

'What about the other feelers you were putting out for me?' she asked.

'Nothing at the moment, I'm afraid. I'm working on getting you a spot in the Celebrity Recipes ads, and I think that could well be a runner. "*When she's not racing her Gazelle in some exotic spot, Tamsin Wells likes nothing better than cooking herself a spaghetti carbonara using our ingredients . . .*" That sort of thing. But of course it's only a one-off, and the difficulty I'm having getting you something more permanent is that your face is just too well known. Everybody thinks of you as the Gazelle girl. I'm going to have to go, Tamsin. There's a call coming through on my other line.'

'Maybe it's an offer for me.'

'Unlikely at this time on a Monday morning,' Marjie said flatly. She had absolutely no sense of humour, Tamsin thought.

'Well?' George said as she clicked the phone off and deposited it in the folds of the duvet. 'That wasn't good news, by the sound of it.'

'No. She woke me up to tell me nobody wants me.'

'I want you.' He leaned over, kissing her on the lips, and she turned her head away slightly.

'Don't, please. I'm not properly awake.'

He sighed, hiding his hurt. 'Do you want a cup of coffee?'

'That would be nice. Is there some made?'

'Should be. I put it on just now, when I finished working out.'

That explained why he was still wearing his towelling robe, she realized. She'd had one of the bedrooms converted into a gym, a mistake as far as she was concerned, since she needed a personal trainer and a health club setting to persuade her to work out, but George used it regularly, and it showed. Though he was in his middle forties, he still had a good physique.

'Haven't you got to work today?' she asked as he came back into the bedroom with the coffee and a glass of orange juice.

'Not until later. I'll get off at about eleven.'

George was a freelance photographer. She'd met him on a magazine shoot ten years ago, and liked him immediately. She'd always liked older men, perhaps they took the place of the father she'd never known. George had been married and divorced; he had two children, a boy and a girl, whom he adored. They lived with their mother in what had been the family home, whilst George had had a one-room flat in a North London mews, which doubled as his studio. When she had first seen it, Tamsin had scarcely been able to believe he could bear to live that way, with everything, the bed included, submerged in photographic paraphernalia and negatives drying on a line over the bath.

George hadn't minded the muddle at all; he couldn't understand what all the fuss Tamsin had made was about. And when he took Tamsin home one night and stayed, it had nothing whatever to do with dissatisfaction with his own pad and everything to do with wanting to be with her. He had begun asking her to marry him about a year into their relationship, but her answer had always been the same.

'No, thank you, George. It's nothing personal. I just don't want to get married.'

George was puzzled as well as hurt. He thought that someone with her background and no family of her own would have jumped at the chance to create a secure relationship. But still Tamsin stubbornly refused to even discuss it, and he still went on asking her whenever the moment seemed right.

It seemed right now. 'Tamsin,' he said, sitting down on the edge of the bed, 'if the work dries up you can always give in and marry me.'

She looked at him over the rim of her juice glass.

'Oh, yes? And what are we going to live on? You might be still working, but every penny you earn goes to support your family.'

'Not for much longer. The mortgage is nearly paid off, and the kids are growing up. Kevin is at college . . .'

'Costing you a bomb . . .'

'And Sarah says she's going to get a job straight from school. They'll be independent soon.'

'Don't you believe it. You'll still be giving them handouts when you're in your dotage.'

'You're a hard-hearted woman, Tamsin.'

'I know.' But it wasn't true. She wasn't hard-hearted at all. It was just that the thought of marriage made her curl up inside, and she really didn't know why. As he so often said, given her background it would have made a great deal more sense if she'd been anxious for security rather than desperate to avoid it. Robert had said she should see a hypnotherapist and try to find out if there was something hidden away in her subconscious that would explain what was almost a phobia, but she hadn't wanted to do that. It smacked too much of the psychiatrist's couch, and she had seen too many of her American friends completely hooked on sessions with their shrink. Besides, there had never been time, until now. Now it looked as if all that might be changing . . .

'You were very late last night,' George said.

'Yes, later than I meant to be. We had a bit of a crisis. A boy got beaten up.'

George's eyes narrowed. He didn't like her going to the hostel late at night; it worried him, and this sounded like the sort of violence he was always afraid she was going to encounter. He had learned long ago, though, that trying to talk her out of it was a waste of breath.

'Did this happen at the hostel?' he asked tersely.

'No, in the street. His name's Jake. Sometimes he comes to us if it's cold and wet, or if he's ill, but usually he sleeps rough. Last night a gang of youths saw him in a doorway and decided to use him as a punch bag.'

'Bastards!'

'I know. Jake managed to stagger to the Mill House. I found him when I was leaving, hanging on to the railings. He was in a terrible state, his face covered in blood, and he could hardly breathe – I think they must have kicked him in the ribs. We had to call an ambulance and the police, and I had to give a statement and well . . . that's why I was so late.'

'Oh, Tamsin. You know I don't like you going to that place on your own.'

'Come with me then.'

He shook his head. 'I'd find it impossible to be civil to those layabouts.'

'They're not layabouts,' she protested. 'They're people, just like you and me, who aren't lucky enough to have a home, for one reason or another. And they certainly don't pose any threat – well, most of them don't. They're too grateful to have a roof over their heads. I just don't know what will become of them if the Mill House has to close. All those poor kids – and the older ones, too, the ones who have been on the street so long they don't even remember where home is. There will be a good few more boxes in Cardboard City, that I do know. And take last night. What would have happened to Jake if we hadn't been there?'

'Presumably someone would have found him and called an ambulance.'

'Would they? I'm not sure. A lot of people would have assumed he was a drunk or out of it on drugs and passed by on the other side. No, somehow we have to keep the Mill House going.'

George said nothing. He was thinking that if the Mill House closed then perhaps Tamsin wouldn't be out half the night when she should be in bed and asleep, and he wouldn't have to lie awake worrying about her.

The phone began to ring again.

'There you are,' he said, 'that's probably your agent ringing back to say they do want you, after all.'

'I doubt it very much.' She reached for the cordless phone, still lying in the folds of the duvet, and clicked it on. 'Hello. Tamsin Wells.'

George took her coffee cup and the glass that had contained the orange juice, and headed for the kitchen. In the doorway he heard her say in a puzzled tone: 'I'm sorry, I don't understand . . .'

He completed his errand and hurried back. Tamsin was still sitting up against the pillows, fingers pressed to her mouth, eyes thoughtful, the phone, obviously disconnected now, still clasped in her free hand.

'Who was that?' he asked.

She pushed back the covers, getting out of bed and reaching for a kimono which hung on the door.

'It was a solicitor,' she said. 'His name is Jon Nicholson and he said he is administering Robert's estate.'

George's face hardened. 'What did he want?'

'I don't know,' Tamsin said. 'But I expect I shall find out later. I've agreed to meet him.'

'Oh,' George said flatly, mechanically. And realized that in death as in life, he was still jealous of Robert Holbrook.

Jon Nicholson was smiling as he replaced the telephone. That was one objective achieved at any rate; he had half expected Tamsin Wells to refuse to see him. He'd even been surprised that she answered the telephone in person; he'd thought someone like her would have a minder to preserve her privacy, and he would have to fight all the way to get to her.

It had, so far, been one of those days, disappointing and frustrating. The first thing this morning he had called to see the private detective Robert Holbrook had been using, and it had not turned up anything like as much as he had hoped. He had found the office easily enough, a peeling door at the side of a furniture shop with a plate bearing the legend 'Brian Knott, Private Investigator and Detective Agency.' The door was locked; Jon had to ring a bell beside the plate and wait whilst someone inside released the catch. Then he climbed a steep flight of stone steps to another door, which was ajar. In a small cupboard of an office a girl with close-cropped bottle-blonde hair was sitting behind a flimsy looking desk. She was smoking a roll-up cigarette, which she made no effort to either put down or put out.

'Yeah?' She said it with a faintly Transatlantic drawl, as if she thought Americanization went with the job.

Jon introduced himself, and asked to see Mr Knott. The girl pouted at him doubtfully, but parked her cigarette in a saucer on her desk and got up from her desk to head for a door that obviously led to the inner sanctum. She was wearing a black scooped-neck top and a little Lycra skirt that was no more than a band of stretchy fabric above black opaque tights. The whole scenario was, Jon thought, too clichéd to be true.

A few moments later, the girl was back. 'Yeah, you can go through,' she said, reaching for her cigarette again.

Brian Knott sat behind a ring-marked desk. He, too, was smoking – a small cigar. As Jon went in he got to his feet, holding out a hand. He was, Jon noticed, middle-aged, stocky and balding, with sideburns and a small moustache, and he was wearing a tweed jacket, striped tie, and neatly pressed trousers. The office might be a cliché, but Brian Knott was not.

'What can I do for you?' he asked. He, too, had a slight drawl, but more the sort that suggested he had a hip flask tucked away somewhere.

Jon explained, and saw his face fall. Clearly he had been hoping Jon had a job for him.

'I'm sorry,' he said tetchily, 'but what passes between me and my clients is strictly confidential.'

'Mr Holbrook is dead, and I am acting to execute his will,' Jon pointed out. 'In order to do that, I need to know whether you were able to trace his fourth grandchild. So can we cut the cloak and dagger stuff?'

Brian Knott took a moment to examine his fingernails. Then he looked up at Jon, pulling a wry face through the smoke from his cigar.

'All right. I suppose there's no harm in telling you, since you seem to know all about this business anyway. The answer to your question is no. I didn't find the person Mr Holbrook asked me to search for. Hardly my fault; he didn't give me much to go on, and the trail is thirty years and more old. I'd have given it my best shot though if he'd given me more time. But he didn't. One minute it was all systems go; he wanted his daughter's illegitimate child found like yesterday. The next he was telling me to drop it. He must have changed his mind, I suppose.'

The skin had begun to prickle on the back of Jon's neck. 'He told you to drop the investigation?'

'Yes, just like that. I had to submit a bill to him, of course. I'd already done some work on his behalf.'

'Such as?'

'Well, I had a word with the solicitors Patricia worked for around the time Mr Holbrook thought the child must have been born. A firm in Bristol . . . Wilson and King, you may know them . . .'

'I've heard of them, yes. Did anyone there remember anything significant?'

'No, or if they did they weren't saying. Most of the staff who worked there in those days have long since left and of the partners, Wilson is dead and King has Alzheimer's. The only one still there who remembered Patricia was a woman who had been the cashier, and is now office manager. But she couldn't be of any help. She thought Patricia did take some leave of absence to look after a sick cousin at one time, but she said the files relating to staff matters had all been destroyed. In the days before computer records, it would all have been wads of carbon copies of letters and so on, and they took up far too much storage space.'

'I have those letters anyway,' Jon said. 'At the moment, though, they haven't been much help. The sick cousin was supposedly in Worcester, and Patricia stayed at an address in Gloucester. I'm trying to check birth registrations and adoption records in that area at the relevant time, but so far I've drawn a blank on both scores.'

'I also spoke to the solicitors Higgs Ormrod, your competitors.' Brian Knott smiled smugly. 'Patricia also worked for them for a time, after she left the Bristol firm and before she married. Apparently Ormrod is related by marriage to the Holbrooks. He had been with a firm in the Midlands but when he moved down here to a promotion that resulted in a partnership he recommended Patricia for a vacancy. If he'd already been practising in the district, she'd have gone there straight from secretarial college instead of the Bristol firm, I shouldn't wonder. From the scenario Mr Holbrook had outlined, it seemed too late in the time frame to be relevant, but I thought it was possible she might have confided in one of her colleagues at Higgs Ormrod and worth a shot.'

'Who did you speak to there?' Jon asked sharply.

'Ormrod himself. I had to be subtle, of course. Mr Holbrook was insistent he wanted complete confidentiality. But I wasn't able to learn anything new, and truth to tell, I wasn't much surprised. As I said before, it was wrong for the time frame.'

'And that's it?'

''Fraid so.' Brian Knott opened a drawer in his desk, took out a business card and slid it across to Jon. 'If I can be of further help, or if you need any enquiries on any other matter, I trust you'll remember me.'

'Yes, of course.'

He *could* hand this investigation over to him, Jon thought. Perhaps that was what he should do, ask Brian Knott to reopen his file and go for it, this time without all the restrictions Robert had placed on him. If they pooled their resources maybe they'd come up with something. But somehow Jon did not feel quite ready to do that. Later, perhaps, if time was running out and he'd made no headway, but not yet. He still had a few leads to follow up – Tamsin Wells for one – and he hadn't finished going through Robert's papers yet. He was rather enjoying the challenge; it made a change from his usual routine, and in any case Kate Morton seemed set on getting to the bottom of the whole thing, and she was better placed than anybody to do it. There was no need yet to waste money on a private investigator. Besides which . . .

Collaborating with her would give him the perfect excuse to see her again. She might have knocked him back last night, but it was early days. He wasn't ready to give up on that one either.

He sat now, drumming on the telephone with his fingers, then made up his mind; he was going to ring Kate. He picked up the telephone again.

'Can you give me an outside line, please, Julie?' He dialled, and Kate answered almost immediately, as if she'd been sitting beside the phone waiting for it to ring. 'It's me – Jon,' he said. 'I'm going to see Tamsin Wells tomorrow. I wondered if you'd like to come with me.'

'Oh! Oh, yes, I would. Tomorrow, you say? I think I can make that.'

Jon felt a smile tugging at the corners of his mouth. And silently thanked Tamsin Wells for more than one reason.

Jessica and Adrian were sitting across the desk from Leslie Lightfoot in the office next door to the one Hugh Ormrod had occupied for almost thirty years. When Jessica had demanded an early appointment, Leslie's secretary had managed to rearrange his appointments to squeeze her in, but Leslie's heart had sunk at the prospect. He was all too aware of the pitfalls that lay ahead. And he'd been right. To be honest, he could see no sensible way of proceeding with what Jessica was demanding.

'I really don't think contesting the will is a very good idea,' he said with all the authority he could muster. 'To begin with, we would need some incontrovertible evidence that Mr Holbrook was not of sound mind in order to have even a chance of succeeding.'

Jessica snorted. 'I should have thought what he did was proof enough.'

Leslie Lightfoot steepled his fingers together. 'Somehow I rather doubt that would be sufficient to convince a court of law. Trying to prove someone was not in possession of their faculties would be difficult, costly, and probably unpleasant. To be honest, I doubt the wisdom of even attempting it.'

Jessica glared, opened her mouth to protest, and he hurried on: 'It's my opinion that you stand to lose far more than you stand to gain. The will clearly states that the executor has one year to find the missing beneficiary. At the end of that time, the fourth share will be divided equally between you, Kate and Miranda. If, as you maintain, there is no fourth child, then you will be assured that share in due course. Contesting the will would only hold things up and might very well cost you a great deal more than that third of a quarter . . .'

'He's right, Jessica,' Adrian said reasonably.

'He's missing the point.' Jessica turned to Leslie fiercely. 'By making this will, Grandpa has cast all kinds of aspersions. I want to lay it to rest once and for all this silly rumour, for Daddy's sake and for the sake of Mummy's memory.'

The two men looked at one another, an exchange of exasperation and resignation and Leslie Lightfoot felt a stab of sympathy for the man who was married to this harridan.

'But have you considered all the unpleasantness you would be stirring up?' he ventured. 'Supposing there was a fourth child, then by making a fuss about the will, you would not only be making it much more likely that the child will be found, but also telling the world your family business. I suggest you think about this very carefully. But my considered advice is that you should forget any idea of contesting.'

Jessica looked ready to argue some more, and Adrian touched her arm. 'Come on, Jessica. We'll talk this through at home. We've taken up quite enough of Mr Lightfoot's time, and in any case, I have to get to work.'

Though she was still incandescent with rage, Jessica was left with little option but to concur.

As they left the office, Leslie Lightfoot sat down heavily, massaging his balding scalp with his fingers.

'Leslie?' It was Hugh, looking around the door. 'How did it go?'

Leslie sighed. 'That is one difficult woman. She's applied to become a magistrate, I hear on the grapevine. Heaven help us all when she gets to be Chairman of the Bench is all I can say.'

'Did you manage to talk them out of contesting?'

'I've put the case against very strongly. And the husband seemed to agree with me. He seems a reasonable chap. I should imagine he'll get her to see sense in the end.'

'I certainly hope so. God only knows what skeletons are going to come rattling out of cupboards before all this is over.' Hugh looked every year of his age suddenly. All this was weighing on him very heavily, Leslie realized. It was impossible to act for a family for so many years without becoming emotionally involved with them, he supposed, even if Robert hadn't trusted him at the end when it had come to making this controversial will.

'It will all work itself out, I'm sure,' he said, with more optimism than he was feeling.

*   *   *

Liz put the telephone down after talking to Laurie O'Neill, her assistant, and stared out of the hotel bedroom window at the clear blue October sky.

She should be going home. She'd only come over for the funeral, for goodness' sake, and it really was time to book a flight back to Florida. But she kept putting it off and she couldn't really understand why. When she'd first arrived she'd felt like a fish out of water, as if she'd been beamed up by aliens and deposited on a strange and hostile planet. But things had changed subtly since then. She'd discovered a nostalgia for the old familiar places; she'd even become quite attached to this hotel room with its creaky boards and noisy plumbing. There was something typically English about it which was calling to a part of her which had been buried so deeply she had forgotten it existed.

And it wasn't only the places, of course. It was the people. Kate, her god-daughter, for a start. They still hadn't managed to get together for a real heart-to-heart. And Tony. He had scarcely been out of her mind since this whole thing had begun. In the last few days she'd seen quite a lot of him, and she hoped she'd see a bit more of him yet. But she was terribly worried for him. If it turned out that Trish had had a child with Jack and never told him, it was going to destroy him. The reason Trish had kept it from him must have been because she knew how deeply it would affect him, and Liz somehow felt she owed it to Trish to be here for him and try to comfort him now. She'd let Trish down twice before, first failing to be her confidante when she'd had this secret child, with all the emotional upheaval that must have entailed, and then again when she'd reached such a pitch of depression that she had taken her own life. She didn't want to let her down a third time by running away now.

And so she had phoned her office in Florida and said she needed a few more days at least. Laurie O'Neill had sounded almost pleased; she had insisted that everything was in hand, and Liz had the feeling that she was enjoying being in charge.

Well, if her business couldn't run itself for a couple of weeks after all these years, it really was a pretty poor show, she thought. And realized that making something other than work her priority really was a most refreshing change.

Ten

The taxi turned into the Mews, bumping unevenly over the cobbles, and pulled into the kerb outside a canary-yellow door flanked by glossy black railings. Whilst Jon paid the driver, Kate stood looking up at the tall old house, fascinated, but also apprehensive. Already a part of her was regretting having accepted Jon's invitation to go with him to meet Tamsin Wells, yet she knew that given the choice she would do the same again. She was too curious about this woman whose existence her grandfather had kept secret; if there were shocks to come, so be it. She'd prepared herself as far as possible for whatever they might be about to discover. But she was still nervous at the prospect of confronting the reality.

The taxi was pulling away; Jon was slipping his wallet into his back pocket and checking his watch.

'We're a bit early. She's not expecting us until midday.'

'Well, that has to be a first for me!' Kate joked. 'I'm usually late for everything.'

'So I'd noticed,' Jon said dryly. 'I suggest we go for a little walk up the Mews and back again whilst we wait.'

'Can't we just get on with it?' Kate asked without much hope.

'I'd rather be on time.'

'We needn't have left at such an unearthly hour then, need we?' she chided. She'd thought from the beginning he'd allowed far more time than they needed, but then, by her own admission, she did have a habit of cutting things too fine. Jon, on the other hand, had everything worked out, and the fact that they hadn't encountered any of the delays he'd allowed for was hardly his fault. There had not been any delays on the motorway, they'd parked without any trouble in a multi-storey car park and got a taxi easily to take them to Torrington Park Mews. Jon had said he'd prefer to do that than have to search for the place, and possibly have problems finding somewhere to park when they did. He was so damned efficient it annoyed her, perhaps because it made her all the more aware of her own short-comings.

She was also feeling tetchy because last night she'd had an altercation with Chris. Unbelievably, he'd phoned to say he'd managed to arrange to be in Bleadon today, and would take her out for lunch. Of course, she'd had to tell him she couldn't make it, and he had sounded offended and hurt, as if he expected her to be ready and waiting whenever he found an hour to spare for her. She had been shocked at the bitterness his reaction had stirred up in her; she really had reached the point where enough was enough. But the prospect of ending the affair was not a pleasant one. Just preferable to continuing as they were.

And added to all that, there was this terrible knot of nervousness in her stomach at the thought of coming face to face with Tamsin Wells.

'It's an interesting place, this,' Jon was saying as they walked slowly along the Mews. 'I suppose once upon a time all these garages would have been stables. It reminds me of the film of *Oliver!* I keep expecting a whole chorus line of milkmaids and flower girls and knife grinders to come bursting round the corner.'

'The cries of London, yes.' She smiled, her tense mood lifting momentarily. 'I'll bet property round here costs an arm and a leg.'

'And Tamsin Wells, no doubt, can afford it. I don't suppose the Gazelle girl is paid in peanuts.'

'Hmm. It would be pretty ironic if she turned out to be the missing beneficiary,' Kate mused. 'At risk of sounding like Jess, I think even I might be a bit miffed to see her get an equal share of Grandpa's estate.'

'Kate, there's something I should tell you. I think there is every possibility that Tamsin Wells *is* the missing beneficiary,' Jon said a little hesitantly.

Kate's heart skipped a beat. 'What makes you say that now?'

'Well . . . I went to the library yesterday, checked her out in *Who's Who.* According to her biographical details, she was brought up in an orphanage. She doesn't seem to have any family. None that are listed anyway.'

'Oh, shit,' Kate said softly.

'It doesn't necessarily mean she *is* the person we're looking for, of course.'

'No.' She huffed impatiently. 'Oh, can't we just get on with it?'

Jon checked his watch. 'I reckon by the time we get back there we'll be just about right.'

And suddenly Kate was shaking all over. This was it. No turning back now. Prepared or not, it was time. Jon rang the doorbell and raised an eyebrow at Kate as they stood back and waited for someone to answer.

She was beautiful, just as beautiful in the flesh as she was on television. That was Kate's first thought as the door was opened by Tamsin herself.

Her hair was thick and shining, cut into a sharp bob, her features were perfect, her eyes almond shaped beneath thick, but beautifully shaped brows. She was wearing jeans and a shirt, but the jeans were obviously designer and the shirt was silk, and they revealed a figure to die for, slender waist, hips without an inch of fat on them, long legs. Strangely she looked much more like she did on television than she had done on the day of the funeral, but then, Kate supposed, a good deal of her had been hidden by her dark glasses and that hat, and infuriatingly the throw-away elegance made Kate feel far more inferior than the obvious glamour had done.

'You must be Jon Nicholson,' she said.

'That's right. And this is . . .'

'Katrina,' she said, and smiled. 'Come in.'

How did she know who I was? Kate wondered furiously as they followed her into a lobby and up a narrow flight of stairs. She saw me at the funeral, presumably, but how did she know which one I was? Had Jon told Tamsin he was bringing me? She made a mental note to ask him, and then thought, why? In a few minutes, unless this was a totally wasted journey, Tamsin Wells would tell them herself just what her connection was with their family. A nerve jumped in her throat.

'Sorry about the stairs,' Tamsin said over her shoulder.

'That's all right. We're young and fit . . . well, fit, anyway,' Jon said and irrationally, Kate bridled.

The stairs led up directly into a large, light studio room. After the feeling of times past which had prevailed outside, it was almost a shock to see the beige wool carpet, the glass Design Centre table, the low sofas with their bright throws, the modern abstract pictures on the walls, the art nouveau lamps. And a chiffonier Kate recognized as having once stood in her grandmother's dining room. She'd wondered where that chiffonier had got to! A sense of outrage burned in her veins.

'Sit down. Oh – can I take your jacket?'

'No, I'm fine, thank you,' Kate said. She wanted to keep her jacket on, not because she was cold, but because it offered the illusion of protection and it was a comfort to be able to thrust her hands into the pockets, fiddle with the spare button and the handkerchief she kept there.

'Well, sit down anyway. Coffee? Or something stronger?'

'Coffee will be fine,' Jon said. 'I have to drive.'

'You drove up? I thought you'd come by train.'

'I'd like something stronger,' Kate said, somewhat defiantly.

'What would you like?'

'What have you got?'

'Just about everything, I think.'

Wouldn't she just!

'In that case, I'd like a g and t.'

'I'll see to it. Excuse me a moment.'

'I'm learning things about you,' Jon said to her slyly, sitting by her side on the low sofa whilst Tamsin was out of the room.

'"What do you mean?'

'Well, you drink gin and tonic, and you're invariably late . . .'

'And I'm learning about you,' she hissed back. 'Smug, censorious and rather rude.'

He laughed.

'It's all right for you,' Kate said ruefully. 'This is just business for you. For me . . . well, it's a great deal more.'

'I know.' His hand covered hers briefly.

'Here we are.' Tamsin was back with the drinks. The coffee smelled good, strong and freshly brewed, but Kate was still glad she'd asked for gin and tonic. She sipped it, a generous measure in a fine crystal tumbler, and felt as immediate a lift as if she'd injected it into a vein.

Tamsin dropped on to a low leather pouffe, and although she was tall and her legs endless, she did it with extreme grace. 'What did you want to see me about? Did Robert leave me something in his will after all?'

Kate looked at her sharply, a little shocked by her directness, but also puzzled by the way she had phrased the question. It was almost as if she was acquainted with the contents of the will, yet surprised at the idea that there might be something for her.

'I'm not quite sure yet,' Jon said carefully. 'The provisions of the will are somewhat unusual, and it's my job to see that Mr Holbrook's wishes are carried out as far as possible.'

'Yes, that's what he would have wanted.'

'He hasn't exactly made that easy, though,' Jon said. 'Since you were at the funeral, I'm assuming you knew Mr Holbrook fairly well, and what I'm trying to ascertain, is . . . in what capacity?'

'Excuse me?' Those beautiful almond-shaped eyes narrowed slightly, and tiny frown lines appeared over the bridge of her perfect little nose.

'I'm trying to ascertain your relationship with Mr Holbrook.'

'Yes, I gathered that. What exactly is it that you are suggesting?'

Jon coloured slightly. 'There is a provision in Mr Holbrook's will concerning an unnamed beneficiary. He believed, rightly or wrongly, that his daughter Patricia had four children rather than just the three from her marriage to Tony Morton, and he wanted that fourth child to share in the estate. The problem is, we don't yet know who that child is, and I asked to see you because . . .'

'Aah! Because you thought I might be that child. I'm sorry, Mr Nicholson, for biting your head off. I thought you were getting at something else entirely. I'm a bit oversensitive about my private life. It comes from living in the public gaze, I expect. But what makes you think I might be the mystery child?'

'Well, you are about the right age, for one thing – or you could be. You obviously cared a great deal about Robert

Holbrook. And you were brought up in a children's home not far from Market Denton. As far as I can make out, you were there because you have no family of your own.'

'My goodness, you have been doing your homework,' she said lightly.

'All part of the job. The one thing that really doesn't fit neatly is that if Robert had traced you and you'd been in contact, why didn't he come back to me and have you included by name? Unless, of course, he simply didn't get around to it before he had his stroke.'

'Well, well!' She wrapped her arms around her long legs. 'I am impressed.'

Kate felt a nerve jump in her throat and hastily took another sip of her gin and tonic. When Jon explained his reasoning like that it sounded quite plausible that this beautiful stranger was her half-sister, her mother's lost child. And yet some inner gut feeling was denying it. Not only because she couldn't believe Trish could have abandoned a baby to be brought up in an orphanage, whatever the pressures on her, but also because it just didn't feel right. There was nothing about Tamsin that looked anything like any of the family, nothing of her grandparents, nothing of herself or Jessica, or Miranda. She could get her looks from her father's side, of course, but somehow Kate didn't think so.

'It will be necessary, of course, to establish proof of identity beyond any shadow of doubt,' Jon was saying. 'A birth certificate is probably the most incontrovertible and straightforward. But . . .'

'Hold on,' Tamsin interrupted him. 'I'm sorry if you thought your search might end with me. I'm afraid it doesn't.'

'Ah.' He stopped, awkward suddenly, aware that he had let himself get carried away. How the hell could he have let that happen? 'I'm sorry, I thought from what you said . . .'

'I said you'd done your homework. I didn't say you'd come up with the right answers. Believe you me, I wish they were, for any number of reasons. But they're not. You'd be right in thinking my real name isn't Tamsin Wells; I adopted it to give myself a whole new persona. But it's not Holbrook either. I was born Charlene Riddle, and my mother was called Maureen. As for the whereabouts of the missing grandchild, I'm afraid I'm as much in the dark as you are.'

'But you knew of its existence.' Jon put down his mug on the glass-topped coffee table and sat forward.

'Yes. Yes, I did know. Robert talked to me about it quite a bit. It was an enormous shock to him. He had no idea until just before Dorrie died that Trish had another child.'

Kate experienced a flash of something midway between resentment and indignation. Bad enough that this woman, this stranger, should have been in the confidence of her beloved grandfather when she had not, infinitely worse, somehow, to hear her refer to Kate's mother and grandmother by the intimate short forms of their names.

'You mean she kept it from him,' she said, and when Jon looked at her sharply, she added: 'The letters I found – Grandma's letters to Mummy when she was in Gloucester – they prove she knew.'

'I think that was what hurt Robert most,' Tamsin said. 'Discovering that for all those years the two people he cared most about in the world had kept this whacking great secret from him.'

'I expect they thought he'd be furious,' Kate said quickly. 'He could be very . . . well, old-fashioned in some ways.'

'I don't think he was old-fashioned at all!' Tamsin said fiercely. 'Principled, yes. And strong-minded. But to keep something like that from him . . . Do you know what he said to me? "What do they think I am, Tamsin, some kind of monster? Was that the sort of father I was?" I bled for him, I did truly. Yes, he probably would have been angry with the man who got her in the family way and then walked away, even if not with her. And yes, he would have been upset. He adored Trish. But to find out after all those years that they'd schemed and connived behind his back, gone through all that and never told him . . . can't you see how hurtful that was for him?'

'So how did he find out?' Kate asked. She was feeling uncomfortable, as if she too had been part of the conspiracy.

'Dorrie finally told him when she was virtually on her death-bed. She couldn't bear to take her secret with her to the grave, I suppose. But she wasn't terribly lucid, she was drifting in and out of consciousness between doses of drugs, and he couldn't get any sense out of her as to what had happened to the child. "It went to a good home," he thought she said, but

he couldn't be sure whether she meant a children's home, as
in the one where I was brought up, or a home with an adoptive family. He didn't even know if the child was a girl or a
boy. He'd asked her, but she couldn't get any sense out of
her.'

She looked from Jon to Kate, pulling a wry little face. 'I've
given you something to think about, I see. Now, would you
like another drink? More coffee?'

'Not for me, thank you,' Jon said, but Kate thought she
could certainly do with another gin. And why not? Today, at
least, she wasn't driving.

'Yes, please.'

Tamsin grinned. 'A woman after my own heart. It's rather
a pity we're not sisters.'

'So Dorothea spilled the beans, but not enough of them.
Then she died and the rest of what she knew died with her,'
Jon said thoughtfully. 'That, presumably, is when Robert came
to me to make a new will, and also employed Mr Knott.'

'Mr Knott? Who's Mr Knott?'

'A private detective.'

'Private detective!' Tamsin slipped a slice of lemon into
Kate's refreshed glass and stood motionless for a moment,
deep in thought, before passing it to Kate.

'Private detective, of course. That's probably how he found
out . . .'

'Found out what?' Jon asked sharply and Kate froze.

Tamsin laughed apologetically. 'Oh, I'm sorry. I didn't mean
to raise your hopes. I don't know anything, really. Except that
Robert *did* find something out. I was out of the country at
the time, on a photo shoot. In Australia, actually. I talked to
Robert on the telephone as often as I could, almost every day,
because I could tell something had upset him. Eventually I
got it out of him that he had learned something about Trish's
child which had been almost as much of a shock as the fact
that she had one at all, but he wouldn't tell me what it was,
not over the phone. He said it would wait until I got home.
But the trouble was, by then Robert had had his stroke.'

'So he never told you what it was he'd learned that had
upset him.'

''Fraid not, and I didn't press him. It seemed to me to be
very important that he shouldn't be upset in any way. In fact,

I couldn't help wondering if it was the stress of it all that had caused him to have a stroke in the first place.'

'My sentiments exactly,' Jon said. 'He was so fit. Something changed all that. And the hell of it is, we still don't know what it was.'

'No, but . . .' Tamsin checked, and for just a moment, her face was totally transparent.

'Nothing.' She had been going to say something else, and decided against it. Jon knew it and Kate knew it, but it was also painfully obvious that she had not the slightest intention of changing her mind a second time.

'Well.' Jon got to his feet. 'I'm very grateful to you for sparing us so much of your time. If you do think of anything else that might be helpful, perhaps you'll let me know.'

Kate, however, remained seated, eyeing Tamsin with suspicion and a tinge of resentment.

'You really do seem to know a great deal about my grandfather, Miss Wells. Had you known him a long time?'

'Quite a long time, yes.'

'Yet we had no idea. How did you come to meet him?'

'That,' Tamsin said, 'is a very long story.'

'I'm sure it is. Were you . . .?'

'His mistress? No. Oh, I can see you don't believe me, and I can't say I blame you. I expect I'd think the same if our situations were reversed. But I promise you, I wasn't, what we had was much deeper than that. A very real friendship.'

'Obviously, since he confided in you; told you things he kept hidden from us.' Kate knew her voice was tight; odd how it hurt. If Tamsin had been his mistress the fact that he had confided in her would be explicable somehow. As it was she was just a woman, more or less Kate's age, who had somehow managed to get closer to the grandfather she had adored more than she ever had.

Tamsin tucked her thumbs into the pockets of her jeans, meeting Kate's gaze head on. 'Sometimes it's easier to talk openly to those who aren't personally involved in a situation, and I do know Robert didn't want to hurt or worry any of you.'

'Then why the hell did he do it?' Kate asked fiercely. 'We're probably never going to find the missing child. It's like looking for a needle in a haystack. And people *have* been hurt, whether Grandpa intended it or not. For what?'

'It was him though, wasn't it? He simply did what he felt he had to do. And as for not finding the missing child, well, it can't be an impossibility because I believe Robert did, or at least had a good idea where he or she could be found.'

And was so shocked by what he discovered that it gave him a stroke, Kate thought bitterly.

'Well, thank you for your time, Miss Wells,' Jon was saying.

'Tamsin.' She smiled at him. 'I'm only sorry I wasn't the person you're looking for, for more reasons than I can name.'

'But you have been a great help. And you will get in touch with me if you think of anything else that might be useful?'

'Yes, but to be honest I can't see that is very likely.'

Heading back down the steep flight of stairs leading down to the front door, and remembering the moment when Tamsin had almost, but not quite, added something else to her revelations, Kate was not entirely sure she believed her.

'Would you like to go somewhere for a bite to eat before we pick up the car?' Jon asked as they emerged into the Mews.

'No, I don't think so. I'd rather get home.'

'Pity.'

'Why, are you hungry?'

'I am rather. We had an early start and I didn't have time for breakfast.'

'Neither did I . . .' No wonder the gin and tonics were going to her head! 'All right, perhaps it would be an idea. Just as long as we get out of town before the rush hour starts.'

'Sure.' He waved at an approaching taxi; it sailed past, its 'For Hire' flag turned down. 'What do you fancy? Chinese, Italian, Thai, Indian again, or good old English pub fare? That's the beauty of London, there's all the choice in the world.'

'I think we should make it either a pub lunch or an Italian. Italian can be quite quick.'

'We'll see what we can find.' Another taxi sailed past, impervious to Jon's waving. 'Everybody is going to lunch by the seems of it. Ah . . .!'

At last a black cab pulled into the kerb. Jon gave the driver the address of the multi-storey car park.

'I thought we were going to eat first,' Kate said.

'Didn't you notice the greasy spoon café on the corner when we were queuing to get in? Looked perfect for a quick bite –

egg, chips and beans. Just right for filling you up for the journey home.' Kate looked at him in amazement and he laughed. 'Only joking. There are some nice places over there. Though I have to say that some of the best meals I've ever eaten have been in transport cafés and roadside trailers. Fred's Diner. The thought of his bacon sarnies makes my mouth water.'

'I'm sure. But all that cholesterol is very bad for you. And disastrous for my diet.'

'You don't need to diet.'

'Don't you believe it! If I didn't watch my weight I'd be as big as a house.' She sighed. 'I wonder if Tamsin Wells has to diet? She's beautiful, isn't she?'

'Not as beautiful as you.'

'Don't lie. It doesn't suit you. And flattery will get you nowhere.'

'Pity. But it's not a lie. If we're trading mottos, I've got one for you. Beauty is in the eye of the beholder.'

Kate felt the flush start at the base of her throat, spreading slowly upwards until her whole face was burning. His meaning was so crystal clear she really didn't know what to say or do.

'Sorry. I've embarrassed you.' Jon grinned at her; a grin that made her suspect he'd embarrassed himself too.'

She forced herself to grin back. 'I'm just not used to compliments. But I think I could get to rather like them.'

'I'm glad to hear it. Here we are . . . this is the place I was thinking of . . . La Bamba . . . How does that look to you?'

'Looks fine from where I'm sitting.'

And not just the restaurant, Kate thought, surprised by the rosy glow that was spreading through her veins like warm treacle.

'Wendy, are you all right?'

Lynne Garrett, going into the small upstairs room above the main offices of Crossways Properties, stopped short, looking anxiously at Wendy, who was slumped in the upright chair behind the small desk with her head in her hands.

Lynne was a part-timer who worked mainly for the Building Society side of the agency. She hadn't been in yesterday, Monday was not one of her 'days', but when she'd come in this afternoon she'd thought how poorly Wendy looked, very pale and drawn, and wondered if she was sickening for something. Lynne had come upstairs now to make a cup of tea, and was shocked to see Wendy just sitting there instead of working busily as she usually did.

'Wendy?' she said again.

Wendy straightened abruptly, making a great business of fiddling with the files that were open on her desk, but she didn't look up.

'It's high time this stuff was all updated. There are properties here that have been off the market for ages.' There was a catch in her voice and it sounded a bit thick, as if she'd been crying, Lynne thought.

'Cup of tea?' she asked.

'If you're making one . . .' But the determined brightness in her voice was too brittle to sustain; her voice cracked again and filled up with tears.

'Wendy, what is the matter? And don't say nothing, because it's obvious there is.'

Wendy blew her nose. 'Oh, it's just me being silly. My hormones playing up, I expect.'

Lynne dunked a teabag in each of two mugs and splashed in some milk.

'Come on, this is me, Auntie Lynne. You'll feel better if you talk about it.'

'I don't want to talk.'

'OK.' The kettle was boiling. Lynne poured water on to the teabags and milk, stirring vigorously with a rather sorry-looking teaspoon. 'Here you are.'

Wendy reached for the mug and her sleeve momentarily fell away from her wrist, revealing an angry bracelet of bruises. Lynne leaned over, tweaking the sleeve back again.

'How on earth did you do that?'

'Oh, I . . .' Wendy broke off, lip trembling, and suddenly Lynne was remembering the cut lip last week, and the stiff way Wendy held herself when she walked as if she was sore all over, and putting two and two together.

'Wendy, is Tim knocking you about?' she asked before she could stop herself.

'No. No, of course not!'

'I think he is. For God's sake, Wendy, I've been there. I know. Peter, my first husband, beat me black and blue.'

'Really?'

'Yes, really. He was a total bastard. It's a long time ago now, thank God, but it's not something you ever forget.'

'Tim's not a bastard.'

Lynne pulled a face. She'd worked for Tim before he was made redundant and she'd never much cared for him. Very arrogant, very full of himself, and yet all too ready to turn nasty with anyone who suggested there might be a better way of doing something or – heaven forbid! – caught him out in some way. She hadn't had him down for a wife beater, it was true, but how did you ever know what people were like behind closed doors? And very often it was the charmers who could be regular Jekyll and Hydes. Her Peter had been a charmer. Until he couldn't get his own way.

'If he's hitting you, he *is* a bastard,' she said flatly.

Wendy was holding her mug of tea very tightly between her hands as if she was trying to warm them, and staring down at the desk. 'He's just having a really bad time. He's never done such a thing before. And he's promised me faithfully he won't do it again. He's really sorry afterwards . . .'

'They always are,' Lynne said flatly. 'But it won't stop it happening again. Once they've started something like that, once they've tasted the power . . . well, that seems to be it. I can't tell you how many times Peter promised me – no more. He'd cry, and tell me he loved me and couldn't live without me, and then something would upset him and it was all happening again. You have to leave him *now*, Wendy, before things get worse.'

Wendy shook her head. 'I couldn't.'

'That's what I said at first. But the attacks just got more and more violent. And more frequent too. In the end . . . Leave him, Wendy, that's my advice. Leave him while the worst you've got is a few bruises and a cut lip.'

'It's not that simple,' Wendy said. 'It's my home, too. My whole life. And I don't want people knowing, either. I'm so ashamed . . .'

'Better that than you should end up in hospital like I did,' Lynne said bluntly. 'Peter damn near killed me. I had a broken jaw, a broken arm, several broken ribs and a punctured lung. He just used me for a punch bag. And the same could happen to you.'

Wendy was silent. Perhaps there was something in what
Lynne said. He'd attacked her now three times in as many
days; last night for no other reason than she'd been late
getting home from work. She knew the reason, of course.
He was suffering from depression and a total crisis of confidence, and he'd got it into his head that she was seeing Ash.
It was the last straw, because she was the one person he felt
had ever really belonged to him, and he was terrified of
losing her.

'He's just insecure,' she said now. 'His mother abandoned
him, and he was brought up in a children's home. He copes
with it very well usually, but it has left the most awful scars.
Can you believe that any woman could do that to their child?
Some people just shouldn't be allowed to have babies.'

And then her eyes were filling with tears again because
she had wanted a baby of her own desperately, but nothing
had happened. Verity had said probably she took after her;
she had found it very difficult to get pregnant, and perhaps
Wendy should seek help. But Tim hadn't wanted to. He was
afraid, Wendy thought, that it might turn out to be his fault.
And perhaps it was for the best. She was the chief bread-
winner now; she couldn't take time off to have a baby, and
if Tim was going to turn violent, she wasn't sure it would
be a good idea to trust him with a baby, even if she could
have one . . .

'So that's another reason I couldn't leave him,' she said,
swallowing her tears. 'I feel sort of responsible for him.'

'Lynne? Where have you got to?'

It was Crispin, who had taken over the management of
the office from Tim, calling up the stairs. Lynne put her
mug down on Wendy's desk and called down the stairs:
'What is it?'

'There are customers wanting to make a withdrawal.'

'Do it yourself!' Lynne muttered under her breath and pulled
a wry face at Wendy. 'Men!'

'Go on, Lynne, I'm OK, really.'

But she was not all right, she thought, as Lynne's high heels
clattered away down the bare wood stairs. She was not all
right at all. Besides hurting all over, she was worried sick,
afraid to go home, afraid not to. And the whole thing was her
own fault. She hadn't been unfaithful to Tim in the physical

sense, but in her heart . . . oh, that was a different matter. She'd never stopped being in love with Ash, and if that wasn't infidelity, what the hell was?

She really deserved it when Tim hit her. She was a faithless woman who asked for everything she got. And to leave him and break his heart because he was treating her the way she deserved to be treated really would be the final injustice.

Eleven

Not long after Kate and Jon had left, Tamsin's phone rang. 'Hi sweetheart, it's me.'

'George. I thought you were working.'

'I am. But the girls have gone to powder their noses and I'm having a nice cold beer. Has the solicitor gone?'

'Yes, just.'

'So, what did he want? Did old Robert leave you something in his will?'

'No, you know he didn't. I told him he wasn't to, and he asked me down there to choose something. I had it in his lifetime – that wonderful chiffonier. I didn't expect anything else, and I didn't get it.'

'So why did the solicitor want to talk to you?'

'Because somebody who doesn't expect it is going to get a share of the estate. A missing grandchild. I think the solicitor thought it might be me. Of course, it's not – more's the pity. It's ironic, really, after telling Robert I was perfectly fine and he must leave everything to his family, I really could do with some money right now. The Mill House is in dreadful straights financially.'

'Tamsin, you're not giving them money you can't afford, are you?' She was silent. 'Tamsin, sweetheart, you have got to be realistic,' he went on. 'If you get the new contract, all well and good. If you don't . . .'

'I know. I'm broke. Oh, well, so what? It's only money. There are more important things in life.'

'Tamsin – I'm going to have to go. The girls are back. I'll see you later.'

'Yes. See you.'

She put the phone down thinking about what she'd just said. There *were* more important things in life than money, but unfortunately you couldn't get very far without it. All very well to pretend to herself and everyone else that her early life had taught her that love and security and a family were the things that mattered, the fact was that money, or the lack of it, changed lives. Without money there was no independence, no freedom of choice, no hope. When Tamsin thought of how it had felt to have to ask for everything she wanted or needed she remembered all too clearly just how awful her life had been before Robert had rescued her, and resurrected a sick feeling in the pit of her stomach.

Nowadays she had money and success, and they were the foundations of her life. Take them away and what would be left? How much of the edifice would crumble?

I speak fine words, Tamsin thought. I like to pretend I'm cavalier and brave, but underneath I am very, very scared. Almost as scared, in a different way, as I was that night when I first met Robert . . .

She was frightened. Very frightened and also very cold. It was November, and the clammy fog had invaded the Portakabin office where she was hiding so that the bare walls and floor felt damp and chill. When she'd first climbed in through an insecure window there had still been enough daylight to see the portable gas heater in the corner and work out how to get it working, but though she'd had all three bars burning for some time the air still felt as cold as ever outside the immediate circle of fierce heat. Now the flame had begun to putter, coughing and dancing, and only the central panel really glowed. The gas was running out, Tamsin knew, and soon it would be gone completely. The darkness was inky too, though if she looked out of the window she could see a horseshoe of orange lights that marked the Ring Road a quarter of a mile or so away, shrouded eerily in mist.

Tamsin shivered, pulling her jacket round her and hugging herself with her arms. There was no warmth really in the jacket – quilted Indian cotton – her jumper looked quite warm but was only acrylic, her jeans struck cold against goose-pimpled flesh, and her fingers, poking out of her fingerless gloves, felt like icicles. She wished she'd thought to bring a blanket with her, but comfort had been the last thing on her mind when she'd run away from the home. Though she'd often thought about it, making vague plans that seemed unreal and impossible, when the moment had come she hadn't remembered a single one of them. She'd wanted only to get away from Owen Grant, quickly, before he could do anything to her again, to get away as far as possible, as soon as possible. And however bad things got, she wasn't going back. Ever.

The gas heater roared ferociously; a blue flame shot up from the red glow and subsided and the pilot light went out. Tamsin swore, one of the choice expressions she'd learned from the other children in the home. But though swearing might relieve her feelings, it wouldn't keep her warm. Tamsin felt her way across the Portakabin, totally dark now that the fire had gone out, to the door. She thought she'd seen a light switch on the wall, and she'd have to risk putting the light on if she wanted to search for some alternative means of keeping warm. Not that it was much of a risk really. The building site was fairly isolated, and at present the only access to it was by way of a half-made-up track. But she would have been missed by now; they would be out looking for her, and a police car cruising this way might just see the light go on. If a policeman did come, she would tell him about Owen. But she didn't suppose he'd believe her. Why should he take her word for it against the word of a respected social worker? They'd be hand in glove, bound to be, and she'd be sent back.

Don't think about it, Tamsin told herself. You've got away, and you're not going back. Ever.

She felt her way across the Portakabin and located the light switch, flipping it down. Fierce white light flickered and illuminated, revealing a desk and chair, filing cabinets, charts affixed to the walls, and two more doors. Tamsin went to one and opened it – a loo, oh bliss! She hadn't fancied creeping outside to answer the call of nature. The other door led into a tiny inner office with another desk, a computer and a metal filing cabinet. Tamsin dragged open the top drawer, discovered it contained nothing but files hanging on metal runners, and jammed it closed again.

She was just about to open the second drawer when she heard a car draw up outside. She froze, heart pounding. Seconds later a door slammed, and then she heard someone moving about in the outer office. Oh my God, they'd found her. And there was nowhere she could hide. Except possibly behind the door. She slipped into the corner, making herself as small as she could, hands pressed against her mouth to silence her uneven breathing, eyes wide with fear.

Footsteps on the metallic floor, then the door was thrown open so violently that the handle pressed into her stomach. Tamsin closed her eyes tightly, as if by not seeing she would not be seen.

'What do you think you are doing?' The voice was low and angry.

Tamsin opened her eyes again, cringing, to see a man with iron-grey hair and a weather-beaten face, wearing a dark green Barbour over an Aran jumper.

'Nothing!' Her voice, coming from the shaking place inside her, sounded defiant rather than afraid. 'I just wanted somewhere to sleep, out of the cold. I'll . . . I'll go now . . .' She tried to slip past him, but he was blocking the doorway.

'Oh, no, you don't! Who are you?'

'Who are *you*?' she returned cheekily.

'I am Robert Holbrook. This is my site office. How did you get in?'

'The window was unfastened.'

'Was it indeed?'

'Yes.' She glared at him mutely, trying to conceal her terror.

'I suppose,' he said, 'that you have run away from home.'

Tamsin swallowed at the knot of panic in her throat. That was it then. All over. Unless she did something quickly. She darted forward, kicking out, but his hand shot out, grabbing her arm. Although she was almost as tall as he was, she was no way strong enough to break free. And the knowing that she was trapped and the knowing that he was far bigger and stronger than she was started a new sort of panic.

'Don't you dare touch me!' she sobbed. He let go of her arm instantly, looking at her in amazement. 'I know what you want,' she grated. 'You men are all the same.'

'Hey!' he said. 'Hang on. I'm not going to hurt you.'

'That's what they all say. I hate you. I hate you all!'

'Goodness me, you are in a state!' He took a step away from her, looking at her narrowly.

And suddenly, although she was still frightened, she could see that he looked genuinely shocked, not at all the way Owen had looked when she had gone to him with her troubles.

'Oh, don't make me go back,' she begged. 'Please don't

make me go back to that place! I don't want to see him again, ever!'

Her teeth were chattering. 'You're cold,' he said. 'Come on, I'll light the fire and make us both a cup of tea.'

'There's no gas left,' she said. 'I had all three bars on and it ran out. I'm sorry . . .'

'Well in that case, you'd better have my coat.' He took off the Barbour and helped her into it. Then he went to a tiny galley at the end of the main room, filled the kettle and plugged it in.

She stood watching him, thinking this was her chance to escape, but not doing anything about it because really she had nowhere to go. And besides . . .

'Don't run off with my coat, will you?' he said over his shoulder.

When he had made the tea, he set the mugs down on the desk and pulled up two chairs.

'Sit down, drink your tea, and tell me what all this is about,' he said.

And to her own utter amazement, Tamsin found herself doing just that.

For almost as long as she could remember she had lived in the home. Almost but not quite. There were some hazy memories of earlier days, but they were a bit like faded snapshots, as if they really had nothing to do with her at all. She could remember a dingy room with a bed and a sink, and a bathroom two floors down that was kept locked, so her mother had to ask for the key before she could give Tamsin a bath. She remembered her mother's perfume, strong and cheap, she now knew, but a scent that evoked a haunting nostalgia. She remembered a shiny white plastic handbag full of lipsticks and earrings that she loved to turn out. And she remembered the night when the people had come and taken her away.

She'd woken up and found herself alone. It wasn't the first time it had happened, and usually, if she went back to sleep, next time she woke Mum would be there. But that night she wasn't. Tamsin tried to go and look for her, but the door was locked. She panicked then, rattling at the handle and screaming because she was trapped, and Mum wasn't there. And then there were footsteps on the stairs and the door was broken open, but there was still no Mum. Just these strangers. She screamed some more, but they took her out into the night, to a strange house where she was made to have a bath and wash her hair. Wash her hair, in the middle of the night! They put her into a horrible scratchy nightdress and took her to a room where there were several other beds with children sleeping in them, and told her she had to spend the night there. She couldn't sleep; she was too frightened and upset, and she knew that something was terribly wrong. She just lay in the dark surrounded by shadowy forms that meant nothing to her because she'd never seen them in daylight and tried not to cry.

Next morning the lady who'd bathed her took her to a small room.

'I want my mum!' Tamsin said.

And then they told her. Her mother was dead. From now on she would be living at the home. Everything was very blurred after that. She remembered crying and feeling ashamed, she remembered being lonely and homesick and desolate. She remembered wondering why her mother had died, but it was years later before she found out, and the person who told her was a boy a year older than she was, who also lived in the home.

His name was Tim Bryant.

Tim Bryant had been in the home on and off all his life. He'd been placed for adoption once, but for some reason his natural mother had delayed signing the papers and the whole thing fell through. Over the years he had been placed with various foster families, but none of them worked out in the long term. Though he could be surprisingly charming, he was also truculent and rebellious and spiteful. He seemed to enjoy tormenting the other children, and he especially disliked Tamsin, or Charlene Riddle, as she was then. Because she was so pretty she seemed to get preferential treatment from everyone and Tim burned with jealous resentment. He could hardly believe his luck when one day, assigned to do some work in Matron's office, he began poking about in the files and came across the newspaper clipping. VICE GIRL STRANGLED read the banner headline, and the story beneath it told of how the body of Maureen Riddle, aged twenty-one, had been found dumped in woodland on the outskirts of town. The knowledge was power to Tim; for weeks he tormented Tamsin with barbed insults, and eventually he told her the whole story. Tamsin would never forget her disbelieving horror or the way Tim had revelled in cheapening all her warm memories of her mother. She would never, ever forgive him, she thought.

The shame was a constant in her heart. Everyone knew the truth, she guessed, and when she grew boobs and the boys started taking too much interest in her in a way she found embarrassing and distasteful she couldn't forget that her mother had sold her body for sex, and thought that they were expecting her to be 'easy' too. She tried to ignore them when they jeered at her to 'give us a feel', and tried to avoid being left alone with any of them.

The one person she couldn't avoid was Owen Grant, the boys' housemaster at the home. One warm September evening Tim had managed to trap her in an otherwise deserted common room, and was trying to get his hands inside her blouse when Owen Grant walked in. Owen ordered them both to his office, where he lectured them both as if they were equally guilty, but when he dismissed Tim, he told Tamsin to stay behind.

'You've had a very tough time, haven't you?' he said.

She couldn't look at him, couldn't meet his eyes, brooding, somehow, behind his gold-rimmed spectacles. Instead she stared down at the carpet.

'I'll look after you,' he said. And the words didn't comfort her at all. They were like a threat, though she couldn't quite see why.

Until he pulled her down on to his knee and began fondling her. He didn't do anything more that night, that came later, insidiously inveigling her into his office on all kinds of pretexts, and Tamsin was too frightened to tell anyone what was happening. She was trapped, totally trapped. She didn't think anyone would believe her and in any case she was too ashamed. But the panic and the shame just built and built until one cold, foggy Sunday in November when she could bear it no longer.

She ran away, with nothing but the clothes she stood up in and a few scraps of food she had saved from lunch and the little bit of pocket money she had saved. She had no idea

where she was going, just that she had to get away from Owen
Grant and from Tim and from everyone who made her life a
misery. And when it had begun to get dark and she'd realized she had nowhere to sleep, she had walked off the road
to the new housing development thinking she might find
shelter there. She'd been in luck. The window of the site office
wasn't properly fastened and she had been able to climb in.

But now it had all gone wrong. She'd been caught, and
she'd be sent back to the home, back to the torture, back to
the misery, back to everything she was so desperate to escape.
And she couldn't bear it. She couldn't . . .

'Don't make me go back. Please!' she said to Robert.

He was looking furious, the lines and furrows in his face
were deeper than before and his mouth was a grim hard line.

'You know you have to go back,' he said. And then: 'But
not tonight. You can come home with me. Then tomorrow
we'll get all this sorted out. Don't look so worried. I'm not
going to hurt you. And in any case, my wife will be there.'

'I'm not worried,' she said, and it was true. Apart from that
first moment when she'd tarred him with the same brush, she
really hadn't thought he would be like Owen Grant or Tim
Bryant. She didn't know why she wasn't afraid, why she
trusted him. She just did.

'Come on then,' he said.

He secured the window she'd crept in at and she followed
him out to his car. As she got into the front passenger seat
she realized she was still wearing his coat. For some reason
it made her feel safer than she'd ever felt in her life.

The house was incredibly big, or so it seemed to Tamsin, as
big, almost, as the home.

'You don't live here all by yourself, do you?' she said,
looking up at the bulk of it, illuminated by security lights
against the backdrop of trees and shrubs.

'Me and my wife, yes.'

'Haven't you got any children?'

'We have a daughter, but she's grown up and married, with
children of her own. Three girls. About your age.'

'Oh.' Lucky girls, she thought. So lucky to have a grandfather like Robert and a place like this to come to.

She was less sure of Dorothea, though, or Dorrie, as he called her. Dorothea was very neat, very proper, and Tamsin thought she was less than pleased that Robert had brought Tamsin home with him. Not that she was unpleasant, quite the contrary. She put on a wonderful spread of cheeses and pickles and cold ham, and she loaned Tamsin a couple of jumpers which she said had belonged to her daughter Patricia. But there was an edge to her manner which belied her kindness, and when she suggested Tamsin should have a bath before going to bed, Tamsin was reminded of the night when she had first been taken to the home, and the feeling that she could not possibly be allowed to soil the sheets just as she was.

She slept late next morning; Robert was not about by the time she surfaced, and it was nearing lunchtime when he returned.

'I suppose you're going to make me go back now,' she said, in a very small voice.

'I'm afraid you have to,' he said. 'You must know that. But I can promise you that things are going to be different from now on.'

'Different how?'

'This man who's been bothering you, this Owen Grant. He won't be bothering you any more.'

'How do you know?'

'Just take my word for it. He won't.'

Her eyes went round. 'You haven't . . . he's not *dead*, is he? You haven't killed him?'

Robert laughed. Actually laughed. 'You see too many films. No, he's just gone, that's all. And I don't think he will be working with vulnerable young people again any time soon.'

Robert visited her sometimes at the home, and took her out, to the zoo, the Museum of Costume, the SS *Great Britain*, Brunel's iron ship which was being renovated in the docks at Bristol. They had coffee at Cawardines and tea in the restaurant of a department store, and once, as a special treat, Kentucky Fried Chicken. She had been right in thinking that Dorothea was less than enthusiastic though. Tamsin was never again taken to the Cedars, and she never met Robert's daughter and granddaughters.

Life at the home was much improved. She felt a bit guilty at first, knowing it was her fault that Owen Grant had lost his job, and wondering if it had been her fault that he had done what he had done. But eventually she began to get over that, and the new housemaster, when he arrived, was no problem at all. He was young and very serious, in spite of having a ponytail and his ears pierced in three places, and Tamsin suspected he didn't much care for girls at all.

How long ago it seemed now! As if all of it had happened to someone else, not her at all. And yet in some ways it might have been just yesterday. The feeling of utter helplessness still haunted her, though she had been far from helpless for years now, and she suspected it would never quite leave her. However successful she had become, there would always be that part of her that remembered. It was just one of the scars her early life had left on her, but she knew she was lucky to have escaped with so few, and that in the main that was thanks to Robert. From that first night when he had found her in his site office, he had always been there for her when she had needed him, not a constant presence but someone she knew she could turn to if the need arose. And she had loved sharing the good times with him too. He had been so delighted with the success she had made of her life, and she thought that in many ways he thought of her as another daughter. She certainly regarded him as the father she had never known.

Oh, Robert, she thought now, why did you have to die? Why did you have to grow old? Everyone has to, of course, but you . . . you were so fit in body and mind, so young at heart. Until Dorothea died . . .

But it wasn't just Dorothea's death that had seen the beginning of his decline. It was what she had told him when she was dying. He had been shocked to the core, and hurt, too, that he had been kept in the dark about what had happened. But he had been determined to find his missing grandchild and determined to leave him or her an equal share in his estate. And Tamsin knew from what he had said that his motivation partly lay in the fact that he was equating Trish's lost baby with Tamsin herself.

'It's twenty years too late now for me to be able to help with the child's upbringing,' he said, and his face was haunted and shadowy, old suddenly. 'But I must do what I can now to put things right.'

'Robert,' she said, reaching for his hands and thinking how cold they felt. 'I'm quite sure the child is just fine. It was probably adopted by a really nice family and has never wanted for anything. Trish and Dorothea would have made sure of that.'

'Would they? I'm beginning to wonder. If they could keep it all from me, how do I know they didn't just bung the child into care? A home like the one you were in? Dorrie never liked me having anything to do with you; you knew that, didn't you? She seemed to want to pretend you didn't exist, and I could never understand why. Now I'm beginning to wonder. Was it a bit too close to home for comfort? Did it remind her of things she didn't want to be reminded of?'

'Oh, Robert, I don't know.' Tamsin sighed. 'Why don't you just try to put it out of your head? There's no way you can find the child after all this time. The only chance would be if he or she applied for their original birth certificate under the new legislation and sought you out.'

'Not me. Trish. And Trish is dead. I have to do what I can, Tamsin, while there's still time.'

She'd shaken her head, sure this would be just a wild goose chase. But Robert *had* found the child, she was sure. Or at least he had found out something which had put him on the track. And whatever it was had upset him so dreadfully he had never been the same again.

As she had told Kate and Jon, she had been in Australia when he had found out whatever it was he had found out, and he hadn't felt able to tell her what it was over the telephone. 'I just can't believe it,' was as far as he had been prepared to go. By the time she got back to England he had had his first stroke and she had been quite certain that it had been brought on by some kind of stress or shock. When she had visited him in hospital, his eyes had been full of bewilderment. Was that what happened when a part of the brain shut down? she had wondered. Was that look simply Robert searching around within himself for something he could no longer find? Or was it that he was trying still to come to terms with whatever it was that, in his own words, he 'just couldn't believe'. Tamsin rather thought it was the latter.

And of course, that wasn't all.

She tipped her head back now, massaging her neck with her fingers and wondering if she had been right to keep silent about the one thing which Robert *had* said to her, clearly and incontrovertibly. But what good could it possibly have done to tell Kate and Jon? The chances were Robert had been wandering, dwelling on old anxieties and a deeply buried sense of totally unjustified yet still very real guilt about his daughter's death? To tell Trish's daughter what he had said would only stir up trouble and cause unnecessary pain. And yet he had seemed dreadfully sure.

He had searched for the words as if his life depended on it, dredging them out of the fog that had descended on his brain, desperate to tell her something. More than once he had said something incomprehensible about 'truth'. And she had held his hand and leaned close, taking the words one by one and storing them up to make a sentence.

'Trish,' he had said. 'She didn't want to die. She didn't do it.'

'What do you mean?' Tamsin said, alarmed. 'Are you saying she didn't commit suicide?'

'No.' He was becoming agitated, but his eyes burned with the same fury as when she had told him about Owen Grant all those years ago. '. . . killed her.'

'Who? Who did you say?' The name had been nothing but a gurgle.

But perhaps he had never enunciated it all. He struggled again, trembling with the effort. But the name he was searching for was lost somewhere in the fog. Robert could not reach it.

Twelve

Kate was feeling incredibly, almost foolishly, happy, and she really did not know why.

Correction, she did know why, she simply could not believe or understand it. Not a thing had changed. She still had a pile of unpaid bills on her desk and no way of settling them and the days the bank manager had allowed her to sort things out were flying by. And all her other problems still existed too, yet somehow they all seemed less oppressive. She had actually enjoyed herself yesterday; she had felt younger and more attractive than she had done for years. And it was all thanks to Jon Nicholson.

Kate took a red reminder from the pile in front of her and speared it on to the letter spike on the corner of her desk. That was foolish too; the bill still had to be paid, mutilated or not, but it gave her enormous satisfaction to see it impaled.

The doorbell jangled; she looked up expectantly, then her mouth fell open with amazement.

'Chris! What are you doing here?'

'That's not much of a welcome! Aren't you pleased to see me?'

'Well, yes, of course. But . . .'

'Since you couldn't manage yesterday I rearranged my visit to Bleadon for today.'

'Well, well!' Perhaps I should be a little less readily available, she thought, and then realized the irony of it. Today wasn't convenient either. 'You're not expecting me to have lunch with you today instead, are you?' she said. 'Because I can't. I've arranged to meet my godmother.'

'Your godmother? Sounds like something out of Grimm's Fairy Tales! Can't you put her off?'

'No, Chris, I can't. She's over here from Florida. She'll be going back in a day or two.'

He should know that, she thought, irritated. I told him, I'm sure. He can't have been listening.

'Don't I even get a cup of coffee?' Chris had adopted a hurt expression. Usually it made her melt; it gave him a rumpled, little-boy-lost look. Today, however, the expression, too, irritated her.

How dare he play the injured party after all the times she'd sat waiting for his call, or rearranged some engagement to fit in with him only to find his family had a prior claim on his time after all. Why the hell should she feel guilty for having a life beyond the one she occasionally shared with him?

'You can have a coffee if you want one.' She went through to the little kitchen at the rear of the shop and he followed her. Janice, one of her girls, was there, washing up mugs she had collected from around the workroom. 'Leave that, Janice, I'll do them,' Kate said.

'Right.' Janice dried her hands, smirking slightly. The girls knew, of course, that Kate and Chris had a relationship – impossible to keep something like that from them – and they also knew he was married.

The moment Janice's back was turned, Chris reached for Kate, but she sidestepped. 'For heaven's sake!'

'What's the matter with you?'

'This is my place of work, Chris. I don't want to canoodle in front of my staff.' She picked up one of the mugs Janice had washed, drying it energetically.

'I'm beginning to wish I'd stayed away today,' Chris said. 'You're in a foul mood, Kate.'

'No, I'm not. I'm perfectly happy. It's just that you make me cross. I'm fed up with being the other woman.'

'Babe, you know it's not easy. As soon as the kids are a bit older we'll be together, you know that.'

'Will we?'

'You know we will.' He reached for her again. 'I love you very, very much. And one day soon we are going to be together properly, I promise.'

This was usually where she melted, when his arms were around her and his breath tickling her cheek and he was whispering words of love. But today she felt untouched by them. She'd heard it all before, too many times, and now she no longer believed them. And she wasn't sure, anyway, that she wanted to be with a man who could cheat on his wife and children, even if he did it because he said he couldn't live without her.

She pushed free again. 'I'm sorry, Chris,' she said, 'but I don't think I can go on waiting for you to make up your mind to leave. I'm not getting any younger and time is ticking away. I want a husband of my own, not someone else's . . . a home, children, before it's too late. This is my life. I've only got one, and I can't go on wasting it.'

'You're saying I'm a waste of your life?' He looked shocked. 'That what we have isn't worth anything?'

'Not exactly . . .'

'That's the way it sounds to me.'

'Well, all right, perhaps that is what I'm saying. A lot of things have happened just recently to make me stop and think. It's as if my whole world has been put in a bag and shaken up, and I don't think I want to go on any longer the way we are. I'm sorry, but there it is.'

'Well.' He looked shaken. 'I never expected *this* when I decided to call in and see you today.'

'I guess that was it, the final straw,' she said. 'You expect me to be ready and waiting whenever you want me, but when I want you, then it's a different story. And what about Anna? Do you really think we are being fair to her?'

'You know our marriage was over a long time ago.'

'Are you quite sure Anna sees it like that? If there really is nothing between you any more, how come you have to pretend I don't exist? Surely the honest thing to do would have been to tell her about us a long time ago. No, I'm sorry, Chris, but I'm fed up with the whole situation and I think it's time we called it a day.'

He turned away impatiently. 'There's no point talking to you in this mood. I'll call you in a day or two.'

'Don't bother.'

He half-turned back. To her surprise he looked to be on the verge of tears.

'You can't end it just like that. Not after all we've been to each other. You've had a pretty horrible few days, and it's making you see things all wrong.'

'I think it's making me see them *right*.'

'Well, I shall call you anyway.'

'If you must, but don't expect me to have changed my mind.'

When he had gone she picked up the tea towel very matter-of-factly and finished drying the mugs. She could hardly believe what she'd just done, and yet, rather than feeling devastated as she would have expected, she felt only a glorious sense of freedom.

About an hour after Chris had left, Kate remembered that she had intended phoning Jess this morning. She checked her watch. Getting hold of her was never easy; the only way was to keep trying on the grounds that she had to return home sometimes to refuel and change her clothes if nothing else. As she had expected, the answering machine came on – Jess, not Adrian, with a typically bossy message – but to her surprise before it had finished there was a click and Jess was on the line in person.

'Good heavens!' Kate said. 'You're there!'

'Well, obviously.'

'No good works this morning?'

'Did you just ring to be sarcastic, or is there something you want to say?'

Kate controlled the urge to giggle. What on earth was the matter with her? Her whole world was falling apart and she was behaving like a silly schoolgirl.

'Jon Nicholson and I went to see Tamsin Wells yesterday,' she said.

'Tamsin Wells?' Jessica sounded totally blank, and Kate remembered with a rush – she knew nothing about it.

'Oh, gosh, Jess, I'm sorry! Jon identified the mystery woman at the funeral as Tamsin Wells, the Gazelle girl, you know? We went to see her because we wondered if . . .'

'Why did he tell *you*? If anyone was to be told, it should have been me! I'm the oldest . . .'

'Oh, Jess, don't get on your high horse, please. He tried to get hold of you, I think, and couldn't. And I'm telling you now. He had an appointment to see her yesterday in London, and I went with him.'

'Why?'

'Why did he go to see her? Because—'

'No, why did you go with him?'

'I just wanted to,' Kate said, her patience running out. 'I thought if she turned out to be our missing half-sister it might be a nice idea for one of the family to be there. But before you kick off, it's all right – she isn't. And I don't think she was Grandpa's mistress either. But she was very close to him. He told her things he never mentioned to us, well, to me, anyway. I'm afraid there's no doubt about it. There was a child who was adopted; Grandma told him about it just before she died. She had a fit of guilty conscience, I suppose.'

Instead of the heated denial Kate had expected, there was a long, pregnant silence. Then Jessica said wearily: 'Why do people *do* that? If they make a decision to keep quiet about something, why can't they stick to it?'

'They don't want to take the secret with them to their graves, I suppose.'

'Or can't live with it any longer. That's how it was with Mum—' She broke off abruptly, and Kate heard the sharp intake of her breath.

'What do you mean?' she asked.

'Oh, nothing.'

'Why did you say it, then?'

'I just thought . . . Mum taking her own life. That's the way it must have been . . .'

'I thought you didn't believe any of this, Jess.'

'I suppose I shall have to if this Tamsin Wells person is prepared to say it's true. You're sure she's not about to try and lay a claim herself?'

'Quite sure.'

'And she didn't say if Grandpa knew . . . well, obviously he didn't, or he'd have named the child in his will.'

'No, but . . .' On the point of telling Jessica that Tamsin Wells had been fairly certain that Robert had discovered the child's identity shortly before his stroke, she changed her mind.

'Well, I suppose we can still hope that Jon Nicholson fails to identify the missing beneficiary in the time allotted,' Jessica said.

'I don't think that's quite the right spirit.'

'Maybe not, but I'm afraid it's how I feel. I just wish Grandpa had let sleeping dogs lie.'

'Well, he didn't,' Kate said.

As she put the phone down she realized she was trembling

slightly. Confrontational Jess could still do that to her some-times, reduce her to the way she'd felt as a child, little sister to Jessica's bossy grown-up ways, yet too big to be spoiled as Miranda had been. But it wasn't that today, she realized. It was less what Jess had said than what she hadn't. What on earth had she meant about Trish? She'd covered it well, explained it away neatly and perfectly reasonably. When Trish had killed herself it probably had been because she could no longer live with her secrets. But that wasn't how it had come out when Jess had first made the remark. It had sounded more as if Trish had revealed the truth first – and Jess knew about it.

You're being ridiculous! Kate told herself. Far from knowing something, until a few minutes ago, Jessica had actually denied the existence of a mystery child. But for some reason, she found her own protestations unconvincing.

'Personal call for you, Wendy.'

'Personal? For me?' Wendy's heart leaped wildly. Ever since she'd seen Ash she hadn't been able to help hoping . . . He'd called her at home after all on the night of the funeral when Tim had refused to get her to the phone. Perhaps he'd call her again. She took the receiver from Lynne. 'Hello?'

'Wendy, it's me. Dad.'

'Dad.' Her heart sank, disappointment settling in her stomach like a lead weight. Why had she thought for even a moment that it might be Ash? She'd met him in the street, hadn't she, the day after he'd telephoned? If he'd had anything to say he would have said it then.

'I'm sorry to call you at work, Wendy, but I wanted a word with you without your mother knowing.'

'Really? Secrets?' She tried to make her voice light.

'Not secrets. Just, well, discretion. I wish you'd call in and see her, Wendy. She's been very down this week, not herself at all. And she was very disappointed you couldn't make it for lunch on Sunday. She does so look forward to seeing you.'

'Dad, I was with her only last Thursday.'

'But that was for the funeral. She doesn't count that. I know you're married, with a life of your own now, but I don't think you realize how much it means to her. You're her world; always have been.'

Wendy bit her lip, feeling the weight of duty that came from being an only child pressing hard down on her shoulders as it always had done. She loved her parents, of course, but knowing her mother's world revolved around her could be a burden as well as a blessing. And there was no way she could visit until her mouth had healed properly.

'I can't make any promises, for a day or two at least,' she said.

'Well, do your best, will you, my love?' There was a rather odd note in his voice, Wendy thought, not anything she could put her finger on, he just didn't sound quite himself. It was rather odd ringing her at work, too. She could never remember him doing such a thing before.

'*You're* all right, are you, Dad?' she asked, concerned suddenly.

'Me? Yes, of course.'

'Are you sure? You don't *sound* all right.'

He laughed, a little self-consciously. 'Oh, I expect Robert's dying has upset me, too. More than I realize.'

'Well, of course it has! You were old friends. And then all that business with the will . . .'

'Robert was perfectly entitled to take his business wherever he liked.'

'Yes, but all the same . . .'

'That Jon Nicholson hasn't been to see you asking questions, has he?'

'No, why should he?' Wendy said, surprised.

'Just wondered . . . He's a pretty thorough chap, I should imagine, and with the bit between his teeth.'

'Dad, I'm going to have to go,' Wendy said. She could see Crispin looking at her pointedly. 'Mustn't keep the phone tied up. Someone might actually want to buy a house!'

'Of course. Goodbye for now. But you will think about what I said?'

'I will. Bye, Dad.'

She put the phone down, frowning. What was behind Hugh phoning her like that? Was Verity really so upset or unwell he was worried about her? Or was it Wendy they were worried about? Did they suspect what was going on between her and Tim? Or concerned that her old affair with Ash might flare up again? Verity had never cared for them seeing one another.

Ash was too like his father, she always said. It had seemed
a pretty lame excuse to Wendy; she couldn't see that Jack
Morton was *that* bad, and in any case, it was hardly fair to
tar Ash with the same brush.

She was standing up for him again, she realized. And if he
so much as crooked his little finger, she knew she'd be there.
No wonder Tim was so suffused with jealousy and hatred!

I'll make it up to him, Wendy thought. I really will find a
way to make it up to him. And knew, even as she thought it,
that she was whistling in the dark.

Kate had arranged to meet Liz in the Plume of Feathers, a
pub within walking distance which enjoyed a good reputation
for bar food. By the time Kate arrived just after half past
twelve, Liz was already there, occupying a window seat, with
two glasses of gin and tonic on the table in front of her and
a couple of large paper carrier bags propped up beside her.

When they had exchanged greetings, she pushed one of the
glasses in Kate's direction. 'I got this in for you. I hope I
made the right choice.'

Kate grinned. 'Well, I shouldn't really be on the alcohol in
the middle of a working day, but I dare say I can force myself.'

'I'm sure you can. Let me move these bags out of your
way.'

'You've been shopping,' Kate said, sipping the g and t gratefully.

'Yes, raiding Tracey's Boutique. I'm running out of things
to wear. I only came equipped for the funeral; staying on longer
wasn't in the original plan. Perhaps we'd better order, though,
before we start chatting. You can't be too long, I take it.'

'Not too long, no,' Kate said regretfully.

They perused the menu cards and the 'specials' board that
hung beside the bar.

'I can thoroughly recommend the fish soup,' Kate said. 'In
fact, I think that's what I'm going to have. It comes with lovely
toasted French bread and grated cheese and a mustard dip –
a meal in itself.'

'Sounds extremely fattening to me,' Liz said. 'I think I shall
stick to a salad, Parma ham and melon, perhaps.'

'You don't need to worry about putting on weight.' Kate
eyed her godmother enviously. 'You're very slim.'

'Only because I do worry about it, believe me! And I shall be eating tonight—' She broke off, looking slightly embarrassed. 'I'm actually having dinner with your father.'

'Oh, really!' Kate was surprised, but also pleased. She worried about Tony, whose social life beyond the country club had seemed to be non-existent since Trish's death. Was it possible that he and Liz . . . ? Was that what the shopping trip for new clothes was in aid of? If it was, she for one would be only too delighted.

'We have been seeing a bit of one another,' Liz said, as if she had asked the questions aloud. 'I rather feel that with things the way they are, he could do with some moral support.'

'Yes, I think he probably could,' Kate said, slightly disappointed.

'Shall we order then? What's the form? Do we have to go to the bar?'

'Yes. I'll see to it.'

'No, this is my treat.'

'Liz . . .'

'I insist.' She slid out of her seat.

Kate sat watching her at the bar telling herself it was stupid to be so sensitive. If her business weren't in trouble, she probably wouldn't have thought twice about Liz buying lunch. As her godmother, it was her habit to treat Kate on the rare occasions they met. But with the situation as it was, it felt like charity.

To make matters worse, the moment she returned to the table Liz said: 'You said you wanted to pick my brains; something to do with your business, I imagine,' and Kate couldn't help feeling that Liz, too, had made the connection.

'I'm not sure there's a lot of point really,' she said, trying to sound nonchalant. 'I'm not doing too well at the moment, no use pretending otherwise. But I don't really think there's anything anyone can do. The recession is to blame; the business just isn't there any more, and I don't know how much longer I can last out.'

'Bad as that?'

''Fraid so. At the moment I'm hanging on by the skin of my teeth. This legacy of Grandpa's might just save the day. Did you know he left more than we first thought? He owned some land which could be ripe for development – if the industry starts to pick up again. On the strength of that, the bank has allowed me a little leeway.'

'Kate.' Liz toyed with her glass. 'Do you really think that's wise?'

'What do you mean . . . wise?'

'Propping up an ailing business with every penny you can lay hands on. Don't you think it might be better to cut your losses? If things are so bad, pouring in the money your grandfather left you might be a bit like pouring water into a bucket that's full of holes. It won't solve anything in the long run, and you'll be left with absolutely nothing.'

'I know that. But I couldn't just cut and run, Liz. I'd be letting down all the people who work for me, and the people I owe money to. I have to keep trying, just as long as there's the faintest glimmer of hope.' Kate sighed. 'In any case, what else could I do?'

'Well, you know there's always a place for you in my outfit.'

'In the States, you mean? That really would be running away, wouldn't it?'

'You don't need to think of it like that. Making a fresh start would be a better description.'

'I'm sorry, I'd see it as running away. Deserting the sinking ship.'

'There are times when that is the only sensible thing to do,' Liz pointed out.

'Maybe I'm not a sensible person.'

Liz smiled. 'I think you are eminently sensible. A bit too loyal and honest for your own good, perhaps. Not really a businesswoman. Which is why I think you'd be better off working for someone else. Your talent is for interior design, not balance sheets. And you definitely lack the killer instinct.'

'Maybe. But I made a commitment. I have to see it through.' She stopped talking abruptly as the barmaid approached their table, slapping condiments and cutlery wrapped in paper napkins on to the bare wood table in front of them. Then, when the girl had left again, she went on: 'It may be, of course, the fourth share of Grandpa's estate will be divided up between the three of us too. We don't seem to be making much progress in finding the missing beneficiary.'

'I'm very glad to hear it.' Liz spoke with such feeling that Kate glanced at her in surprise, and she picked up the cutlery parcel, twisting it round between her hands. 'I just wish your Grandfather had let sleeping dogs lie, Kate. I'm sure he meant well, but it's causing a great deal of trouble and heartache, and for what?'

Kate ran her finger round the rim of her glass. 'Strangely enough, Liz, it means something to me that somewhere I have a half-brother or sister I don't even know . . . may never know.'

'That's it exactly,' Liz said smartly. 'If your mother had a child before she was married, that child is now an adult person, who has grown up in a totally different environment to you. You didn't know they existed; they don't know you exist. You have nothing in common. All this can only cause trouble.'

'But perhaps they need . . .'

'Be realistic, Kate. Most adopted children are very much wanted. They are showered with blessings – love, care, money probably. Adoption agencies are very fussy about making sure prospective parents can afford to do right by the children placed in their care. They're vetted to high heaven, for goodness' sake. Every aspect of their lives is put under the microscope. And in the sixties, the criteria were even stricter than they are today. They had to be the right age, the right religion, in a stable marriage, home-owners, with a secure income. If Trish put a baby up for adoption, the chances are that baby was placed with perfect parents and is now set up for life. He or she probably needs your grandfather's legacy far less than you do.'

'That really isn't the point.'

'I still think only trouble can come out of pursuing this,' Liz said firmly. Too firmly, Kate thought.

The waitress was back. 'Parma ham and melon.'

'Mine, thank you.'

'And fish soup.'

'Mine.' Kate looked at the enormous bowl of steaming soup and wondered how she was going to get through it. Her appetite had suddenly disappeared. There was something she needed to ask.

'Liz,' she said, spreading a little dip on her crouton and dipping it in the grated cheese, 'was Mum involved with Uncle Jack?'

The silence was laden, Liz's shock palpable. 'Why do you ask that?' she said at last.

Kate put the crouton down on her side plate, quite unable to put it into her mouth. 'I found some photographs amongst some things Mum had left at Grandpa's house. Photographs of a very young Uncle Jack. And I couldn't help wondering?'

'I see.' Liz smiled slightly. 'I suppose in that case there's no point denying it. She did go out with Jack for a time before she married your father. But there is absolutely no reason to suppose that he might have been the father.'

She said it with such vehemence that her denial had precisely the opposite effect to the one she had intended.

'Oh my God, Liz, that's exactly what you do think, isn't it?' Kate said. 'That Jack – that Jack and Mum—'

'No, of course not!' Liz said quickly. 'Not for one moment.'

'You do. That's why you are so anxious to hush the whole thing up, why you're so cross with Grandpa for raking it all up after all these years. You think that if Mum had a baby before she married Dad, the chances are that Uncle Jack was the father. Oh, I can see now why she kept it so quiet! What a can of worms!'

'Kate, you're jumping to conclusions . . .'

'But didn't Dad *know?*' Kate demanded. 'Didn't he *suspect?*'

'He knew Trish and Jack used to go out together, of course he did. That was no secret. He met Trish through Jack. As to anything else, I don't know.'

Kate felt sick. The gin seemed to be curdling in her stomach. She'd known of course from the moment she'd found the photographs that Jack had to be in the frame for the father of Trish's illegitimate child; she just hadn't wanted to admit it. It was too horrible, incestuous almost, though she knew that was a purely emotional reaction. But she could see that this would make the whole thing doubly painful for her father, especially if Trish had never told him the truth. Why? Why hadn't she told him the truth? If he'd known about her and Jack then surely it would have been only a small step to confessing he had made her pregnant? Unless . . . no, don't go there!

And what about Jack? Had he known the truth all these years? Was he just pretending he was as much in the dark as anyone about an illegitimate child? And when had it happened? Had he and Trish continued their affair after he was married to Sandra, or even after Trish had married Tony, and that was the reason for all the secrecy? But if that were the case, then Tony must have known too.

So many questions suddenly, and all arising from one answer that had been staring her in the face. No wonder she had tried to close her mind to it!

'Perhaps you can see now why I am so anxious this should all blow over quickly,' Liz said, abandoning all pretence of denial. 'I don't know that Jack is the father, but I have to accept that if there is a child, then there is a very good chance that he was. She was very much in love with him.'

The gin pinched at Kate's stomach again. She pressed her hand to her mouth against the rising nausea. What was the matter with her, for heaven's sake? Trish had been a flesh and blood woman, not a plaster saint. But knowing it didn't make the revelation any easier to take. Her mother in love with Uncle Jack, having a sexual relationship with him. Perhaps after she was married to her father. Kate thought of all the times the family had been together, for parties, for Christmas, for family outings, and suddenly they were tainted by this huge cloud of guilty passion. What had been going on that they didn't know about? And had it, in the end, had anything to do with Trish's suicide?

'I'm going to have this out with him,' she said fiercely.

'Kate, no. There's no point. I've already spoken to him, and he denies all knowledge.'

'You've *asked* him?'

'Not asked him, no. I really didn't want to know, as I suspect you don't really. But I did warn him to keep quiet if there was anything. For your father's sake. And he assured me there was nothing to keep quiet about.'

'Did you believe him?'

'I'm not sure. One never is, really, with Jack. But I don't think he *will* say anything. He has his own marriage to think of, remember. I don't suppose Sandra would be exactly over the moon about it. Always providing she's not in on it already.'

'God, what a mess!'

'Exactly. Which is why I think we must hope that the search for the child is unsuccessful and the whole thing blows over. The last thing we want is someone else asking awkward questions and maybe even producing embarrassing legal documents.'

'I suppose not.'

'Have your soup,' Liz said. 'It's getting cold.'

How could she be so pragmatic? Kate wondered, and found herself remembering that in the beginning Liz had tried to discount the whole thing, whilst all the time she had known a great deal more than she was saying. Again she wondered whether there were others pretending ignorance when they actually knew different. Uncle Jack, Auntie Sandra, her father, Jess . . .

Why did I add Jess to the list? Kate wondered, surprised by her own train of thought, and almost immediately supplied the answer. Jess was the one who had been the most adamant there was no child, yet when that was more or less proved beyond doubt, she had made that very odd remark about Mummy. Just as if there were something she *did* know. Had known all the time . . .

'I'm sorry our lunch has turned out like this,' Liz said.

'Not your fault. Mine, for asking awkward questions.'

But she was glad, all the same, that she had. Little as she liked the truth that was emerging, it was better that she knew it. That was the best way to protect the vulnerable from being hurt. Especially her father. As far as Kate was concerned, he was the one who really mattered.

But at least she wasn't the only one concerned with his welfare. Kate looked across the table at Liz, with her lovely serene face and the stack of carrier bags containing clothes obviously bought with a purpose, and knew that Liz too cared a great deal more for Tony than she was about to admit.

Thirteen

'Oh, Ashley, you're back! Did you have a nice walk?' Sandra asked, pouring herself a large Bacardi.

'Cold,' Ash said. He unwound his old college scarf, letting it hang loose over his waxed jacket and threw his mother a disapproving look. 'Isn't it a bit early in the day for that?'

'Oh, don't be such a bore, Ashley!' Sandra topped up her glass with diet Coke and raised it at him challengingly. 'With my elder son home for the first time in ages, I feel like celebrating.'

'Sounds like an excuse to me,' Ash said equably.

'I don't need an excuse. At my age, if I feel like a drink I shall have one.' She reached for her cigarettes and lighter, stacked neatly on the corner of the sideboard. 'I suppose you disapprove of me smoking, too.'

'I wish you didn't, yes. But I don't suppose that is going to stop you.'

'Very true. Everything in moderation, I say. That's the key.'

'As long as that's the way it stays. You don't want to turn into an alcoholic.'

'Like Trish did, you mean?' Sandra smiled slightly. The subject of Trish had never been far from her mind these last days. Truth to tell, she was enjoying all the furore Robert's will had created, the speculation and the discomfort. It created a welcome diversion in a life that had become, in recent years, frankly boring. 'Don't worry, I won't. I always thought she turned to the bottle to drown some secret sorrow. Now we know what is was, don't we? A love child. Lost to her. No wonder she drank. No wonder she . . . Did you know there's talk that she went to Gloucester to have it, having told her employers she was looking after a cousin in Worcester? I mean, where did they dream these places up?'

'Ma, let it drop, can't you?'

'But it's the most exciting thing that's happened around here for years! Why don't you want to talk about it? No, don't answer that, let me guess.' She lit her cigarette and pointed it at him, bobbing it up and down between her fingers in time with her words. 'Everyone's wondering what became of the child. But you are more concerned about who the father is, aren't you? I've noticed how cool you've been with Jack. You –' she extended the cigarette as if it were a gun – 'think it was him.'

'Mother, for God's sake!'

'Oh, dear, I've shocked you again.' Sandra's lips curved into her familiar mischievous smirk and she sipped her Bacardi and Coke. 'I'm a realist, Ash. Trish was besotted with your father, and he . . . well, I've never been under any illusions about him. He sowed a great many wild oats, I'm afraid. That was part of the attraction as far as I was concerned. The challenge of taming him. And I think I've pretty well succeeded. It took me the best part of thirty years, but it's a long while now since he had a fling. It may just be that he's getting better at concealing them, of course. Or growing old. That could be in. But I can tell you, Ashley, in his heyday no woman was safe from him. There must be—'

'Stop this mother!' Ash's tone was closer to a snarl than she had ever heard it.

'Sweetheart, baby, I'm only speaking the truth.'

'Well, I don't want to hear it. You talking like that is sordid and disgusting.' He wound the scarf round his neck again. 'I'm going for another walk.'

'Ash, don't go.' Sandra dumped her cigarette in an ashtray and went to him, catching hold of him by the arms. 'I didn't mean to upset you. I want to make the most of what time we've got. This time next week you'll be back in Saudi.'

'And a bloody good job too.' Ash shook himself free and strode out, leaving Sandra staring after him in dismay. Then, as she heard the front door slam, she shrugged resignedly.

Perhaps she shouldn't have said what she'd said; obviously it had hit a raw nerve. But she had noticed that Ash was behaving very coolly towards his father, and she had thought that if she brought it out into the open, let him know that she'd long ago accepted Jack's failings, that it might help. Seemingly not.

Ah, well, he was a grown man now, he'd have to work through his hang-ups himself, or not, as the case may be.

Sandra rescued her cigarette, reached for her drink, and returned to the delicious speculation as to the details of Trish's lost child.

Kate sat at the kitchen table with her laptop in front of her. Since talking to Liz at lunchtime she had been pondering the next move in the search for her mother's missing child, and it had seemed to her the only clue she had lay in the address at which Trish had stayed in Gloucester. She no longer had the letters Dorothea had written to her there; Jon had taken them, along with the other papers, and she supposed he would eventually get around to pursuing that lead himself. But first he was checking out the registers of births and the adoption agencies, which might well take some time. It wasn't even as though finding the missing beneficiary was a full-time job for him; he had work for other clients to distract him. Today, he'd told her, he had a full diary of appointments, and tomorrow he was in court defending some otherwise perfectly respectable householder who had finally snapped at the continuous loud music blaring over the fence from his neighbour's garden and taken the law into his own hands, taking a sledge hammer to the ghetto blaster and punching its owner on the nose. There was no way she could expect Jon's undivided attention, but she was impatient for results, so she had decided to try to follow up this one on her own.

The address where Trish had stayed was etched on her brain: 15 Osbourne Terrace, Gloucester. She remembered the name of the landlady too, Mrs Millett. Without a great deal of hope she had set out to access the electoral roll; thirty years was a long time and Mrs Millett could be long dead, or moved away. She wasn't too confident of her ability to find what she was looking for either; she really wasn't very computer literate. She had one at work, of course, but she'd only ever used it for word processing and spreadsheets, and the new computer was a recent acquisition, purchased only just before she'd realized she really shouldn't be spending money on such luxuries. But to her amazement, after a couple of frustrating hours, she had found the site she was looking for. And struck gold.

Mrs Millett, it seemed, still lived at No 15, Osbourne Terrace.

Something midway between excitement and apprehension bubbled in Kate's stomach and she pressed her hand to her mouth, staring at the screen and trying to decide what to do next. She should tell Jon, she supposed, and leave it to him. But it would probably be next week before he could follow it up. In the meantime . . .

I'll go myself, Kate thought. I might get further, anyway, than if I turn up with a solicitor.

She pushed the laptop to the back of the table and fetched her road atlas. Simple enough to get to Gloucester, just get on the motorway and head north. And then what? Stop at a garage and buy a local A–Z?

She'd go tomorrow, she decided. Strike while the iron was hot. Should she tell Jess and Miranda what she planned? Jess had been pretty miffed only to have heard about the visit to Tamsin Wells after the event. But the prospect of having either of her sisters along was not an enticing one. And Mrs Millett might need careful handling; Jessica would only rub her up the wrong way.

What about Ash? She wondered, and dismissed that too. Ash had promised to get in touch with her and hadn't. In fact he'd barely spoken two words to her. He'd changed, and it hurt. No, she wasn't going to ask a favour of him now.

Kate reached for the phone and called her senior assistant.

'Look, I'm really sorry to ring you at home, but do you think you can manage without me tomorrow? There's something I really have to do . . .'

Osbourne Terrace was very much as Kate had imagined it would be. Ranks of terraced houses, probably built around the turn of the century, faced one another across a narrow street. Each house was fronted by a tiny garden, some of which had been concreted over to provide just enough space to park a small car. Others had been modernized with pebbles replacing grass, some were carefully tended with rose bushes and winter bedding, some overgrown and untidy.

The garden of Number 15 was one of the tidy ones. It was fronted with a low stone wall and a gate; what looked like a peony bush stood sentry beside a freshly painted front door with a polished brass knocker in the shape of a fox's head.

Pristine net curtains shielded the downstairs window, but a vase of yellow chrysanthemums stood on the sill in front of them.

Kate hesitated for a moment, her heart thumping unevenly. Turning up like this, unannounced, was a long shot. She had no choice; she didn't have a telephone number. And she'd come all this way; she couldn't chicken out now. Before she could change her mind, she lifted the fox-head knocker and rapped sharply.

For what seemed like an age there was no sound from within the house and Kate was about to knock again when she heard the rattle of curtain rings on a pole, and the door swung open. An elderly woman stood there, peering curiously up at Kate. She was tiny, well under five feet, Kate guessed, and she wore a blue and white checked nylon coat overall over a pair of black crimplene trousers. Wisps of snow-white hair escaped from a maroon-coloured beret.

'Mrs Millet?' Kate said.

'That's me. And if you're a Jehovah's Witness, or trying to sell double glazing, I'm not interested, thank you.'

Kate took a deep breath. 'No, it's nothing like that. My name is Kate Morton. I'm sorry to just descend on you like this, but I really want to talk to you about a lodger you had back in the sixties.'

The lines and creases in the woman's small shrunken face deepened, so that she resembled nothing more than a deflating balloon.

'I had a lot of lodgers back then. They came and went.'

'Well, yes, but I'm hoping you might remember this one. She was quite young, probably still in her teens, and she was pregnant. I believe she probably had her baby from this house. Her name was Patricia Holbrook – Trish, everyone called her.'

The old woman frowned, but her eyes were bright and clear behind her pink plastic-framed spectacles.

'Trish. Yes, that was her name.'

'You do remember her?'

'Well, of course I do! I'm hardly likely to forget. Went off to hospital in a taxi in the middle of the night when the baby came.'

Kate's heart lurched. 'I know this is an imposition, but please . . . could I ask you some questions about her?' Mrs

Millett was looking at her with narrow suspicion. 'I should have explained at the start,' Kate said. 'I'm her daughter.'

It was Open Sesame. Mrs Millett opened the door wider against a heavy chenille curtain and Kate stepped into a tiny hall dominated by a huge print in a wooden frame that Kate recognized as a pencil portrait of John Bunyan. His eyes seemed to follow her as she crossed the hall. Had they also followed her mother? She imagined so; John Bunyan looked as if he had occupied this space on the wall for a very long time.

Mrs Millet opened a door to what was clearly the 'front room'. It was spotlessly clean, with lace antimacassars on the squat little three-piece suite and the occasional table polished and gleaming, but it was also very cold, as if it was rarely used. Mrs Millett crossed to the hearth where a two-bar electric coal-effect fire stood in the grate, and flicked a switch. Instantly the bars began to glow, giving off a hot, dusty smell.

'Sit down.' Mrs Millett indicated one of the pair of easy chairs and when Kate sat, she perched in the other, smoothing her nylon overall over her knees with gnarled hands.

'Well,' she said in a quavering voice filled with wonder. 'So you are the baby that was born from this house.'

'Oh, no, that wasn't me,' Kate said apologetically. 'But it *is* that baby I want to talk about. We have only recently learned of its existence and we are trying to find out what happened to it. That's why I'm here. I'm hoping perhaps you may be able to help.'

'Oh, I doubt that.' The shrewd little eyes fixed on Kate's face. 'Can't your mother tell you?'

'I'm afraid my mother is dead,' Kate said.

'Oh, dear, I'm sorry to hear that.' She did look genuinely sorry, and shocked too. 'A growth, was it? You know . . . *cancer*?' She mouthed the word silently, as if to speak it aloud was some kind of curse.

'No, an accident,' Kate said. She had no intention of going into details. 'She was already dead before we learned about the baby, and so was her mother, my grandmother, who seems to have been the only other one in the family to have known about it.'

'Her mother . . . oh, yes. She came with Trish the day she moved in, I remember. Very upset she was at leaving her;

I don't think Trish had ever been away from home before, and in her condition . . . But there you are. You make your bed, you have to lie in it.' There was disapproval in her tone; Kate realized she was glimpsing the moral climate her mother had come up against thirty years ago.

'But you were still willing to have her as a lodger?' she said.

'I wasn't altogether happy about it,' Mrs Millett admitted. 'I laid down strict rules. No men friends to visit. And the front door to be locked by ten at night. She didn't go far, though. The pictures, sometimes, if there was a film on that she wanted to see, and that was about it. I don't suppose she felt like parading herself in her condition. And she didn't have any visitors at all, except for the social worker.'

Kate sat forward, very alert suddenly. 'The social worker?'

'Well, yes. It was her that contacted me in the first place to see if I'd have Trish here. Like I say, I wasn't sure about it. Most of my lodgers were respectable folk, moving into the area to work and wanting somewhere to stay till they found a place of their own, that kind of thing. But they knew I had the room vacant just then, and this Mrs Smith came to see me, and I couldn't afford to turn her down. I was a widow, and letting the room gave me that bit extra to make ends meet. A nice woman, she was, and expecting herself. I couldn't help but think - what a difference! There was she, happily married and really looking forward to her baby – you only had to look at her to see it – and there was Trish, worried half to death, and dreading it. She said to me once: "I don't know if I can go through with it, Mrs M," (she always called me Mrs M) and I said: "Well, you should have thought of that before you went letting yourself down, shouldn't you?"'

Kate's heart contracted at the thought of her mother, alone and scared, being preached at by a stranger. She could imagine all too clearly how the stuffy little house must have felt like a prison, and yet how Trish must have dreaded reaching the end of her sentence because it would mean giving up the baby she had carried for nine long months.

'How long was Trish with you?' she asked.

'Just the three months.' Mrs Millett twisted her puffy hands together in her lap. 'And I looked after her well. When she came, she was hardly showing at all. Strapped herself up, I dare say, to hide it. But once she got here she didn't have to pretend, and I fed her up a treat. A good cooked breakfast every day, meat and two veg at dinnertime and a high tea with a bit of ham or a tin of salmon. No one could ever say I didn't give my lodgers value for money.'

The fierce heat from the electric fire was scorching Kate's legs and her face, too, felt hot and dry. She shifted a little in her seat.

'So, she was here right up until the baby was born,' she said, trying to draw Mrs Millett back to the relevant facts.

'Yes, she was. Like I say, she had to get a taxi in the middle of the night to take her to the hospital. Why she didn't call an ambulance, I don't know, but she didn't. She knocked on my bedroom door at four in the morning and said she was off. I'm only a light sleeper, mind you, and I'd been half expecting it. I could see she was uncomfortable the day before, shifting about like a cat on hot bricks. Well, that was the last I ever saw of her, going off in that taxi.'

'She never came back?' Kate asked.

Mrs Millett shook her head. 'Never. After all I'd done for her. The welfare lady, Mrs Smith, came and collected her things. Packed them all up to go. Not that she had much, but all the same. And it was Mrs Smith paid me up to the end of the month, too. I said there was no need, but she insisted and I wasn't going to argue. It took me till after the Christmas before I could let that room again.'

'So you don't know what happened to the baby?' Kate asked.

'Well, it was adopted, I suppose. Straight from the hospital, I shouldn't wonder. Mrs Smith arranged all that. Trish did tell me once there was a couple all lined up and waiting. If it was a girl, she said. They wanted a girl.'

'And if it had turned out to be a boy?'

'I wouldn't know. Maybe they'd still take it, and maybe they wouldn't.'

'And was it a girl?'

'Do you know, I never asked,' Mrs Millett said. 'I meant to, when Mrs Smith came for Trish's stuff, but she was very cool with me that day, very businesslike. She packed the case, sorted out the money, and that was it. And I was feeling a bit put out, too, that Trish had gone just like that. I didn't feel like showing any interest. Now, if there's nothing else, I'd best be getting on. It's my bingo this afternoon, and I've got my bit of dinner to cook . . .'

'There is just one thing.' Kate hesitated. 'You must have talked to Trish quite a bit while she was here . . .'

Mrs Millett, getting up from her chair, snorted.

'Not so as you'd notice. We were never what you might call friendly. She kept herself to herself pretty much. Watched a bit of tele – she liked *The Man From UNCLE*, and I'd sometimes watch it with her, though it was a lot of rubbish from what I could see of it.'

'She never talked about the baby's father?' Kate persisted.

'No, she did not! Well, she wouldn't, would she, with him getting her in that condition and then buggering off and leaving her to face the music?'

The swear word sat oddly with the woman's strict, old-fashioned morals, and Kate fastened on to it.

'He left her in the lurch,' she paraphrased. 'Was that because he was a married man?'

'Well, that I couldn't say.' Mrs Millett was at the door now, opening it. 'Could have been married, I suppose. Men in the forces often conveniently forget they've got a wife and responsibilities, and lead the girls on, letting them think they're single. It happened all the time in the war, didn't it, especially the Americans . . .'

'He was in the forces?' Kate was holding her breath.

'RAF. Stationed somewhere local to where she lived, if I remember rightly.'

'She told you that?'

'No, like I said, she didn't even mention him. But she did write to him a couple of times. I posted one of the letters for her.'

'How do you know he was the father?' Kate persisted. The information might not take her any closer to finding the missing child, but it was important, all the same, because it would take Jack out of the frame.

'I know because the letters came back, return to sender, after she'd gone.' Mrs Millett looked slightly shamefaced suddenly. 'I was going to send them on to her, but I never did have a home address for her. I thought she might have put it in the letters to this chap, so I opened them to see.'

Liar! Kate thought. You opened them because you were nosey.

'You read the letters,' she said.

'Only so as to find out how to get hold of her,' Mrs Millett said defensively.

'And what did they say?' Kate pressed her.

'Oh, I can't remember that now! Just the sort of thing you'd expect. That she was having his baby and thought he ought to know. She was hoping he'd do the right thing by her, I expect. Make an honest woman of her. And if he didn't, she'd have to give the baby up to a good home.'

For someone who'd only been looking for an address, Mrs Millett seemed to know a lot about what the letters had said, Kate thought.

'You don't still have them, I suppose?' she asked.

'Good lord, no. It was donkey's years ago. And it's no good you asking me what the chap's name was either, though I do know he was an SAC – Senior Aircraftsman. I noticed that because my sister's boy was an SAC when he was doing his National Service back in the fifties.'

'It doesn't matter,' Kate said, not wanting Mrs Millett to go off on some long story. And it was true, it didn't matter. Trish hadn't been able to trace him thirty years ago and he had no more idea of the whereabouts of his child than any of them. Like them, he hadn't even known of its existence. The only thing that mattered was that the father of Trish's baby hadn't, it seemed, been Jack.

Though she was no nearer to finding her missing sibling, Kate felt free, a bird let out of a cage of anxiety. It was some unknown RAF boy who had made her mother pregnant, and awful though the whole story was it was the most enormous relief that Tony would not have to come to terms with the fact that the father of his beloved wife's baby had been his own brother.

She did, however, have one piece of information that might prove useful. As soon as she got home, Kate phoned Jon's office.

He was still in court, his secretary said, and Kate wasn't sure whether to be disappointed or relieved. She wasn't sure how he would react when he learned she had gone off to Gloucester investigating off her own bat.

'Can I leave a message for him?' she said. 'Will you tell him that I think social services, or whatever they were called back in the sixties, was involved in placing Trish Morton's illegitimate baby? The social worker on the case was called Mrs Smith. She was pregnant herself at the time, so it's likely she left soon afterwards – women usually did in those days when they started a family. But I would think it must all be in the archives somewhere, and there's a chance, anyway, that she may have gone back to work when her children started school.'

'I'll pass that on to Mr Nicholson,' the secretary said primly. 'Thank you for calling.'

Next, Kate rang Tony. From what Liz had said, it was playing on his mind, too, that Jack might well have been the father of Trish's child, and she was anxious that he should have his fears allayed as soon as possible. Since he'd never mentioned such a possibility to her, she had to be careful what she said, of course, but simply relaying the conversation she'd had with Mrs Millett should do the trick. It proved beyond doubt, of course, that Trish had given birth to a secret child, but in all honesty Kate thought they'd all more or less accepted that from the moment the will had been read. The important thing was that Tony should know that his brother had not been the father.

'Oh, my poor Trish,' Tony said when Kate told him, but she could hear the relief in his voice all the same.

'You never heard her mention being involved with an RAF chap, did you?' Kate asked.

'Never. But there were a lot of RAF stations all over the place at that time,' Tony said. 'The chaps would go to local dance halls on a Saturday night, and Trish liked to go dancing. That's how she met him, I expect. As for being *involved* . . . it doesn't sound as though she knew much about him. It was more of a fling, I'd say, with disastrous consequences.'

'A one-night stand, even.' Kate wasn't sure if that made it better or worse. 'Perhaps he didn't even tell her his right name. But that hardly matters now. At least we know . . .' She broke off, realizing she was straying towards dangerous ground. 'It's the child we're looking for, not the father.'

'And we're no further on with that.'

'Not necessarily.' She told him about the social worker,

Mrs Smith. 'Jon Nicholson is on the case, and I think we'll have to leave that to him. He's the one with the Open Sesame when it comes to official records. And I really must devote some time to my business. For all the good it will do.'

'Don't give up, Kate.'

'I won't. I told Liz . . .'

'Talking of Liz,' Tony said, 'she's staying with me for a few days.'

Kate almost dropped the phone. 'Liz is?'

'It seemed silly for her to be paying for a hotel when I've got plenty of room, and it wasn't ideal in any case.' Tony sounded slightly defensive, slightly embarrassed. But also, Kate thought, happier than she'd heard him in a long while.

'Good for you, Dad,' she said.

And meant it.

This wasn't going to be the easiest of relationships, with Liz's life on one side of the Atlantic and her father's on the other. But it was the first time Tony had shown the slightest interest in a woman since her mother's death, a really good sign. It wasn't right to shut himself off the way he had. Her mother wouldn't have wanted that for him, and neither did Kate.

And she rather thought that Mum would have been as pleased as she was that the person who had finally managed to make a crack in his defensive shell was her old and dear friend, Liz Langley.

Fourteen

Tamsin's hand hovered over the telephone. It had been playing on her mind that she hadn't told Kate and Jon about the strange things Robert had said to her the last time she had seen him before he died. 'Trish didn't want to die. She didn't do it . . . Killed her . . .' The name he'd been searching for lost in the woolly recesses of his mind, or mumbled so incoherently she hadn't been able to catch it.

It probably meant nothing. Over and over she'd told herself that he had been rambling, lost in a muddled world where old anxieties and regrets surfaced in the same way that the worries of the day, in grotesque forms and disguises, creep into ones dreams. Trish had drowned, in what the coroner had recorded as an accident, but given her emotional fragility, Robert and the other close family members had suspected she had taken her own life. Somewhere in the confusion that had overtaken him when the stroke had affected his brain and reality and imaginings had blurred, he had sought for an explanation that exonerated him from, as he saw it, failing his only daughter in her hour of need, and become convinced that someone else was responsible.

But supposing it wasn't that at all? Supposing he hadn't been wandering, but briefly lucid? Supposing he had been trying to tell her something that he had discovered as a result of the investigation he had undertaken? Supposing someone else had been responsible for Trish's death? For her *murder*, for that was what it would have been. If someone had killed her . . .

No, it was too far fetched, like something out of a melodramatic novel or a film. What possible reason could anyone have had for killing Trish that was connected in some way to Robert's search for her missing child? It couldn't be . . .

And yet Tamsin couldn't get it out of her head. If Robert

hadn't been wandering, if he'd been trying to pass on what he knew, she was the only one with an inkling about it. She should have at least mentioned it and left them to make up their own minds as to whether it had meant anything or not.

But who to tell? The solicitor, who was not personally involved in any of this, but might feel duty bound to tell the police? Or Kate? She'd liked Kate. She was very much Robert's granddaughter. Tamsin thought that if they had met under different circumstances they might well have become friends. And she had seemed eminently level headed; she didn't seem at all the sort of person to become hysterical about it. The trouble was, she had the solicitor's telephone number, but not Kate's. She'd have to try and find it through directory enquiries.

As she reached for the telephone it rang, making her jump. She picked it up.

'Tamsin Wells.'

'Tamsin. Sweetie. Good news. I've just had a call from a German agency. The girl they had lined up for a shoot tomorrow has been involved in an accident, likely to be unavailable for some time. They want you.'

Tamsin experienced the old rush of adrenalin. 'Who? When?'

'It's a television commercial, but it will also show in cinemas. There's just one snag.'

'Wheel it on.'

'You have to be in Munich first thing tomorrow morning.'

Wendy had cooked what she had thought was a perfectly nice supper. Not exactly a gourmet meal; when she'd been at work all day she was too tired to go in for all the frills, but she'd picked up some smoked haddock from the fishmongers, potatoes and carrots from the mini-market, and found enough parsley in her little herb garden to make a parsley sauce. She was just giving it a last stir when Tim came through from the lounge where he'd been watching television.

'What the hell is that awful stink?' he demanded bad-temperedly.

'Fish,' Wendy said, nodding towards the pan where the haddock was poaching. 'It does make a bit of a smell, I know, but . . .'

'A *bit* of a smell? It's disgusting!'

'It's fish.'

'And what's that muck?'

'Parsley sauce.' She started pouring it from the saucepan into a jug.

'God, we used to have that stuff in the home. Lumpy, horrible gloop.'

'It's not lumpy.'

'Let me have a look.' Tim made a grab for the pan, Wendy held on to it, and before she knew it the Pyrex jug, already half-full of hot, thick sauce, was knocked flying. She squealed as it scalded her ankles and feet, and pooled on the tiled floor.

'You clumsy bitch!' Tim yelled. His jeans and slippers were splattered too. 'Look what you've done now!'

'I couldn't help it! Oh, my foot . . .' She was heading for the sink and a cloth to wipe it off when Tim hit her, a back-handed flip in her face. Wendy sidestepped, her shoe skidded in the puddle of spilled sauce, and she fell, jarring her shoulder against the cupboard and landing in a shaken, painful heap with one leg twisted awkwardly beneath her.

'Get up!' Tim shouted. 'That was your own stupid fault. I hardly touched you.'

'I know . . . I know . . .'

'And I wouldn't have had to at all if you cooked me a decent meal. I'll bet you wouldn't serve up muck like this for your precious Ashley.'

'Tim, please.' She was cowering, anticipating the next blow or kick.

'You'd do *him* a nice steak with all the trimmings.' He was turning away.

'Perhaps we would be able to afford steak,' Wendy muttered.

Tim swung round. 'What did you say?'

'Nothing . . . nothing . . .' Wendy was trying to get up. Tim grabbed her by the hair, dragging her to her feet.

'I know what you said. Well, I'm sick of being compared to that poncy bastard.' He lashed out at her again and this time there was nothing Wendy could do to defend herself. 'You want him?' Tim ground out. 'You go to him! See how he likes your bloody whinging. I've had it with you.'

Wendy staggered back as he released her, crashing against the corner unit. Her knees gave way beneath her and she slid slowly down, dazed and limp as a broken doll.

'Go on, go to him if that's what you want.' When she didn't move, he grabbed her by the hair again, yanking her up on to her knees and half-throwing her towards the door.

'Tim, please . . . I'm sorry, I'm sorry . . .' She was sobbing, blood trickling down her chin from where her own teeth had sunk into her lower lip with the force of his blow.

'Too late for sorry.' He pushed her again and again in the small of the back, driving her along the hall. There were a few moments' hiatus as he grabbed her keys from their hook and opened the front door. 'Come on, you bitch.' He caught hold of her again, roughly, forcing her across the drive to her car and into the front passenger seat.

'Tim, what are you doing?' she squealed.

'Taking you to your precious Ash.' He was in the driver's seat now, jamming the key into the ignition, slapping the gear-stick into first.

She didn't know what he was talking about; he was making no sense. He was drunk, too; he shouldn't be driving. But Wendy was too shocked and too frightened to protest again. She tried to get her seat belt around her; failed. The car shot forward, tyres screeching in protest, and veered wildly across the road.

'Tim, please,' she sobbed softly.

He ignored her and Wendy shrunk into her seat in mute terror as he hit the main road, driving like a maniac, narrowly avoiding parked vehicles and oncoming traffic. There was a cyclist with no lights on his bicycle; at the last moment Tim saw him in the glare of his headlamps and swerved round him. The traffic lights were on red; he went straight through, but fortunately there was nothing coming in the opposite direction.

'Stop! Please, stop!' Wendy screamed.

Tim's only reply was a low growl that sounded more like a predatory animal than a human being.

They were out of town now, careering along the middle of a narrow lane. Through a mist of pain and terror, Wendy recognized it as the road that led to Jack and Sandra's house. The exclusive cul-de-sac of three executive homes loomed on their left, their windows and an old-fashioned lamp standard in one of the gardens glowing normality into the dark. Tim swung into the turning, jerked to an abrupt halt.

'Tim, you can't!' Wendy gasped, horrified.

For answer he leaned across her, opening the door on her side of the car. Then, before she could fully grasp what he intended to do, he gave her a mighty shove. Wendy teetered and he pushed her again so that she went sideways out of the car, landing on her shoulder on the path, one leg still hooked into the well of the car.

'There you are, Ash – delivered!' Tim sneered. He thrust Wendy's leg out of the car, wrenching her knee, and pulled the door shut, but not properly. As he screamed away it flew wide open, flapping wildly. Briefly Tim stopped, slamming it shut again, and then he was gone, roaring back down the lane.

Running footsteps. Dazed, Wendy struggled into a sitting position.

'Are you all right?' It was a man with a golden retriever on a leash. He sounded as shocked as Wendy felt. He must have been walking his dog and seen her deposited on the pavement like a sack of garbage.

'I don't know . . .' Her voice was shaky, disjointed. She managed to get up, the man steadying her. She was hurting all over and she had lost a shoe, so the pavement felt cold and hard beneath her one bare foot.

What the hell was she going to do? She was hurt and miles from home. And she couldn't go back anyway. If she did, Tim would kill her.

'The Mortons,' she said. 'Please . . . tell the Mortons . . .'

And then everything seemed to have gone a long way off and the darkness of the night was closing in on her.

'Wendy! My God – Wendy!'

Ash's voice. Ash's arms around her. The roughness of his jersey was stinging her poor sore mouth and she didn't care. Ash . . . oh, Ash!

'What's happened to you?'

'Tim – he threw me out of the car.'

'Let's get you inside. Can you walk?'

'I've lost a shoe.'

'Come on, lean on me.' He supported her for a few faltering steps; tried to pick her up.

'You can't carry me,' she protested. 'I'm too heavy. You'll hurt yourself.'

'I'll give you a hand.' The stranger who was still hovering, let go the dog's leash and he and Ash hoisted Wendy on to their crossed arms.

The front door of the house was ajar; they got her inside. Wendy leaned her head into Ash and when they set her down she folded in against him.

'Thanks,' he said to the man with the golden retriever, who, looking anxious and curious, reluctantly retreated through the door, closing it after him. Ash supported Wendy into the lounge, sat her down in one of the huge leather armchairs and dropped to his haunches beside her.

'Wendy, what the hell has happened to you?'

'Tim . . .'

'And he's hit you too!' His fingers hovered over her bruised face and bleeding lip. 'My God, I'll kill him!'

For all her pain, for all that she was still shocked and shaking now from head to foot, there was a warm place somewhere deep inside. Wendy felt she had come home. Ash was looking at her the way he used to look at her, the tenderness in his eyes contrasting with the furious set of his mouth. For a brief moment she felt once again as if their hearts and souls were reaching out to one another, touching. Then the spell was shattered by a shrill voice from the doorway.

'Ashley? What on earth is going on?'

Sandra stood there, wearing a cream silk robe and high-heeled feathered mules. Her hair, scooped up at the back, hung in damp tendrils around a face which, for once, lacked any make-up. The scent of magnolia wafted in with her; obviously she had been taking a bath. Her eyes, surprisingly small without their kohl liner or mascara, fastened in disbelief on Wendy.

'Wendy! Oh my God! Has there been an accident?'

'Not an accident, no.' Ash's voice was shaking with barely contained rage. 'Tim did this to her.'

'Tim?' Sandra seemed incapable of anything but monosyllables.

'He's beaten her up and dumped her outside our house.'

'Why?' Sandra wailed.

'Because he's a total bastard.'

'No, why here? I heard all the commotion – I was in the bath. This is appalling! Are you hurt, Wendy?'

'I think I'm OK.' Wendy's mouth was beginning to feel stiff, and talking was difficult as well as painful.

'You must go to hospital – get checked over.' Sandra reached for the telephone. 'I'll call an ambulance.'

'Oh, no! No, please!' Wendy protested. On top of every-thing else, she was now horribly embarrassed. 'I don't want an ambulance.'

'Then Ashley will take you.'

'I don't want to go to hospital. I just want . . .' She broke off. *I want to go home* . . . she had been about to say. But her home was no longer a haven but a place of torture. She couldn't go home. What was she going to do? Where was she going to go?

'We'll take you to your mother's house, then.' Sandra answered the question for her. Again Wendy's heart sank. She didn't want to go to her mother's house either. She didn't want Verity and Hugh to see her in this state. The shame flooded her again and tears filled her eyes.

'Couldn't I . . . ?' She hesitated, hardly daring to ask. 'Couldn't I . . . just stay here for a little while?'

She looked pleadingly at Ash, seeking for the comfort he had offered her a few moments ago.

And saw the shutters come up in his face, felt him with-draw as if she had struck him the way Tim had struck her. She winced inwardly, her heart as raw as her poor bleeding lip.

'Mum's right,' he said, and his voice was different too. 'You should go to hospital, just to make sure you're not seri-ously hurt. And then . . . well, is there a friend you could go to if you don't want to go to your mother's?'

'I don't know, let me think . . .' Her brain felt like cold porridge.

'I also think,' Ash said, 'that we should tell the police.'

'No!' Wendy was appalled.

'He's assaulted you, and it's not the first time it's happened either, is it?' Ash was still furious, she could see, but the tender-ness had disappeared as if it had never been. The memory of it, however, and the way it had made her feel, unleashed a wash of guilt.

'I deserved it,' she said wretchedly. 'It's all my own fault. I make him angry.'

'That's no excuse.'

'It's certainly not,' Sandra said. 'Heaven knows, I make Jack angry, but he'd never . . . Well, he wouldn't do it more than once!' She looked at Wendy narrowly. 'But I still don't understand. Ashley, get Wendy a brandy, or a cup of tea, or something.'

'Which?' Ash cocked an eyebrow at Wendy.

'Tea, please.'

'Make it strong and sweet,' Sandra instructed him.

The minute he was out of earshot, she sat down in a chair opposite Wendy.

'Has Ash got anything to do with this, Wendy?'

'No.' Wendy's eyes fell away. They were telling a different story.

'He has, hasn't he?'

'No, not really. I mean, there's nothing . . . But Tim thinks there is. He thinks that something is still going on between us, that I'm still in love with Ash.'

'And are you?'

'It was all over a long time ago, you know that,' Wendy hedged.

'Why?' Sandra asked sharply, and when Wendy looked puzzled, she went on: 'Why did you end it? I always thought you were made for each other. And Ash was totally gutted.'

'He was the one who ended it, not me,' Wendy said. 'As for why, I never found out. He just sent me a letter, saying it was over. And went off to the Middle East.'

Sandra was staring at her in total disbelief. 'I know he went to the Middle East. I thought he took the job there to get over you. I've never seen him as wretched as he was when the two of you split up. And I could have sworn . . .'

That he was still in love with you, she was about to say, but broke off as Ash appeared in the doorway with a mug of tea. Seemingly unaware that he had been the subject of their conversation, he handed the mug to Wendy.

'Strong and sweet, as ordered.' But there was a tautness in his tone, and his avoidance of her was almost tangible, passing the mug to her carefully, handle first, and quickly retreating to put a safe distance between them.

'So,' Sandra said, 'if you won't go to hospital, and you won't go to your mother's, what are we going to do with you?'

'There's a girl I work with,' Wendy said, nursing the mug of tea between her hands, which were still shaking a little, letting it warm her. 'She was in a similar situation once. Maybe . . .'

'You shouldn't be with strangers,' Sandra said, and for a moment Wendy thought she was about to say that Wendy could, after all, stay with them. Clearly Ash thought the same, and he was having none of it.

'What about Kate?' he suggested.

'Kate! Yes, that's a good idea,' Sandra said, but she sounded distinctly disappointed.

Was she miffed at being divorced from the action? Wendy wondered. Or did it have anything to do with the conversation they'd been having when Ash was out of the room? Shallow she might be, a born mischief-maker she certainly was, but Sandra adored her sons, especially Ash. His happiness was paramount where she was concerned. But she was labouring under a misapprehension if she thought that getting back together with Wendy would make him happy. Clearly he couldn't wait to get her out of his sight.

'I'll ring Kate,' he said, and left the room to make the call from the telephone in the hall, where, presumably, he could explain what had happened without Wendy overhearing his pleas for Kate to take her in.

Kate was soaking in the bath when the telephone rang. She groaned. Why did it always happen that just as you'd begun to relax and unwind someone decided it was a good moment to call? And chances were it was Chris, trying to get her to change her mind about ending their affair. There was nothing like rejection to spur someone into realizing they wanted what they were about to lose. But her mind was made up. Nothing was going to change. The minute he had her back where he wanted her, everything would go back to being as it had been before, and she didn't want that. Actually, she no longer wanted *him*. Years of waiting, hoping, longing, had tarnished the bright allure and now her eyes were wide open. Chris had deceived his wife and used her. She'd never be able to trust him, and she could see now the self-centred duplicity and the weakness that the rose-tinted spectacles had once obscured.

Besides which, there was Jon.

Perhaps it was Jon ringing, Kate thought, brightening, as she pulled on her towelling bathrobe and ran down the stairs. She had, after all, left a message for him . . . She grabbed the phone. 'Hello?'

But it wasn't Jon, and it wasn't Chris.

'Kate,' the low, disembodied voice said. 'It's Ash here.'

'Ash!'

'I was beginning to think you were out.'

'I was in the bath. You're still in England, then? Not headed off back to sunnier climes?'

'A couple more days.'

'I thought you were going to ring me before now.'

'Yes, sorry about that . . .' She waited for him to explain the omission. Instead, he said: 'Kate, we've got a bit of a problem and we're wondering if you can help.'

She frowned. 'If I can. What sort of problem?'

'We've got Wendy here. She's in a bit of a state. Tim has beaten her up and thrown her out – literally. She doesn't want to go home to her mother's – doesn't want her to see the damage Tim's done, I suppose – and obviously she can't go back to her own place. Is there any chance she could come to you, for tonight at least, until she can sort something out?'

'Tim's beaten her up?' Kate was shocked. 'I can't believe it!'

'True, I'm afraid. And I'm pretty sure it's not the first time. If I laid hands on him, I'd kill him. I know it's a lot to ask, Kate, but . . .'

'Of course she can come here,' Kate said. 'The bed in the spare room is made up and . . . will you bring her, or do you want me to come over for her?'

'I'll bring her to you. You're a star, Kate.'

Kate bit her lip. She didn't feel like a star. She was fond of Wendy, but to be honest, she didn't really want her here just now. She had enough on her plate at the moment. But what could she do?

'OK, see you in what . . . half an hour, an hour?' she said.

'About that.'

'In that case,' Kate said, 'I'd better get dressed and be ready for her.'

'I haven't got a single thing with me,' Wendy said. 'Not a toothbrush, not a change of clothes, nothing.'

She was huddled in the front passenger seat of Ash's car, arms wrapped around her aching body.

'I'm sure Kate will lend you what you need.' Ash was concentrating on the road.

'I shall have to go home sometime. It's everything, my bag, my purse . . . everything. But I'm really scared.' Wendy sounded close to tears.

'You really should go to the police,' Ash said.

'Yes, I suppose I should,' Wendy said in a small voice, and lapsed into crushed silence, utterly broken and wretched.

Bad enough what Tim had done to her. Bad enough that she should be left in this humiliating position. Bad enough that her fragile world had finally shattered. But what was really destroying her was Ash's cold, hard attitude. For a few blissful moments when he had first come out of the house and seen her bloody, beaten and scared out of her wits, she had really thought that after all he cared for her. But he didn't. He couldn't wait to get shot of her, it seemed.

Overwhelmed by wretchedness, Wendy bowed her head to her chest and let the tears flow.

Fifteen

When Ash returned home, Sandra was waiting for him. She had dressed now, in her velour leisure suit, and she was smoking a cigarette. The inevitable glass of Bacardi and coke was on the occasional table beside her.

'So, you've installed Wendy with Kate?' she asked.

'Temporarily, yes. Wendy is still saying that tomorrow she'll try to arrange to go to this friend of hers from work who had apparently gone through a similar experience with an abusive husband. And Kate thinks she should get legal advice.'

'Someone from her father's firm? She won't want that, surely?'

'No, the solicitor Robert went to when he remade his will. It seems he and Kate have become quite friendly.'

'Ah, well . . .' Sandra clearly had other things on her mind. 'I am going to ask you something, Ashley. What happened between you and Wendy?'

He shrugged, looking puzzled and impatient. 'What do you mean, what happened between us? I took her to Kate's and left her there, that's all.'

'No, not tonight. Years ago, when you split up. I always assumed it was Wendy who ended it. You were so broken up by the whole thing, and you still are. Don't try to pretend you're not, darling. I know you too well.'

Ash went to the drinks tray and poured himself a whisky from the crystal decanter.

'I'm fond of her, of course I am. And I don't like to see any woman in the state she was in.'

'Ah.' Sandra stubbed out her cigarette. 'She's not just any woman, though, is she?'

Ash stiffened. 'I'd be outraged at wife beating no matter who it was.' He tossed back his drink.

'I'm sure you would, darling. But still, this is Wendy we're talking about. Wendy, whom you adored, and still do. Why did you end it with her and chase off to Saudi, that's what I want to know. And why are you still shutting her out now?'

'She's married to someone else,' Ash snapped.

'Who is using her as a punch bag. Why aren't you in there on a white charger rescuing her?'

'Oh, for heaven's sake!'

'No, I'm serious. You might fool the world, Ashley, but you can't fool me. I know how you feel about Wendy. Why the hell, now you know the state of affairs between her and Tim, don't you try to make amends? It would be perfect really. You could take her back to the Middle East with you, right away from any unpleasantness.'

'Mother, stop, please. It is not going to happen.'

'But why, Ashley? Why are you so set against it when . . .?'

'You really want to know?' Ash slammed down his whisky tumbler. 'Believe me, Mother, you don't.'

Sandra's eyes narrowed. She took out another cigarette and lit it.

'What is this, Ashley?'

'I've said enough – too much.' Ash turned away abruptly.

'Don't walk out on me!' Sandra's voice was shrill. 'I want to know what you are talking about. I want to know the reason you turned your back on Wendy when you are clearly still in love with her. I demand to know!'

He turned back, wondering briefly if she had guessed the truth.

'All right,' he said, 'I'll tell you the reason, and I think you'll see why. You will also see why I have never explained before, to you, to Wendy, to anyone.' His hands were clenched to fists. He still couldn't quite bring himself to speak the words.

'Go on,' Sandra challenged him.

'OK. What would you say if I told you Wendy is my sister?'

He knew at once he'd been wrong in thinking Sandra had thought she knew what he was going to say. Her complete surprise was evident, shock and disbelief making her mouth drop open.'

'What did you say?'

'Dad is Wendy's father. Or so I'm told.'

'By whom?'

'Does it matter?'

'Well, yes, actually. If it was your father who told you this.'

'It wasn't. it's hardly likely he'd admit to me that he'd had an affair with Verity.'

Sandra's jaw dropped even further. And then, unbelievably, she began to laugh.

'It's hardly funny,' Ash said harshly.

'Funny?' Sandra laughed again, pressing her hand to her mouth. 'It's hysterical! Your father – and *Verity*? Oh, he's had his affairs, I know, and plenty of them. I learned to turn a blind eye years ago. But *Verity*! Really, Ashley, that is the most ridiculous thing I have ever heard in my life! It's priceless! Your father never gave Verity so much as a second glance.'

'Didn't you used to socialize together?'

'Well, yes, on occasion. But Verity was a boring old frump even then.'

'Perhaps he regarded it as a challenge. Or perhaps she's a dark horse.'

'I'm sorry,' Sandra said, 'I simply don't believe it. Almost anyone else I would believe. But not Verity. Not in a million years.'

'I must agree, I found it pretty incredible myself,' Ash snapped. 'But it wasn't something I was prepared to take a chance on. It would have been incest, for God's sake. Already was, as a matter of fact. I did the only thing I could do, ended it, and put as much distance as I could between Wendy and myself.'

Sandra shook her head, utterly sober now. 'For heaven's sake, Ashley, why didn't you speak to me or your father about this?'

'I didn't want anybody getting hurt.'

'But you have been, and so has Wendy. You've never got over this, either of you.'

'Better that than she should know she had slept with her own brother.'

Sandra slammed her glass down on the table. 'This is utter nonsense, Ashley. And I want to know who it was who told you. It was sour grapes, it must have been. Someone who wanted to cause trouble, come between you. Who was it, Ashley? I demand to know.'

For a moment Ash was very still. Then he crossed to the

drinks cabinet and poured himself another whisky.

'Very well, if you must know, it was Verity herself.' He emptied the glass in one gulp. 'That is the reason I was so sure it must be true. Why would Verity make up something like that?'

Sandra gazed heavenward, sighing loudly. 'Well, I would have thought it was obvious. She was intent on breaking up the pair of you. She never approved, if I remember rightly.'

'And now you know the reason.'

'Nonsense!' Sandra said roundly. 'Nobody was good enough for her precious Wendy, that was her thinking. And because of Jack's reputation as a philanderer, she came up with this idea – the one thing she knew would put a stop to it once and for all. Well, just look where her interference got her! Poor Wendy married to a wife beater.'

'It's what she told me,' Ash said flatly. 'And I had no reason to disbelieve her.'

Sandra snorted. 'I am going to get to the bottom of this, Ashley, if it's the last thing I do.'

'Mother, don't make trouble,' Ash warned. 'How is Wendy going to feel, finding out the man she's always thought of as her father isn't her father at all? That her mother had an affair with Dad?'

'No worse than she already feels, I should imagine, thinking you simply abandoned her.' Sandra's eyes were flashing dangerously. 'And if it is just a story Verity made up to stop you and Wendy seeing one another, as I'm sure it is, then maybe it's not too late to put things right.'

She saw the momentary hope light Ash's eyes and her heart bled for him. Why the hell hadn't he said something long before this? But she knew the reason. Ash had been protecting her as well as Wendy. The road to hell is paved with good intentions, as the saying goes.

But he was wrong, she was sure of it. She knew Jack, knew his taste in women. She'd had a lifetime of experience. She'd learned to spot the competition very early on, and she'd scarcely ever been wrong. Jack had thought he was good at hiding his flings, but he wasn't. He'd got away with them because Sandra had allowed him to, accepting that the leopard would never change its spots and preferring to let the affairs run their course rather than forcing a showdown that would mean the risk of losing everything she held dear – her marriage, her lifestyle, the man himself. A philanderer Jack might be, but she loved him in spite of it. Maybe because of it. The wandering eye was part of his attraction and created a frisson which affected Sandra like an aphrodisiac.

But to imagine him with Verity was, frankly, disgusting. It was a step too far. She simply could not believe it. He would never sleep with Verity, even if he'd had too much to drink.

Into her mind flashed a game they'd used to play. Rating women by how many drinks you'd have to down before you'd go to bed with them on a scale of one to ten. Verity had definitely been a ten-pinter. She remembered Jack saying so. 'Verity? Oh my God, ten pints and the rest! Poor old Hugh. I feel sorry for him.'

'Ashley,' she said with determination, 'just leave this to me.'

Kate was totally shocked at the state Wendy was in. It wasn't just the physical damage, though that was bad enough: cut lip, bruise beginning to shadow one side of her face, cuts and grazes to her hands and knees, ricked ankle, shivering in spasms, skirt covered in dirt, tights in tatters. Worse, in Kate's opinion, was the cowed and beaten way she looked, as if her spirit had died and there was nothing left but an empty husk. Wendy was normally warm and vibrant, a bit reserved maybe, but mostly sunny. Now she had totally gone into herself and seemed beyond caring about anything.

Kate fixed her a hot drink, adding a dash of brandy, and ran her a bath. She looked out some pyjamas, a change of underwear and a white waffle robe that she kept for visitors. Then, when Wendy had undressed, she put her muddy skirt and blouse in the washing machine. She would gladly have loaned Wendy some of her own clothes, but she wasn't sure they would fit. Wendy looked to be a good two sizes bigger than she was. She might just get into a pair of jogging pants with their elasticated waistband, but she would probably feel better able to face the day ahead wearing her own things.

Apathetic as Wendy was, it was impossible to discuss plans with her, so when she was settled in a hot bath laced with fragrant oil, Kate decided to take matters into her own hands and contact Jon. He was the best person to advise on a course of action, she told herself, and admitted that, actually her motives were not totally altruistic. She very much wanted to speak to him, and for reasons which had nothing to do with Wendy.

As well as his office number, Jon had given her his home number and the one for his mobile. Highly privileged, she thought, and felt a stab of guilt. But she didn't let it deter her. There was no reply from the home number, just the answering machine. Kate left a message that she was trying to contact him and dialled the number of his mobile. Again, just the messaging service. Damn! She left another message, did a spot of clearing up, and went to check on Wendy.

'Are you all right?' she called through the door. For a long moment there was silence. 'Wendy?' she called, alarmed.

'I'm OK.' She didn't sound it; her voice was thick as though she had been crying. But at least she was alive.

From downstairs the telephone began to ring. Kate ran down and picked it up.

'Kate. You've been trying to get hold of me.'

Jon. Her heart did a silly, skittish leap.

'Yes. I'm really sorry to bother you out of office hours . . .'

'No bother. Some calls I am always happy to take. Were you going to invite me out for a drink?'

'Actually no,' Kate said regretfully, feeling guilty again. 'I have an unexpected visitor. And a big problem. I'm looking for advice, really.'

Why didn't I say I'd have loved to out for a drink, but with Wendy here I can't . . . oh, well, too late now.

'Fire away.'

Kate explained the situation. Jon was silent for a moment. Then: 'I'm no expert on family law, but my advice would be to do nothing until you've spoken to someone who is. I'll have a word in the morning with Stella Bradshaw, an associate who deals with that sort of thing, if you'd like me to, and I'm sure she'll find a window to see Wendy as a matter of urgency.' He hesitated. 'Surely, though, there must be someone at her father's firm who could deal with this?'

'She doesn't want her mother and father to know.'

'They're going to have to, surely?'

'I suppose they are, eventually. But when it comes down

to the ins and outs, all the gory details, I have a feeling she'd rather talk to someone with no personal involvement.'

'That's up to her, I guess,' Jon said, 'but given that Hugh has already had his nose put out of joint over Robert's deflection, I shouldn't imagine he'd be too happy about his own daughter consulting the opposition.'

'Oh, shit, you're right.' Kate sighed. 'It's going to cause one hell of an upset. I'll talk it over with her in the morning. I don't think she's in any state to come to any decision tonight. I shouldn't have taken it upon myself to call you, really, but this has landed at my door, literally, and I don't know what to do for the best.'

'I'm glad you did,' Jon said, and her heart leapt, stupidly, wildly, as if she were a teenager again. Then he said: 'Speaking of the matter of Robert's will, I was going to call you tomorrow anyway,' and it dropped again like a stone. For the moment she'd thought his pleasure was a personal sentiment.

'Oh, right.' She made her tone determinedly casual.

'Yes. I got your message about the social worker who was visiting Trish in Gloucester, and followed it up right away.'

'And?'

'It's a bit of a puzzle actually. They have no record of a Patricia Holbrook having been in their care.'

'Perhaps she didn't use her own name,' Kate suggested. 'Or her file's been lost. The sixties was well before the system was computerized, after all.'

'That's true. But even more puzzling, they have no record of a Mrs Smith working for them as a case officer.'

'That's ridiculous,' Kate said. 'Trish's landlady was absolutely clear about her visiting. She even remembered that she was pregnant herself. Could it have been that she was locally based, and followed up on the case when Trish went to Gloucester in hiding, as it were?'

'Possible, I suppose. But pretty unlikely I'd say. If Trish did make the initial arrangements through the local branch they would almost certainly have handed over to Gloucestershire at some point. They'd never have sanctioned their social worker to do hundred mile-odd round trips to check up on a single case.'

'It does seem a bit much,' Kate agreed.

'Anyway, the bottom line is we seem to have come up against another brick wall,' Jon said.

'We're never going to find the missing child, are we?' Kate said despairingly.

'It's early days yet.'

'But we've already thrown everything at it.'

'Nil desperandum.'

Wendy appeared at the top of the stairs, wearing Kate's dressing gown.

'I'm going to have to go,' Kate said.

'OK. And about that drink that you *didn't* suggest. Let's make it soon, yes?'

Kate's heart lifted again. 'Absolutely.'

Jack, as was his habit, did not arrive home until after the club had closed its doors. He enjoyed the socializing, supporting the indoor bowls team, chatting in the members' bar, even raiding the kitchen where the chef could usually rustle him up a plate of something delicious left over from the restaurant. It was a good thing one of them was a social animal, he often said. If it were up to Tony it would be left to the staff to create the ambience the club prided itself on. Generally by the time he let himself into the house, Sandra was in bed, either reading or resting her eyes under pads soaked with some expensive refreshing lotion that promised to eradicate lines, dark circles and puffiness, so when he saw the lights were still on in the lounge, he assumed it would be Ash. Since his son had come home they'd had a few sessions lasting into the wee small hours over a shared bottle of whisky.

He was surprised, then, to find not Ash, but Sandra, curled up on the big leather sofa with a glass of Bacardi on the coffee table beside her and a late-night film showing on the television.

'What are you doing still up?' he asked.

She arched an eyebrow at him. 'Why shouldn't I be?'

'No reason.' He glanced at the TV. 'Are you watching this?'

'Not really. Turn it off, will you?'

He did, puzzled. 'Are you all right, Sandra?'

'I'm fine. Though it has been one hell of an evening.'

'Why? What's happened?'

'I'll tell you in a minute. First, I want to ask you something. Did you ever have an affair with Verity?'

'*What?*' Jack's jaw dropped; he looked utterly dumbstruck.

'Verity Ormrod. Did you ever have an affair with her?'

'You are joking!'

'Not at all. Apparently, Verity told Ash that you and she had had an affair, and that you were Wendy's father. That's the reason Ash finished with her and went off to Saudi Arabia. I'd like to hear your side of it.'

'I don't have a side. I'm totally gobsmacked. Why the hell would Verity say something like that? Good God, I've never so much as looked twice at the woman!'

Sandra smirked, reaching for her glass.

'No, to be honest, I didn't really think you had. But given your track record, I had to ask, just to be sure.'

'What do you mean, my track record?'

'Oh, come on, Jack, you and I both know that monogamy doesn't really suit you.' Sandra sipped her Bacardi, looking at him wickedly over the rim of her glass and rather enjoying herself.

'Sandra, I don't cheat on you.'

'Not now, maybe,' she conceded. 'You're getting just the teensiest bit past it. Though if some gorgeous dolly bird were to throw herself at you, I'm not sure you'd put up too much of a fight.'

'For goodness' sake!'

'It's OK, darling. I'm used to your little ways. But Verity . . . I must say, I took that as a personal insult. I mean, if you actually fancied *Verity*. Well, it doesn't say much for your taste in women. Doesn't say much for *me*, come to that.'

'I do not fancy Verity!' Jack exploded. 'I never have, and I never would, not in a million years.'

'Then you'd better tell your son that. It seems to me that Verity's fantasies and your reputation have gone some way to ruining his life, and Wendy's too. But there's just a chance there might be a window of opportunity to put things right. Ash is here, and Wendy appears to have left Tim, or been kicked out, pretty violently.'

'What the hell are you talking about?'

'Wendy. She turned up here tonight in a dreadful state . . .'

She went on to relate the events of the evening, from the time

Wendy had arrived, dumped like an unwanted parcel outside their door, to the conversation she had had with Ash.

'I think Verity has some explaining to do,' she mused.

'Sandra, don't get involved. You can take my word for it, the whole thing is nonsense. I am certainly not Wendy's father.'

'Hmm.' Sandra's eyes were narrowed. She'd spent the evening wondering why on earth Verity should invent such an unlikely story, and the only possibility she'd come up with was the one she'd put to Ash, that Verity had been set on breaking them up and come up with the one sure way of doing it. But it didn't ring true somehow. Sandra had the feeling that there was something she was missing. And suddenly a different scenario had suggested itself to her, so startling that it ran through her in shock waves. She needed time to think it through, but . . . Sandra's fingers, clasped tightly around the glass, were tingling and inside her was an enormous pool of utter stillness.

'Let Verity stew in her own juice,' Jack said.

But Sandra was not at all sure she was going to be able to do that.

It was adding up. It was all adding up. The more she thought about it, the more sense it made. It was outrageous, of course, absolutely outrageous. But there was a horribly undeniable ring of truth somewhere at the heart of it and all kinds of long-forgotten snippets of the past were popping up in her mind to reinforce the scenario that had suggested itself to her.

'Oh, God, no!' she murmured. 'Please, no!'

Jack was snoring beside her, but she was still wide awake, and sick with anxiety. Ironic, really, this sort of intrigue was just the sort of thing she would normally have revelled in. But this time it was too close to home; people were going to be hurt, and one of those who would be hurt most was her beloved son, Ash. She'd opened a can of worms, and no mistake . . . if she was right.

Sandra's last thought before she finally fell into a troubled sleep was that come hell or high water, she was going to get to the bottom of it.

Sixteen

'I don't know what to do,' Wendy said wretchedly. 'I just don't know what to do.'

She was sitting in Kate's kitchen, hunched over a cup of strong, freshly brewed coffee, still wearing Kate's dressing gown though it was now well past nine in the morning. She and Kate had both been up for more than two hours and the coffee pot had been in constant use. Kate was fretting that she should have long since been at her desk, but she couldn't leave Wendy until they'd sorted something out, and in any case, when the chips were down what the hell did it matter? She wasn't likely to be able to save her business in a couple of lost hours, and probably not at all. And in the event, seeing the mess Wendy's life was in somehow put it into perspective. There were things that were more important than a pile of unpaid bills.

'You're adamant you don't want to go to your mum and dad?' Kate asked Wendy for the umpteenth time.

'No, I can't, Kate. Not until I've sorted something out, at least. Mum will just take over. She'll make me feel like an imbecilic child, as well as a failure.'

'Then let me ring Jon's associate, the one who specializes in family law.'

A tear squeezed out of the corner of Wendy's eye and rolled down her cheek.

'I don't want to tell *anybody*. And I don't want to get Tim into trouble. It's not his fault, it's mine.'

'How do you make that out?' Kate asked bluntly.

'Because . . . because I'm still in love with Ash, and Tim can't bear it. He's had the most awful life, Kate, first the children's home, and then losing his job and everything. I'm all he's got. He depends on me. And I've let him down.'

'Nonsense,' Kate said. 'There's no excuse for the way

he's been treating you. And you have got to stop blaming yourself.'

'I can't.'

'You have to. You certainly can't go back to him.'

'I have to go back sometime. All my things are there. But I'm really scared. Honestly, Kate, I thought he was going to kill me.'

'You're lucky he didn't. He can't be allowed to get away with it, Wendy.'

'I don't want to put him through any more.'

'You're right about one thing,' Kate said, giving up the argument. 'Somehow we are going to have to get your belongings, the things that matter, anyway. A change of clothes, your credit cards and purse.' A thought struck her. 'Do you have joint accounts? Tim could clean them out, leaving you with nothing. I really do think you need to speak to a solicitor, and soon.'

'He wouldn't do that.'

'How do you know he wouldn't? Wendy, you've got to be sensible.'

'I will have to go to the house, though.' Wendy was going round in circles. 'I expect he's calmed down by now. But . . .' She chewed her lip. 'But would you come with me?'

Kate shrank inwardly. She really didn't like the idea, but she didn't suppose Tim would do anything terrible if she was there. His rages were probably for Wendy alone, when there were no witnesses.

'If that's what you want,' she said reluctantly. 'Why don't you get dressed, your own clothes are washed and dry, and we'll go over now. Then, when we see what sort of reception we get, it will help us decide what we have to do next.'

'OK.' Wendy pulled a tissue out of the box on the table between them and blew her nose. 'Let's do it. My clothes are where?'

'Hanging over the ironing board. I pressed them last night after they came out of the tumble drier and before I went to bed.'

'Oh, Kate, thank you. What would I have done without you? How can I ever repay you?'

'By leaving that bastard and getting back your life,' Kate said shortly.

*   *   *

'Let's get this over with then,' Kate said.

Wendy had come back downstairs after getting dressed in her own clothes and a pair of Kate's tights, since hers had been torn to shreds. Shoes were something of a problem; Wendy had lost one of hers, and she took a size larger than Kate, but they solved it with a pair of slingback sandals. Wendy's feet might be overlapping the heels at the back, but at least her toes weren't squashed double. By the time Kate had loaned her a coat she looked reasonably presentable, especially since she had made the effort to put on a little make-up that did something to hide her pallor and the dark circles beneath her eyes.

Kate felt jittery but determined as they drove across town. Just let Tim try anything this morning and she'd make sure he ended up in police custody, she thought grimly.

The curtains were still drawn at the windows of Wendy's house and there were no signs of life. Wendy's car was on the driveway with one of its front wheels resting in a flowerbed, evidence that Tim had not been in proper control when he parked it.

'Perhaps he's still in bed,' Wendy said. If Tim had gone on drinking after unceremoniously dumping her last night, it was a distinct possibility.

'And you don't have a key,' Kate said.

'There's one under the flower pot by the door.' Wendy bent to retrieve it.

'Perhaps we should ring first,' Kate suggested. 'If Tim wakes up and hears us in the house it might set him off again.'

Wendy's chin came up, the first sign of a defiance Kate had thought had been beaten out of her.

'It's my house. I'm not ringing the doorbell of my own house.' She fitted the key into the lock, opened the door and stepped inside.

They went through to the kitchen. Everything was exactly as it had been when Tim had launched his attack, the smoked haddock still in the pan where it had been poaching, the vegetables in their dishes and the puddle of cold congealed parsley sauce spread across the floor. But there was a flat carton which had obviously contained pizza on the kitchen table, along with a couple of empty beer cans.

'He really didn't want fish,' Wendy said miserably. 'That's what started it all.'

'He beat you up because you cooked fish for his tea?' Kate said in disbelief.

'I should have thought. I know it's not his favourite.'

'Wendy, don't start that again!' Kate warned her. 'Let's get your things and go. There's your bag, look, on the chair.'

'I'm going to have to go upstairs,' Wendy said nervously.

'Come on then.' Kate was tossing up whether it would be better to call out and warn Tim of their presence or hope he was in such a stupor they could get in and out of the bedroom without him knowing.

In the event, they trooped quietly up the stairs. The bedroom door was ajar; Wendy pushed it open and went inside whilst Kate waited on the landing.

'Oh!' It was a gasp of surprise.

'What?' Kate called.

'He's not here! The bed hasn't been slept in.'

Kate entered the bedroom. In the dim light filtering through the still-drawn curtains she could see the un-rumpled duvet pulled up over the stacked pillows.

'Where can he be?' Wendy sounded concerned, worried even.

'Never mind that. Just get your things and let's get out of here while the going's good. Have you got a suitcase?'

'On top of the wardrobe . . .' Wendy drew back the curtains, peering up and down the street. 'I can't understand it, Kate. He never goes out this early and the car's still here . . .'

Kate hefted the suitcase down on to the bed and opened it. 'Come on, Wendy. I don't want to be caught here if you do. Now, what do you want to take?'

Somewhat distractedly Wendy pulled clothes from drawers and the wardrobe and Kate folded and packed them, one ear cocked for the sound of the front door opening. It didn't. They toured the house collecting toiletries and personal items without interruption, but Kate's unease was mounting rather than subsiding.

'Is that everything?'

Wendy sighed. 'For the moment, I suppose.'

'Come on then, let's get going.'

Wendy hesitated, the picture of indecision. Then, to Kate's surprise, she yanked off her wedding ring and put it on the dressing table.

'I don't think I'll be needing that any more,' she said, and the defiance was back in her voice.

They went back downstairs and outside, and Wendy pulled the door shut behind her.

'Do you think you could drop me at the office? If I'm going to get my life back on track, I think I ought to go to work.'

'Oh, Wendy.' Kate hesitated. 'You really do have an awful lot to sort out. The solicitor . . .'

'Later,' Wendy said. 'I can't face it right now. I just want a couple of hours of something like normality.'

With all this hanging over her, Kate could not see that it would be possible for Wendy to immerse herself in reality, as she called it, but Kate was not about to argue.

'It's your decision, Wendy,' she said, relieved that she, too, would be free to put in an appearance, albeit rather late, at her own business.

Sandra parked at the kerb outside Verity and Hugh's home and marched up the path. The double garage was open, she could see Verity's Polo parked inside, but there was a space where Hugh's car spent the night. He must be at work, she assumed. Well, good. What she had to say was for Verity's ears alone. She straightened her poncho, raised a gloved hand and rang the bell. After just a few moments she heard footsteps in the hall and the door was opened by Verity herself. She wore twin set and pearls, a tweed skirt and dark green tights that only served to draw attention to the sturdiness of her legs. Though she was in the house, she was not wearing slippers, but stout sensible shoes – the reason the approaching footsteps had been so clearly audible.

'Sandra!' Verity was clearly surprised; apart from family gatherings, their paths seldom crossed.

Sandra's lips tightened into a cold smile.

'Verity. I think you and I need to talk. May I come in?'

'Well, yes . . .' Verity stood aside and Sandra went into a hall that smelled of lavender polish. Immaculate. Everything about Verity always was. Yet the place was singularly lacking in warmth. There might be flowers in the vases and guest soap in the bathroom, but the house didn't feel like a home. Sandra was not surprised Wendy had not wanted to come here last night, battered and bloody. But she did think Verity should know about it.

And she had a few questions to ask Verity too. The answers to which might well be dynamite. Or which might set her mind at rest.

'Can I get you a coffee?' Verity enquired, showing Sandra into the sitting room and indicating that she should take one of the brocaded armchairs.

'No, thank you.'

'Something stronger, perhaps?' Verity suggested archly.

'Nothing, thank you.'

'So.' Verity perched herself on the edge of a matching chair, facing Sandra across a huge fireplace with an ornamental screen masking the fact that Verity seldom allowed it to be used for the purpose for which it had been intended. Fires meant mess, ashes in the grate and dust gathering in the furnishings; Verity preferred to rely on the somewhat anti-quated central heating. 'What's all this about, Sandra? Not more nonsense about Trish's missing child, I hope.'

'It's about *your* child,' Sandra said acidly. 'I thought you should know that she turned up at my home last night in a dreadful state. She and Tim had had a bust-up and he had thrown her out. After giving her a beating, I might add.'

Verity's hand flew to her mouth; above it her smooth face became paunchy with anxiety.

'Oh my goodness, I knew it! I knew something was going on. She hasn't been herself for months. But . . . why did she come to you, Sandra? Why didn't she come here, to us?'

'Perhaps,' Sandra said, 'that is something you should ask yourself, Verity.'

'This is her home. We are her parents.'

Sandra's lips tightened a shade. 'Do you mind if I smoke?'

Verity bristled. 'Actually, I'd rather you didn't.'

'Well, I'm sorry, but I really do need to.' Sandra got out a cigar-ette and lit it, ignoring Verity's obvious disapproval. 'Do you have an ashtray?'

Verity opened the doors of the mahogany sideboard and got out a heavy crystal ashtray which she placed on the arm of Sandra's chair.

'I hope,' she said, 'that the reason she came to you has nothing to do with the fact that Ashley is there.'

'As it happens, I think it had everything to do with it.' Sandra drew on her cigarette. 'It's also why I want to talk to you. Ashley told me something last night that he's never mentioned to anyone before. Something that you told him at the time that he and Wendy were going out together.'

Verity blanched. She had become very still, yet beneath her smooth face Sandra caught the sudden trembling of her jowls. Her mouth opened, as if she was about to speak, but no words came.

'I can see you know what I'm talking about, Verity,' Sandra said tautly.

'He didn't . . .' Verity was struggling for words, looking like nothing so much as a goldfish dropped from its bowl. 'He didn't tell you this in front of Wendy, did he?'

Sandra's eyes narrowed.

'You're not bothered that he said it to *me,* given the nature of the information?' She laughed bitterly. 'No, I don't suppose you would be. The answer to your question is no, Ashley, being the honourable man he is, didn't tell me this until after he had taken Wendy to Kate's. That's where she is now, by the way; where she spent the night. I expect you were trading on Ashley's total decency when you said . . . what you said to him. He would never do anything to hurt Wendy, and you knew that. You knew that he wouldn't burden her with the guilt of incest. He'd rather she simply thought he'd got tired of her than he would inflict that on her.'

'I had to put a stop to it!' Verity snapped. 'You must see that.'

Sandra ground her cigarette out in the crystal ashtray.

'But why did you lie, Verity? Why did you tell Ashley you had had an affair with Jack?'

'I didn't,' Verity protested.

'Ashley says you did. Or led him to believe it. But we both know that's not the case. You never had an affair with Jack. Oh, I know he's a philanderer. I'm under no illusion about that. He has had affairs, quite a few of them, in his time. But not with you. Never with you. And I want to know why you said he did.'

'I never said I had an affair with Jack,' Verity repeated. A dull flush had risen in her cheeks, her hands were clenched to fists. 'I told him that Jack was Wendy's father.'

'Ah, now we're getting to it!' Sandra's eyes were glinting. All the theories that had taken shape in her mind during the long hours of the night were there, milling around in a horrible choking fog of intrigue and deceit almost beyond belief. 'Why did you tell him that? Was it a way of putting a stop to Ashley and Wendy as a couple? Did you just make it up in order to make him stop seeing her?'

Verity drew herself up. 'I don't want to talk about this.'

'No, I don't suppose you do, but you're going to, dammit! My son's happiness is at stake here. And your daughter's, if it comes to that. If she is your daughter.'

Verity clutched at her throat. She was pale now, all colour drained from her face.

'As I see it, Verity, there are a limited number of interpretations of your behaviour here, given that we both know that Jack would never father a child by you in a million years,' Sandra went on. 'Option one – Wendy is your daughter, yours and Hugh's, and the story you told Ashley to make him split up with Wendy was a barefaced lie. Or, option two. You told the truth – Jack *is* Wendy's father, and the relationship between her and Ashley would indeed have been an incestuous one. In that case, she is certainly not your child.'

'I don't know what you are talking about!' Verity turned her back on Sandra, straightening cushions with a jerky, bustling action as if a burst of domesticity could make this all go away. 'And that cigarette ash smells disgusting!' She grabbed the ashtray from the arm of Sandra's chair. 'I want you to go, Sandra. Now.'

Sandra shook her head. She would have been enjoying this if it had not been for the fact that she had the most horrible feeling that her beloved Ash was going to be the loser here. But she had gone too far to stop now. She had to know the truth.

'I've been doing a lot of thinking, Verity, adding up titbits from the past that never seemed important before. I don't like the conclusion I've come to, and I don't know how the hell you got away with it. But I'm going to tell you straight out what I think. I think Wendy is Trish's missing child. And you believe that Jack is her father.'

For a long moment her eyes held Verity's and her stomach plummeted even though what she saw in Verity's face was what she had expected. She had been right. The guilt and the horror of discovery was written all over Verity. Wendy was not her child at all. She was Trish's missing baby. Trish's – and Jack's. Shaking all over suddenly, Sandra bent forward to fish her cigarettes out of her bag. Damn Verity – she needed one!

She barely saw the flash of light reflected in the hundreds of facets of crystal. She barely felt pain as it connected with the base of her skull. She was aware only of a moment of heart-stopping shock as she pitched heavily forward on to the hearthrug.

'Oh, Sandra, why did you have to come here?' Verity muttered brokenly as she lowered the ashtray, sticky now with Sandra's blood, and stared at it almost unseeingly.

She might be in her office, but Kate was finding it almost impossible to concentrate. There was just too much going on in her head. The missing child, Wendy's problems, Jon. Every time she thought of him, the blood sang in her veins and in spite of everything she felt ridiculously happy. Ridiculous since absolutely nothing had happened between them yet, and maybe never would. A few teasing remarks, a feeling of belonging when they were together, was really no foundation for her optimism. The closeness might exist only in her imagination, be nothing more than wishful thinking, and the things he'd said . . . For all she knew he could be a ladies' man who simply enjoyed chatting up every female who crossed his path. But somehow she didn't think so. Or was that wishful thinking too?

The bell on the shop door jangled; Kate glanced up. Through the Venetian blind covered window that separated her office from the display area, Kate saw a smartly dressed woman. A customer! Glory be! She pushed back her chair and went out into the shop, striving for the combination of friendliness and efficiency that was her trademark.

'Good morning. Can I help?'

'I hope so. I need some new curtain nets, and as I was passing, I decided to look in and see what you have.'

Curtain nets. Kate's heart sank. Any business was better than none, but a few metres of curtain net were not going to go far enough to solve her financial problems.

'We have a good range,' Kate said, hiding her disappoint-ment. 'There – and another stand just there . . . And if you don't see anything that's quite right for you, I could always order in something especially.'

'Oh, I'm sure one of these will be fine.' The woman was flicking through the sample lengths.

'Did you want white or ivory? Or there's a beautiful cream with an inset of ecru—' The bell jangled again. To her surprise, Kate saw that it was Jessica. Jessica never visited her at the studio. Even if she was in town and practically passing the door, she always claimed to be in too much of a rush to call in.

Kate smiled at her benignly, still in business mode.

'I'll be with you in a moment. Would you like to go through to my office?'

Jessica frowned, irritated, no doubt, by not having her sister's full and undivided attention immediately, but she did as Kate had suggested.

The customer was dithering; Kate, desperately hoping she wasn't about to lose the sale, hovered patiently, a smile pinned firmly to her lips. The customer heaved a sigh and let the length of net she had been inspecting fall back between the others.

'I don't know. I really don't know.'

Oh, bother!

'What I'm wondering is if I should get the whole room done whilst I'm about it. It really does need updating, and it seems silly to do it piecemeal . . . You do design consultancy, don't you?'

'Absolutely. I can come to your house and advise, and when you've decided what you would like, we can supply everything, from carpets and wall-covering to art works and lighting, so you don't have to be dealing with a number of different outlets.' Kate could feel a pulse beating at the base of her throat. 'Would you like to book an appointment? I'll just get my diary so we can arrange a convenient time.'

She went into her office where Jessica was pacing impatiently.

'Won't be long,' she said, picking up her desk diary and glad that she'd had the foresight to make bogus entries on the otherwise blank pages. It gave a client confidence if they thought you were busy. 'Sit down, why don't you? Or make a cup of coffee. You know where everything is.'

A few minutes later she was back, the appointment made. Unless something went horribly wrong, this was looking good. The address the customer had given her was on an estate of executive homes in a neighbouring village – plenty of money there! After all her disappointments and frustrations, Kate was almost afraid to allow herself to get too excited, but if she did a good job this could well be the start of a revival of her fortunes. And she would do a good job. She'd make sure of that.

'Sorry about that, Jess,' she said cheerfully. 'Business has to come first, though.'

Jessica didn't reply directly. Her manner was tense and edgy, not unusual in itself, but especially marked today.

'We need to talk, Kate.'

Kate frowned. 'About what, exactly?'

Again, Jessica avoided the question.

'I haven't been entirely honest with you, Kate. There's something . . . well, I've kept it to myself for a very long time. I hoped for everyone's sake it would never come out. Even after we learned the contents of Grandpa's will, I hoped it would just go away. But I don't think it's going to. I've been wrestling with my conscience, and I really think I should share it with you, at least. Then we can decide together what we ought to do about it.'

'What are you talking about, Jess?' Kate asked. But she thought she knew, and a moment later her suspicions were confirmed.

'Mum talked to me just before she died,' Jess said. 'Unburdened herself, really. I've known for the last twenty years that she had a baby before she married Dad. And I've known what happened to that baby.'

'What!' Kate stared at her sister, shocked, yet at the same time remembering her suspicion that there was a reason why Jessica had tried so vehemently to deny the existence of a secret child. That she had known more than she was saying. 'Why haven't you said something before this? Why have you let us run round in circles, searching?'

'Because it's a tinder box,' Jessica said. 'I think, as you do, that it was finding out the truth that caused Grandpa to have his stroke, and that's just the start of it. A lot of people are going to get hurt, Kate. That's the reason I've said nothing, why I tried to persuade you to let the whole thing drop. It's why I'm still reluctant to tell what I know, to you or anyone.'

'Go on,' Kate said grimly. 'You can't stop now.'

'OK.' Jessica levelled her gaze with her sister's. 'What would you say if I told you that Wendy was Mum's missing child?'

Sandra stirred, groaned. 'Help me, please!'

Verity's mouth worked convulsively, then tightened. For the moment she had no idea how she was going to explain Sandra lying, badly injured, on her hearthrug, but she'd think of something. An intruder. A burglary gone wrong. She'd come up with some explanation and they'd believe her. They always did. Though she said it herself, she was a most convincing liar. It was her respectability that helped her to get away it, she presumed. Everyone thought she was far too respectable – and dull – to have anything to hide. And her determination was the other factor. With her mind made up, Verity was the most stubborn of schemers.

She was certainly determined now. She couldn't have let Sandra go making those accusations. Couldn't let her bring down the whole edifice of deceit. What in the world would people think if they knew the truth? No, Sandra had to be stopped. The only pity of it was that she hadn't killed her outright when she'd struck her with the ashtray. It had been a spur of the moment thing, of course, just like that other time. But that had passed over with no problem. No one had thought for a moment to suspect her. This . . . well, this was going to be more difficult. It would take more effort. More thought.

But of one thing she was in no doubt whatever. Sandra must not be allowed to leave this house and spread her mischief-making allegations. Verity simply had to work out a plan to ensure she did not.

Seventeen

'Oh my God,' Kate said. 'Are you sure about this?'

'Absolutely.' Jessica's tone was laden with certainty, her expression so serious that Kate was left in no doubt but that she was speaking the truth.

'Tell me.'

'We're not going to be interrupted again, are we?'

'Hang on.' Kate buzzed through to the upstairs workroom. 'Dee, could you come down and mind the shop for a bit, please? I'm tied up at the moment with important business.' She replaced the phone and turned to Jessica. 'Go on.'

'Right.' Now that the moment had come, Jessica scarcely knew where to start. She huffed a little, plumped herself down in the visitor's chair, got up again. 'You remember the terrible depressions Mum used to suffer from?'

'As if I could forget.'

'She'd never say what was wrong, would she?'

'No, I just thought of them as "Mum's moods".'

'And so did I. Until she told me different. It wasn't that long before she died. I got in from school early; we'd been given a free period that we could use for private study, at home if we liked. They used to do that sometimes when we were in the sixth form.'

'Yes, I remember. Go on.'

'I got home and found Mum crying. There was nobody else there; she was alone in the house. I asked her what was the matter, and at first she just hedged, pretending it was nothing, as she usually did. And then she turned really strange. She put her arms round me and held me so tight it frightened me, and she was sobbing as if her heart would break. She was talking what seemed like gobbledegook to me. "Thank God I've got you three," that sort of thing. And then she said: "But she's mine, too. Oh, do you know what it's like for me? What torture? Seeing her grow up, and her not knowing." I didn't know what on earth she was talking about. "I have to tell her," she said. "I can't keep it to myself any longer." And I said: "Who, Mum?" and she said: "Wendy." Can you imagine how shocked I was, Kate? I mean, *Wendy*, our sister!'

Kate shook her head, reeling. She could well imagine how Jessica must have felt; she was feeling just the same. Wendy – Trish's lost child? Her mother and father were Verity and Hugh. It made no sense at all. How could Wendy be Trish's and nobody know?

'What else did she say?' she asked.

'Nothing, then. I couldn't stay and listen. I went off up to my room. But I didn't get much private study done, I can tell you. It was all going round and round in my head. I kept telling myself she'd gone off her head; I really thought she'd finally lost it completely. And then she came up and said she wanted to talk to me. I was scared stiff; I knew it was going to be something I didn't want to hear. But she wouldn't stop. She said it had to come out, and I was nearly grown-up and she wanted me to understand. But I wasn't to say anything to anyone until she'd had the chance to tell them herself, and she'd have to pick her moment. That not even Dad knew the truth, and he had to hear it from her, not from me.'

Jessica bowed her head, as if the weight of what her mother had confided in her was still weighing heavily upon her.

'It was bizarre; it was as if she'd bottled it all up for all those years, and now she'd started talking about it, she just couldn't stop. She told me that she'd become pregnant when she was not much older than I was then. The father was this RAF chap she met at a dance; I don't think it was a serious relationship, more like a one-night stand, or a quick fling in the alley at the back of the dance hall. She told me she was trying to get over Jack, who'd dumped her for Sandra and this stranger made her feel wanted. Anyway, by the time she discovered she was pregnant, he was out of the picture. He'd been posted away somewhere, and he didn't answer her letters.'

No, they came back marked 'Return to Sender', Kate thought, but she said nothing. She didn't want to interrupt Jessica's story.

'Well, Mum told me she was scared to death,' Jessica went

on. 'Out of her mind with worry. An illegitimate baby in the sixties was still a terrible stigma, a matter for shame. And Grandpa was very strict and old-fashioned. Mum was terrified of him finding out. It would have been bad enough if Jack, or some other steady boyfriend *had* been the father, but a boy she scarcely knew . . . She kept it to herself as long as she could, but in the end she had to confide in her mother. And Grandma Dorothea took charge of the situation.'

'But how on earth did they manage to keep Grandpa in the dark?' Kate asked.

'As luck would have it he was away quite a lot at the time. His company had a big, important contract for a housing development in Dorset, and he was overseeing it personally. In any case, Trish concealed the fact that she was pregnant right up until the last couple of months. A first baby doesn't necessarily show as much as subsequent ones, and by strapping herself up and wearing loose clothes she only looked as if she'd put on a bit of extra weight. When she couldn't hide it any longer she went to stay in lodgings in Gloucester and came up with various excuses to explain her absence. She got time off from the solicitors in Bristol where she worked by inventing a fictitious cousin who was ill and needed live-in help; though I think her bosses might have known the truth, her colleagues were fobbed off with the sick relative tale. And they told Grandpa she was going on a training course of some sort. According to what Mum told me, he never questioned it. She went to Gloucester, had the baby there, and then came home again as if nothing had happened.'

'It must have been terrible for her,' Kate said, appalled. 'No wonder she was . . . the way she was. But I just can't get my head round it. Are you saying Verity and Hugh adopted the baby? Jon checked all the registers in Gloucester and drew blanks. Did Mum use a false name? And how could the baby be just handed over and no questions asked, and no paper trail left behind? I was under the impression the authorities were as thorough then as they are now, even more so, maybe, when it comes to vetting adoptive parents. And what about Wendy? Surely she would be bound to know she was adopted? When she needed her birth certificate to get a passport, or when she was married, she'd see it was only a short form and question it, even if they'd never told her before. I just don't see how they could possibly keep something like that from her. She must have had her suspicions at the very least that she had been adopted.'

Jessica shook her head. 'She wasn't.'

'Wasn't what?'

'She wasn't adopted. That's where the real skulduggery comes in. She was passed off right from the outset as Verity's baby. Her birth was registered by Hugh with Verity as the mother and himself as the father.'

'*What?*' Kate could scarcely believe what she was hearing.

'I know. It beggars belief, doesn't it? Verity and Hugh had been trying to start a family for some time, it seems, without success. Dorothea knew that; knew they were getting desperate. When Trish fell pregnant, Dorothea went to them, and between them they hatched up this plan. At the time Verity and Hugh were living in the Midlands, where Hugh was working as a junior solicitor. That's presumably the reason they settled on Gloucester as a suitable place for Trish to go into hiding to give birth; far enough away for them not to arouse suspicion, near enough to be accessible. Verity pretended to be pregnant; while poor Trish was strapping herself up to hide her growing girth, Verity was adding layers of padding. She used to visit Trish in Gloucester, I understand, to make sure everything was still going according to plan.'

'Oh my God,' Kate said. 'Mrs Smith, the pregnant social worker. No wonder no one at social services had ever heard of her.'

'What?' Jess looked puzzled.

'It doesn't matter.' Kate waved a dismissive hand. 'Go on.'

'Well, after her baby was born, Trish made some excuse so as not to register the birth when the registrar visited the hospital. As soon as she was discharged she handed her over to Verity, who had, presumably binned her padding, and the birth of a baby girl was registered in their names. At the register office local to where they were living. And that's about it, as far as they were concerned. They brought Wendy up as their own child and nobody suspected a thing. But Trish . . . Trish just couldn't put it behind her.'

'I'm not surprised!' Kate said, horrified. 'It must be bad

enough to give away your own baby, but to have to watch her grow up, not knowing who she really is must have been torture. Perhaps she'd have stood a chance if Verity and Hugh had stayed in the Midlands, but to have them move back here right on the doorstep . . . No wonder poor Mum used to go into those depressions. She was being torn apart.'

'I know.' Jessica paused, her eyes going far away as if she was reliving the day when Trish had finally unburdened herself. 'She told me she just couldn't stand it any longer. That she wanted to come clean so that Wendy could become part of our family.'

I love all my children equally. All four of them . . . Once again, Kate heard her mother's voice that night when they had been playing the Truth Game. Had she been on the point of spilling the beans that night, and lost her nerve? Whatever, ten years had gone by before she confided the whole story to Jessica, perhaps as a sort of rehearsal for telling everyone else. Ten more long years when everything in her had been crying out to hold Wendy in her arms and never let her go . . .

'And just to make things even worse, Verity had been led to believe that Jack was the father of Trish's baby. I suppose Grandma must have thought she might baulk at taking on the result of a one-night stand with an unknown airman, and she wanted to preserve as much of Trish's reputation as she could – she didn't want Verity and Hugh to see her as promiscuous. So the whole situation was absolute dynamite.'

'Oh, poor Mum!' Kate groaned. 'It must have been terrible for her. And what a dilemma! Suffer in silence, or tell the truth and set off all the repercussions that were bound to follow.'

'Exactly,' Jess said. 'It would have been all hell let loose. Not only from a family point of view, but legally too. I mean, Hugh, a respected solicitor, breaking the law like that. Goodness only knows what the penalty would be. He would have been struck off, at the very least, I should imagine. He and Verity might even have gone to prison. I didn't realize the full implications at the time, of course, but I do now. And for all that she was desperate to tell the truth, I suppose Mum did too. And I think it is why she killed herself. She couldn't leave things as they were, and she couldn't bring herself to blow the whole thing wide open either. She simply couldn't see any way out, and so she ended it all.'

Kate nodded grimly. 'You're probably right.'

'Well.' Jessica let her breath out on a sigh, reverting to her usual brisk self. 'Now you know. I've kept quiet all these years because I knew I'd be opening up a can of worms. It's just a pity that Grandma Dorothea felt she had to share her secret with Grandpa rather than taking it to her grave. And that he felt he couldn't let it rest until he'd made some effort to find the missing child and put things right. All without saying anything to anyone. If I'd known Grandma had told him half a story, I could have filled in the blanks, and I'm sure he would have thought it best to let sleeping dogs lie. But he didn't. He went ahead in his own sweet way, and now we're left with this mess.' Her eyes met Kate's squarely. 'So, what are we going to do? Tell the truth and shame the devil, or keep quiet and let it all blow over?'

Kate ran a hand through her hair.

'I don't know, Jess. We really should put Miranda in the picture, I suppose, but you know how indiscreet she is. I'm all for honesty, but this is going to wreck lives, isn't it? Verity and Hugh must be going through purgatory, and I'm not sure Wendy is in any state to deal with the shock on top of everything she's been going through. Perhaps we should just let it die the death, and when the year's up and no missing beneficiary has been found, we can quietly give Wendy the fourth share and say we think it's what Grandpa would have wanted.' She hesitated. 'The only trouble is, I think she could do with the money *now*. She and Tim . . .'

She went on to tell Jessica of the events of the previous evening.

'Does Verity know about all this?' Jessica asked when she had finished.

'No. Wendy didn't want her to.'

'Interesting.' Jess's mouth pursed. 'Verity was so desperate to have her, and yet when Wendy really needs help, she's the last person she feels she can turn to.'

'Ours not to reason why.'

'No, but . . . Don't you think she should know what's been going on?'

'That's up to Wendy. It's really not our business.'

'And all the other stuff? Should we at least put her in the picture? See what she has to say?'

'Maybe. I don't know, Jess. I need time to think . . .' *And time to think if I should fill Jon in or not . . .*

The telephone shrilled. 'Damn. I should have taken it off the hook.' Kate reached for it. 'Hello?'

'Kate. This is Tamsin Wells. You came to see me.'

'Yes, I know who you are, of course.'

'There's something I should have mentioned, except that it didn't seem to make any sense. When I went to see Robert in hospital after he had his stroke, he was pretty incomprehensible. But he did seem to be trying to tell me something and I'm wondering if what he said might make any sense to you.'

On the point of saying that it really didn't matter any more, Kate changed her mind and waited.

'He seemed to be trying to say that Trish didn't commit suicide,' Tamsin went on. 'Understandable he should want to think that, of course, but since the inquest verdict was accidental death, I'd have thought he would have reverted to that. As I say, he *was* very confused, but it was strange all the same.'

'What?' Kate asked, intrigued.

'He seemed to be trying to say that someone killed her. The trouble was I couldn't hear the name; he was really struggling to get it out, or else it was lost somewhere in the foggy part of his brain. And he was going on about "truth", too, except that he said it in French, which seemed very odd. I mean, I've heard of people speaking in a foreign language when they come out of a coma, even if they've never spoken it naturally before, and Robert was well-travelled and educated. But all the same, I did find it surprising.'

Kate had never heard her grandfather speaking French, although she supposed he could, a bit at least, if he chose. And she, too, had heard of the phenomenon of the most unexpected people doing just such a thing when they woke from a period of unconsciousness, even if as they recovered the ability deserted them once more.

'Grandpa was speaking *French*?' she said wonderingly.

'Yes. He didn't say "truth". He said "*vérité*".'

*   *   *

An accident. She'd have to say it was an accident. That Sandra had fallen and hit her head on the stone fire surround. But that was no good. Her blood was on the ashtray and the hearthrug. Well, Verity could always dispose of the ashtray, and say she'd pulled Sandra on to the rug to make her more comfortable, but there'd have to be blood on the fire surround.

Perspiration pouring from her, Verity got beneath Sandra's shoulders and heaved her round. Blood trickled obligingly over the fender. Trouble was, Sandra was still alive. Drifting in and out of consciousness, but alive. If she survived she might not remember anything of what had happened, but then again, she might. Verity couldn't take the chance. She was going to have to make sure Sandra was dead when they found her, and the only way to do that was to strike her again, exacerbate the wound and ensure it was fatal. Smashing her head against the fire surround would add to the authenticity of the 'evidence', and she didn't think anyone would look at it too closely. Why should they doubt her version of events? She was an upstanding pillar of the community, the very embodiment of respectability. And to all intents and purposes, there was no earthly reason why she should wish Sandra harm.

Verity bent over Sandra. The blood was thundering in her ears and she felt dizzy. *Do it. Just do it. For Wendy. For Hugh.* She laid a hand on each side of Sandra's head, trying to summon up the strength of will to translate her plan into action. Then Sandra's eyes flickered and Verity gasped and shrank away.

She couldn't do it. Not in cold blood. When she'd struck Sandra with the ashtray it had been in a moment of blind panic and rage, a reflex reaction, almost, against the threat of her secret being revealed.

Just as it had been before, when she had pushed Trish into the lake.

Verity sat back on her heels, covering her face with her hands, but there was no way she could shut out the image that had haunted her down the years. Trish floundering, the water soaking her heavy coat, dragging her down, the alcohol she'd consumed impeding her still further. And she'd never been much of a swimmer, anyway.

'I have to tell the truth,' she had said, her voice a little slurred, but not so much as to mask the ring of determination. 'I'm sorry, Verity, but I can't go on living this lie and I thought I owed it to you to tell you first, so that you'd be prepared.'

'You can't!' Verity had cried, horrified. 'Trish, you can't! Think of Wendy! It will destroy her!'

'She's eighteen years old, Verity. A young woman. She deserves the truth.'

'And what about Hugh? What will happen to him – and to me? We broke the law, Trish. What we did was very serious. And you, and your mother . . . you were culpable too. You concealed a birth, colluded . . .'

'I can't help that,' Trish had said. 'Whatever the consequences, I just can't go on like this any longer. It's driving me insane.'

She had crumpled then, stretching out her arms as if reaching for something, then wrapping them around herself. Her face was contorted with anguish, tears running down her face and falling on to the backs of her hands.

'I want my baby!' she wailed, and somehow Verity knew it was the echo of a cry Trish had uttered many times before.

'Trish, you've got three lovely daughters!'

'I know, but it doesn't make any difference. Oh, Verity, I should never have done it. I want to hold Wendy in my arms. Like I did when she was born. She was beautiful, wasn't she? And she still is. She's grown into such a beautiful girl. Oh, Wendy, Wendy . . . my baby. My darling little first born baby.'

'You are drunk, Trish.'

'Maybe I am. But it's how I feel. How I've always felt. And I can't keep it to myself any longer, Verity. I'm sorry, I'm really sorry, but I'm going to tell Tony tonight, and the girls, and then—'

That was when Verity pushed her.

She closed her eyes now, remembering. Trish's gasp of surprise. The almighty splash. The gurgling sounds. The cries for help. Verity had turned her back and run, but she could never leave them behind.

No one had suspected. No one had even known she'd been there that day. Accidental death, the coroner had said. Suicide, the family had suspected. Certainly the level of alcohol in Trish's blood had pointed to one or the other.

It had taken Robert to discover the truth. Oh, why had Dorothea had to break the silence of the years and confess that she had helped Trish conceal the birth of her illegitimate baby? Why? At least she hadn't revealed the baby's identity, but Robert had been determined to find out, and Robert with the bit between his teeth was a force to be reckoned with. They'd been worried to death, she and Hugh, that their secret was going to be exposed in the most public way, and she'd taken it upon herself to try to persuade him to let the matter drop. She'd talked to him, reasoned with him, and he'd agreed to call off the private detective he'd hired to find the missing child. But she'd still been worried. She'd gone to see him again, and somehow, and she didn't know how on earth she could have been so careless, she'd let slip that she was with Trish on the day she died.

'She didn't kill herself, Robert,' she had said. 'It was an accident, just as they found at the inquest. She slipped . . .'

Robert's face was a mask of horror. And then anger. 'You could have saved her, Verity. My Trish need not have died!'

It was that flash of overwhelming anger that had caused him to have the stroke, she supposed. She watched, trembling, breathing heavily, as he collapsed before her eyes. And felt nothing but the most enormous relief.

'I didn't want to save her, Robert,' she said, bitterly, triumphantly almost. 'I couldn't let her tell the truth. You must see that. I wanted to make sure she never would.'

The doorbell was ringing. Verity heard it as if from a long way off, and then the sound of the handle rattling. Who in the world could it be? It was too soon, too soon for Sandra to be discovered. She had to get to the door, send whoever it was away. She had to appear normal. But she didn't feel normal. She felt very odd indeed. Her heart was pumping in her chest and the blood hammering at her temples. Verity tried to rise, but her knees were buckling beneath her. And everything was going a long way off, darkness closing in like the tide washing in on a beach. She could hear it roaring in her ears. But she could see nothing. Nothing at all.

She didn't hear the voices either, Kate's and Jessica's, calling her name, and Sandra's. She didn't hear them frantically trying to rouse her, or phoning for an ambulance. And she didn't hear Sandra, concussed but alive, sobbing out fractured details of what had happened. Like Robert before her, Verity had suffered a massive stroke. From which she would never recover.

Epilogue

The Christmas tree, decorated with candle-lights and scarlet ribbons, was tall enough that the star on its topmost branch almost touched the ceiling of the drawing room, and an ever-green garland draped along the length of the fireplace over-mantel.

Kate stood back in the doorway, casting a critical eye over the room and smiling with satisfaction. It looked exactly as it had looked in those long-gone days when she and her sisters had gathered here at the Cedars with the rest of the family to celebrate Christmas, and that was what she had intended. She wanted to recreate the warmth and the gaiety, the magic that they had all experienced here in their grand-parents' home. She'd done it for her children, Lucy, eight years old and still at least *pretending* to believe in Father Christmas, and Noah, six, who was so excited he could scarcely sit still for two minutes at a stretch, and for the rest of the family too. It was the first time they would all have been together for Christmas for many years, and she was determined to make it an occasion to remember. Nostalgic for the older members of the family, precious memories for the little ones to store away.

The Cedars was her home now; had been ever since she and Jon had married. Kate had hated the thought of it being sold to strangers, this house that Grandpa had built for Grandma, and where they had all shared such happy times, and the others had felt the same. They had delayed putting it on the market and when, after a whirlwind courtship, Jon had asked her to marry him, they had raised the money to buy her sisters out. The huge commitment had worried Kate at the time. Though her share of Grandpa's estate had come in time to save her ailing business, the months of uncertainty had left their scars, and she had a deep-rooted fear of seeing the debts begin to mount again. But Jon had done his sums and said that if the worst came to the worst, with a little belt-tightening his salary would cover the mortgage, and they'd decided to go for it.

'You'll always regret it if we don't,' Jon had said. 'And it will be a wonderful place to bring up our family.'

Now, Kate thanked her stars that they'd taken the risk. Nothing had been as hard as she had feared; Jon's practice had gone from strength to strength, and slowly her own business had picked up, the orders rolling in as her reputation grew and the stranglehold of the recession eased. Nowadays it was thriving. She'd been able to take on another assistant to handle the business side, leaving her free to concentrate on design projects – and her growing family. And she had a superb consultant, too, in Liz.

Though to all intents and purposes Liz still lived in America, she was a frequent visitor to England for longer and longer periods, always staying with Tony. And since he had taken early retirement, he had spent more and more time in Florida. Kate would never be surprised if they decided to get married, but so far it hadn't happened. Both of them seemed perfectly happy with the way things were and that, Kate thought, was really all that mattered.

'Mummy! Mummy!' The front door had opened; the children were running across the hall. Jon had taken them out to look for holly and mistletoe, now they were back, their faces rosy beneath their bobble hats, their arms full of sprigs of clustering berries.

'I'm here,' Kate called. 'Come and see.'

They stopped in the doorway beside her, eyes widening.

'Wow!' That was Noah.

'You've done the tree! Oh, Mummy, I wanted to help! I always help!' Lucy sounded peeved.

'I really wanted to do it myself this year,' Kate said. 'You can put up the mistletoe if Daddy helps you. And you've got your paper chains to make.' She smiled down at the children. 'What do you think, though? Do you like it?'

'It's . . . well, it's wow.' Noah.

'Yeah, it's fine,' Lucy agreed, sounding a little less petulant.

'It's just like it used to be when I was a little girl. But you must be very careful with the ornaments. They're very fragile, not like the shatterproof ones we have today.'

'We'll be really careful, Mummy.'

'And Bob is not to come in here bounding about either.' Bob was their golden retriever, named by Noah after Bob the Builder, his favourite cartoon character when they'd got the dog as a puppy three years ago. A very apt name, Kate had thought, amused.

Jon came into the room, unzipping his jacket. 'Come on, kids. Let's get this holly and mistletoe sorted.' He took in the tree and the garlands. 'Great job, Kate.'

'I must admit, I'm rather pleased with it.' She smiled at him and their eyes met in a look of love. A love that had its seeds in a meeting under the most stressful circumstances and blossomed and grown now to a closeness that seemed as if it had always been. She found it almost impossible now to believe that she had once been in love with anyone else, wasted years of her life on a man who had belonged to someone else. But maybe Chris had been caretaking her heart, keeping it safe from involvement with anyone who wasn't Jon.

'Happy Christmas, Mr Nicholson,' she said.

He dropped a kiss on her cheek. 'Happy Christmas, my love.'

'It will be,' Kate said with confidence.

Wendy and Ash walked through the airport arrivals lounge and emerged shivering into the biting December night.

'Oh my God, I'd forgotten just how cold England can be!' Wendy gasped through chattering teeth.

'Bracing.'

'Cold. Freezing!' Wendy huddled into the collar of her jacket. '*Please* let your father be waiting for us!'

'He will be.' Ash steered the trolley, laden with their cases and assorted Christmas presents, around the corner to the spot where Jack had said he would meet them. And sure enough there he was, expectantly watching the flow of passengers for their familiar faces.

'Ah, there you are! Great to see you. Good flight?'

'As OK as they get,' Ash said. 'How are you?'

'Oh, fine. Better when we get home and I can have a

Christmas tipple. Haven't had one all day. You can't be too careful at this time of year. The police and their breath-alysers are everywhere.'

'Let's hope you're not still topped up to the limit from yesterday then,' Ash said good-humouredly. 'Mum not with you?'

'No, she's busy writing last-minute cards to people we thought we'd dropped from our list, but who sent ones to us anyway.'

'She's OK though, is she?' Wendy asked anxiously.

Ten years had done nothing to assuage the terrible guilt she felt over Verity's attack on Sandra. She hadn't been to blame, everyone had assured her of that, but it didn't make her feel any better. It was because of her that Verity had done what she had done, and though she now knew different, she still thought of Verity as her mother.

Thank God, Sandra had not only survived, but made what everyone said was a miraculous recovery. 'Our Sandra is a hard nut to crack,' Jack would joke coarsely when the worst of it was over, though in the first days after the attack, when she had lain seriously ill in a hospital bed, he had been beside himself with worry. For all his philandering ways, he was devoted to Sandra, and coming so close to losing her had brought home to him just how much she meant to him.

Thank God, too, that both she and Verity had been wrong in assuming that Jack was the father of Trish's illegitimate daughter. Whilst Verity had been led to believe that was the case, Sandra, putting together the fragments of the past, had been unable to think of any other explanation. But Kate, backed up by Jessica, had been able to set the record straight, and Ash, released from the nightmare of believing she was his sister, had been free to help Wendy through the traumatic time with all the love he had fought so hard to deny.

Wendy did not know how she would have coped without him. Bad enough that she should be grieving for the woman who had raised her as her own child, on top of that she had not only had to come to terms with the shocking discovery that she was not who she had always thought she was at all, and also the knowledge that Verity had inflicted terrible injury on Sandra in a desperate effort to keep her secret. Kate and Jessica had agreed to keep the fact that she had also been responsible for Trish's death, to themselves, however. What good would it do to toss it into the public arena now? Verity was dead of a massive brain haemorrhage, and nothing would bring Trish back. In any case, they had no proof, and the accusation, ten years after the event, would only cause distress to the most vulnerable.

So Wendy had remained in ignorance that she had inadvertently been the cause of her real mother's death, and with Ash's loving support she had been able, gradually, to get over her shock and grief.

It had been a terrible time for her, though, no denying it. Though she was accepted warmly into the bosom of the family, she still felt oddly disembodied and rootless, as if the foundations of her world had collapsed, leaving her floating in a vacuum of space and time. And before she had had the chance to recharge her batteries, Hugh too had died. The loss of his wife of forty years, together with the shame and worry that what they had done would become public, he had collapsed a few months later with a massive heart attack and was dead before he reached hospital, despite the best efforts of the paramedics to save him.

Then there was Tim. He had been missing for several days, having walked out of his home with nothing but the clothes he stood up in, and Wendy was dreadfully afraid for his safety. In spite of the way he had treated her, she still couldn't help feeling responsible for him. She couldn't rid herself of the feeling that she'd given him a raw deal and that was the reason he had behaved the way he had. And she still loved him, too. Not in the way she loved Ash, of course, but love none the less. She was enormously relieved when he finally surfaced in Bristol and even more relieved that he seemed to be making an effort to get his life back on track. An old friend there had offered him a job with his estate agency and Tim had taken him up on it. Now, ten years later, he was managing a branch in a seaside town, and apparently doing very well. The boom years had returned to the housing market, and Tim had made good use of them.

There was no way, of course, that she would have gone back to him after what he had done, even if she hadn't had Ash. The divorce had gone through, and she and Ash had married, and she had gone back to the Middle East with him.

It seemed a long time now since she had lived in England, and she and Ash were blissfully happy. Their only regret was that no children had come along, but they accepted it, and did not allow it to overshadow the life they shared. For too long they had yearned for one another, now they were together they felt truly blessed and made the most of every precious moment.

She might be shivering in the chill of the English winter, her ears blocked and buzzing as they always did after flying and her skin feeling taut and dry, but Wendy glowed with an inner contentment that came from having finally reached the place in her life where she truly wanted to be.

'Come on then,' Jack said. 'Let's get you home.'

Jessica was rolling pastry for yet another batch of mince pies, wearing a dark blue cook's apron that, for all her best efforts, was dusted with flour. Scarcely could she get one trayful out of the oven than they had disappeared into the mouths of her two hungry sons, she thought ruefully. At this rate she'd be baking from now until Christmas Day.

'Why don't you buy a couple of boxes at Sainsbury's?' Adrian had suggested, but that wasn't Jess's style. The boys might not notice the difference, but she liked to think they did. And anyway, goodness only knew what chemicals were used in the commercial variety.

The kitchen door opened and Dominic came in on a blast of pop music. He was nineteen now, tall and, in Jessica's opinion, very handsome, though she did wish he wouldn't gel his hair into those silly spikes that made it look as though he'd just got out of bed.

'Oh, great, Mum!' He helped himself to one of the previous batch of mince pies cooling on the wire rack, stuffing it practically whole into his mouth.

'Dominic!' Jessica chided him. 'We shall be having dinner soon.'

'That's OK. I'm starving.'

'What do you want anyway?' Jessica asked. 'I'm very busy.'

Dominic swallowed his mouthful of mince pie.

'Do you remember those cufflinks we got to choose when Grandpa Robert died?'

'Well, yes, of course I remember.'

'Where are they?'

'Upstairs, in one of my drawers. Why?'

'I've got to dress up tomorrow night. Emma's mum and dad are taking us out for a special meal at some posh restaurant.' Emma was his girlfriend; he'd been seeing her for six months now, something of a record for him. 'I thought I'd wear that double cuff shirt you got me for my birthday. And it hasn't got buttons on the sleeves.'

Jessica found herself smiling. She'd almost given up hope of Dominic ever wearing the shirt; he seemed to live in casual sweatshirts and jeans. Now here he was actually asking for Robert's cufflinks!

'I remember the day you chose them,' she said. 'You swore you'd never, ever, wear cufflinks.'

'I was only a kid then, wasn't I?'

'Yes,' she said. 'You were. I'll look them out for you when I've got these pies in the oven.'

'Cool.'

Jessica was still smiling as she stamped out circles with the pastry cutter. With a little luck she might be able to persuade him to wear them on Christmas Day, too. Since they were all going to Kate and Jon's, which was Grandpa's old home, it seemed very fitting. And it would be nice to see him looking really smart, too.

Where had the years gone? she wondered. It seemed just yesterday that two little boys were racing round the garden, now they were young men.

But young men she was very proud of. And she thought that if he could see them, Grandpa would be, too.

No one on the soup run had recognized Tamsin and why would they? The closest most of them ever came to watching television was through the window of an electricals store. But it was the way Tamsin liked it. She could go scarcely anywhere there days without people staring, nudging and pointing. Her face was even more well known nowadays than it had been at the height of her career as the Gazelle girl. Big stores had come to realize that 'grey power' were probably the biggest spenders and a huge multi-national chain had taken her on to front their advertising. The cosmetics companies had been chasing her, too, promoting her as the flawless and ever-youthful way the older woman could look if they purchased their range of products.

No, these days Tamsin was well able to afford to support the Mill House and any other charity for the homeless that appealed to her, though George, bless him, had managed to talk her into getting sound financial advice this time around to make wise investments for the future. And she still loved to help out there too, unnoticed, almost, certainly unsung.

Life had been good to her, and she had not been selfish with her good fortune. Tamsin never forgot her early years, and never ceased to be grateful to Robert Holbrook for giving her the chance to make something of herself. If she could do the same for others, then she felt her experience would not be wasted.

There was a girl in the queue tonight about the same age Tamsin herself had been when she had run away from the home. At least, Tamsin thought she was. It was hard to tell these days. But the pinched face beneath the hoodie looked incredibly young to her and the desperation in the girl's eyes tore at her heart. She was just a child, somebody's daughter, somebody's sister, and yet here she was wrapping her hands around the polystyrene mug to warm them and looking at Tamsin with eyes that knew too much, yet longed only to be an innocent again.

Tamsin pulled her aside. 'Have you got anywhere to sleep tonight?'

The girl's mouth set defiantly. 'I'll find somewhere.'

Tamsin felt her heart breaking.

'It's Christmas. And I know a place where you'll be made very welcome. You'll have a warm bed and good food, and nobody will bother you there,' she said, wishing with all her heart that she could take the girl home with her, and knowing she could not. But she would talk to the girl later, if she could persuade her to come to the Mill House, try to find out why she was on the streets in this bitter weather. She might even be able to persuade her to go home, or at least let her parents know she was safe, even if she didn't want to be found. Some you could help, some you could not. It was a hard lesson, but for all the times she had been hurt and let down, Tamsin knew she would never stop trying.

This time, she thought, she stood a chance. The girl's mouth trembled and tears filled her eyes. 'OK,' she said, and Tamsin knew she was enormously relieved that someone with honourable intentions had taken an interest in her.

If she could save just one little soul who was as lost and frightened as she had once been, it would be the best Christmas present she could ask for.

Christmas Day and the whole family had gathered at the Cedars. Liz and Jessica had given Kate a hand in the kitchen, and Ash and Wendy had helped carry the platters of steaming vegetables through to the dining room where the table was laid with time honoured crystal as well as candles, crackers and party poppers. Now they were all around the table; Jack and Sandra, Tony and Liz, Jessica and Adrian, Kate and Jon, Miranda and her partner Andrew, Dominic and William, the children fitted in between them.

Jon had carved the turkey; it sat in thick slices on their plates surrounded by all the trimmings.

'A toast for the cook!' Jack said, raising his glass. 'Good work, Kate!'

They all raised their own glasses. 'The cook!' they echoed.

'There's another toast I'd like to make,' Kate said. Her face was a little flushed from the heat of the kitchen; she looked rosy and happy. 'I'd like us to remember those who we have loved and are no longer with us, and before anyone calls me maudlin, it's a happy toast. I'd like to specially mention Grandpa Robert and Grandma Dorothea. This was their home, and they always made Christmas special for us when we were children. I'd like to think I'm keeping up the tradition this year and I'd like to think that if they can see us now, they approve.'

'Well said, Kate!' That was Jessica. 'Here goes then – Grandpa and Grandma.'

Again everyone responded, even the children, raising their glasses of orange juice and clinking them together with the adults.

Kate caught Jon's eye and smiled. Just look at them, that smile said.

She was satisfied, too. This had worked out exactly as she had planned, and so far everything was going really well.

My family, she thought, looking around the table. We went

through the mill, but we all emerged stronger. And happier. Perhaps the glass of sherry she'd had whilst she was making the gravy had gone to her head and made her sentimental, but if you couldn't be sentimental at Christmas, when could you?

She raised her glass again and this time her toast was a silent one.

Mum. Dear Mum, who loved all her children equally. I'll never forget you.

And then the first crackers were being pulled, and party poppers shooting paper streamers at the elaborate light fittings, and Kate relaxed into blissful contentment.